L.P. HARTLEY

NML/FF

We hope you enjoy this book. Please return or renew it by the due date.

You can renew it at www.norfolk.gov.uk/libraries or by using our free library app.

Otherwise you can phone 0344 800 8020 - please have your library card and PIN ready.

You can sign up for email reminders too.

14/7/22
27/9/22

D1427564

NORFOLK COUNTY COUNCIL
LIBRARY AND INFORMATION SERVICE

Other Books By L. P. Hartley include:

L. P. Hartley

The Brickfield

JOHN MURRAY

First published in Great Britain in 1964 by Hamish Hamilton Ltd

This paperback edition first published in 2012 by John Murray (Publishers)
An Hachette UK Company

1

© The Trustees of the Estate of Annie Norah Hartley 1964

The moral right of the Author of the Work has been asserted in
accordance with the Copyright, Designs and Patents Act 1988.
All rights reserved. Apart from any use permitted under UK copyright
law no part of this publication may be reproduced, stored in a retrieval
system, or transmitted, in any form or by any means without the prior
written permission of the publisher, nor be otherwise circulated in any
form of binding or cover other than that in which it is published and
without a similar condition being imposed on the subsequent purchaser.

All characters in this publication are fictitious and any resemblance to
real persons, living or dead, is purely coincidental.

A CIP catalogue record for this title is available from the British Library

ISBN 978-1-84854-780-3
E-book ISBN 978-1-84854-781-0

Typeset in Sabon by Hewer Text UK Ltd, Edinburgh

Printed and bound by Clays Ltd, St Ives plc

John Murray policy is to use papers that are natural, renewable and
recyclable products and made from wood grown in sustainable forests.
The logging and manufacturing processes are expected to conform to the
environmental regulations of the country of origin.

John Murray (Publishers)
338 Euston Road
London NW1 3BH

www.johnmurray.co.uk

To Mary Wellesley

I

'I'm flattered, of course,' the young man said, 'but why ask me, when you have several friends who know you and your work much better than I do?'

The grey-headed author sighed.

'Most of my friends are my contemporaries,' he replied. 'They haven't had heart attacks, it's true, as I have, but all the same, they might not outlive me, whereas you, I hope, will outlive me many years. How old are you, Denys?'

'Twenty-eight.'

'And I'm sixty-seven, nearly forty years your senior. When did you come to be my secretary? You see how bad my memory is.'

'It will be three years in March.'

'So long – how time flies! Well, you've been a comfort to me, a great comfort.'

'And you to me, Mr. Mardick.'

'Nice of you to say so, Denys. And by the way – I've often been meaning to say this – would it be against discipline, or your sense of fitness, would you have any objection, I mean – to calling me by my Christian name?'

'Oh no, sir,' said the young man promptly. 'I should

like to. To tell you the truth, I sometimes do, behind your back.'

Mr. Mardick smiled.

'Well, say it then.'

'Richard.'

'You said it rather experimentally, and as if it was a hot potato in your mouth, but you must struggle to get used to it. Try to think I'm not present, and you are saying to some friends of yours, "that old so-and-so, Richard—"'

'Oh, Richard, I never should.'

'That's all right then. We understand each other. And you really are prepared to take on the job of being my literary executor?'

'More than prepared. I'm honoured.'

'I can't think that. There aren't many *manuscrits inédits* or typescripts – I never was a copious writer, as you know, and the sin of burying my talent, or hiding its light, has never been one of mine. By hook or crook, I have published nearly everything I wrote, since I wrote *The Imperfect Witness*. You won't have many posthumous works to deal with—'

'I don't want to think of you in the past tense.'

'Some day you'll have to. But there are legions of letters. I hate destroying letters – it's as if you were trying to wipe somebody out of existence. But to spare you, I may leave instructions that you can burn the lot, unread.'

'But surely some of them are important?' Denys asked.

2

'To me, perhaps, but not . . . not to posterity.'

'Posterity?'

'The word slipped out. Oh dear, how vain you must think me. Of course posterity won't be interested in me, and yet—'

'And yet?' The young man prompted his employer, perhaps with a shade too much confidence.

'People might want to know something about me. Most of my books are forgotten, as you know. But *The Imperfect Witness* still sells after nearly forty years.'

'It sold seven hundred and sixteen copies last year, Richard.'

'That book's always been their favourite, I suppose because they can identify themselves with the hero, though why they should want to, when he was such a cad—'

'It's easier to identify oneself with a cad than with a really nice man, if such there be, and cads are popular,' said Denys, stretching out his long legs comfortably.

'I know people say that, but—'

'Would you like to identify yourself with the Prince Consort, Richard?'

'I might have, if I'd lived then. Would you rather have been Jack the Ripper?'

'Well, he had more fun.'

'It depends what you mean by fun,' the novelist said, with mock severity in which, however, there was a hint of disapproval. 'But as we're neither of us cads—'

'Speak for yourself, sir.'

' "Richard", you should say. And I speak for you

3

too, my dear fellow. But where were we? What were we talking about?'

'Cads.'

'Yes, but before that?'

'About the sale of your books, with special reference to *The Imperfect Witness*.'

'Now I remember. I had asked you to be my literary executor. And there was something else I wanted to ask you.'

'Yes?'

The young man rose and stood with his back to the fireplace, in which was an electric fire that imitated coal. The heat it gave out did not seem to belong to it and the light and shade that flickered across its craggy front hadn't the expression and personality that a coal fire has. Denys was so tall that his head overtopped the black-faced sphinxes on the broad Regency mirror that spanned the chimney-piece. He took a gold cigarette-case from one pocket and a gold lighter from another. His movements were deliberate and marked by a conscious elegance; an appreciable time elapsed before he puffed out the first cloud of smoke. Suddenly he remembered and bent down and held the case out to his friend.

'Won't you have one?'

Richard shook his head.

'Doctor's orders. You've still got the case, I see.'

'Yes, and the lighter too. Did you think I should have pawned them?'

'I might have to ask for them back.'

'Even the gods cannot recall their gifts,' said Denys,

4

slowly restoring the cigarette-case to his pocket. 'Was that what you were going to ask me?'

'No, it wasn't. How is your financial situation, by the way?'

Denys shrugged his shoulders.

'Oh, fairly healthy, but these golden accessories give rather a false impression. When I flaunt them in a shop, the counter-jumpers think I've come to buy it.'

'No doubt you have.'

'They certainly make it easier for me to get credit.'

Richard smiled.

'I'm glad of that. Credit is what matters. Which brings me to—'

'What you were going to ask me?'

'Yes, in a way.'

A look that was half impatience, half distaste, crossed Richard's face; the look of someone who, having publicly pledged himself to a disagreeable task, thereby arousing expectation, must now perform it or lose face. Calling his own bluff, he said, 'Do you think people will *want* to know about me?'

'Know about you?'

'The facts of my life and so on.'

'You've always said there weren't any except those listed in *Who's Who*. I know them by heart, of course, I've had to supply them to so many of your fans. Shall I refresh your memory?'

'Do, dear boy.'

'Well then. Mardick, John Richard. Born 29th Jan 18—'

'You needn't rub that in.'

'If you interrupt me, I shall forget,' Denys complained. 'I can reel it off like a prayer – a prayer to you, so long as I don't stop anywhere. "Born at Fosdyke, Cambs, only son of Walter Lusby Mardick. Educated St. Peter's School, Medehamstead, and All Hallows College, Oxford (scholar). Served First World War (R.A.M.C.) Unmarried". I suppose you are unmarried?'

'Yes, of course. As you are.'

' "Has travelled extensively—" '

'That's not really true. I've only travelled extensively between England and Italy.'

'Please don't interrupt me. Publications: *The Imperfect Witness*, of course, and then *O Sunflower*—'

'I think we can take them as read,' the author broke in. 'Their names make me so self-conscious. *O Sunflower*, indeed! So like a young man to think himself weary of Time! If it was now – No, spare me the others.'

'Then I shall have to say them over to myself, or I shall forget the last part.'

Denys' lips moved rapidly for a few moments. '*The Tired Heart*, 1957', he wound up aloud.

'That was prophetic,' Richard said.

'Or tempting Providence.'

'Well now,' Denys said. 'Recreations: swimming, rowing and climbing.'

There was a pause.

'I shall have to alter that in the next entry, if there is one, to "Bath-chair comforts and back-seat driving".'

'Don't be so depressing, or you'll make me sorry I ever told you the facts of your life. Now! Address: Flat 15, 99 Suffolk Gate, S.W.7. That's where we are now, in case you've forgotten. Clubs: Everest, Euthanaseum.'

'Is that all?' the novelist asked.

'I think so. I may have made a slip, because you would keep interrupting, but I think it's all. Can I sit down now? I feel quite tired.'

'You just wanted to elongate yourself. I never asked you to stand up,' said Richard.

'No, but I sometimes do, out of respect for my employer.'

Denys disposed himself in a chair and with the same elaborate gesture as before, lit another cigarette. He fixed on Richard a long, speculative stare, which seemed to be neither taking in nor giving out. Suddenly it would be extinguished, like the revolving lantern of a lighthouse, but while it was still turned on you could neither ignore it nor comfortably meet it, you had to turn away. Richard liked looking at Denys – at his baby-blue eyes, source of the stare, his slightly upturned nose, his long oval face, his complexion as delicate as a woman's.

'It isn't much to go on,' Richard said.

'Not much? You *are* ungrateful. I thought it was a mouthful. You wouldn't find anyone else to cover you as copiously as I have.'

'I don't like that phrase "cover you",' said Richard, 'it's too journalistic, and besides—'

'Besides what?'

7

'You haven't really covered me.'

'What have I left exposed?'

'I think we'd better drop that metaphor,' Richard Mardick said. 'It's rather . . . rather misleading. The main point is: is it likely that someone will want to write about me?'

'More than likely, Richard.'

'In that case, would you do it?'

The young man opened his blue eyes wide. Normally his face was inexpressive; he might have kept it still so as not to wrinkle it. When he did register an emotion, it had an almost theatrical effect.

'Of course I should,' he said. 'And anyhow, your wishes are my commands. But it would have to be a very short book, wouldn't it, just a memoir?'

'I suppose so. But I could tell you more than *Who's Who* does, and then there are the letters written to me, and letters of mine, which my friends may have kept—'

'But why don't you ask one of them to do it? They know the set-up so much better than I do. I only know you in your rôle of employer and benefactor, and—'

'Yes, yes,' said Richard hastily. 'There are several people who know me, in some ways, better than you do, and have known me longer. But I'd rather you did it.'

'I should be charmed. All the same I don't like talking about it, biographizing on your grave. Let's have a drink and talk of something else.'

'A drink by all means. Help yourself, my boy. No, not for me – I have to ration myself, as you know. A bore, but there it is. But while we're on the subject, let's have it out – I'd rather not go back to it again. Now take your time – I know you don't like hurrying, and it's not good for me, either.'

He turned in his chair and watched his secretary's long fingers hovering selectively above the bottles.

At last Denys came back, the whisky in his glass a deep shade of orange.

'Isn't that rather strong?'

'Well, it was you who got me into those bad ways, you who corrupted me. Until you came along, I never—'

'All right, all right,' said Richard.

'And besides, I have to nerve myself for what you're going to tell me.'

'I'm not sure I am going to tell you,' Richard muttered. 'It's like this. If anyone writes about me, I'd rather it was you. You could put a notice in the paper saying you were my literary executor and were going to write a memoir of me, and would anyone who had letters of mine send them to you—'

'Oh dear, I hate all this,' said Denys.

'Yes, but we must be practical. Then when you've got the material, you can decide whether or not you want to write it. I rather hope you won't.'

'I don't quite follow.'

'Well, you'll have the material, and as long as you have it, no one else can use it. You can always be *going* to write the memoir—'

'But how shall I make up my mind?'

'You'll have to use your discretion.'

'I never had very much, you know.'

'Oh, but you will have, by that time. The doctor didn't contemplate my immediate decease. He said he just couldn't tell. Oh yes, he was quite frank with me; you'll find out, when you get older, that people can be frank with you and you with them.'

'You haven't been very frank with me so far,' the young man said, sipping his whisky.

'No, that's to come, at least I think it is.'

'You don't really trust me.'

'Of course I trust you – you're one of the few human beings whom I do trust. Otherwise I wouldn't have asked you – well! But I don't quite trust myself. I mean I don't know whether my impulse to tell you is a sound one.'

'You make it all seem very portentous,' the young man said.

'It is to me. But would it be, to someone else?'

'I can't hazard a guess, unless you tell me.'

'You see, I'm in an odd position, not exactly under sentence of death, but nearly. I haven't any future, to speak of, not as other men even of my age have. I couldn't write now, even if I tried. Imagination is a wasting asset, it dwindles with one's other powers.'

'Couldn't I supply you with some emotions to be recollected in tranquillity?' Denys asked.

'It would be fatal if you did. No excitement, the doctor said, pleasurable or otherwise. And above all, don't get angry. I'm not an angry type, but one never knows, so try not to provoke me, Denys. What I mean is, there's nothing more, in the way of emotion, that I can safely learn: resignation is my lot. The Experience Account is closed. But I want to know how I stand, to have a point of view about myself. Richard Mardick to get used to the new conditions and be *ready* – you might say. The readiness is all.'

'Hamlet.'

'Now you're showing off. But in little, I share some of his faults. Life's dropped out of my hands. I can't pick it up again and I don't want to. I don't want anything new to happen to me, no more problems. A novel *is* a problem, you know, a severe mental and emotional strain; and if it isn't, it's no good – at least in my case. That's why so many novelists, even mediocre ones like me, die before their time. I couldn't face another novel. I should like to relax, and wait like an autumn leaf, to fall. No more readjustments; no more trying to tune in to the present age and wondering what the young people of today are thinking. I believe I have your affection—'

The young man drained his glass.

'Of course you have,' he said.

'– And that gives me a kind of security – emotional security – in which I might put forth a few late autumn flowers, strictly for home use, not for sale.'

'You wouldn't need a secretary then,' said Denys.

'Oh yes, I should. I should have plenty of letters to write, and as I shouldn't be working, I should need companionship more than ever. But your glass is empty,' he added, noticing that Denys was making ineffectual attempts to drain it a second time. 'Fill it up, won't you, though I don't really think you ought to. It's only half-past six, still two hours to dinner-time. You mustn't get sozzled.'

Denys rose with his air that was at once languorous and resolute, and said, 'Don't forget you were going to tell me something.'

But when he had replenished his glass, a silence fell.

'I'm waiting,' he said.

Thus reminded, Richard took the plunge, but into shallow water.

'It isn't easy to explain,' he said, 'it's for the sake of the synthesis, the harmony, the integration, if you like, though it's a dreadful word – in my thoughts and feelings. Am I being unbearably egotistic?'

'Not more than usual.'

'I don't want to have to look back at my life as if it was a jigsaw puzzle with one piece of the pattern – the most important piece – always missing. I know what the piece is, but other people don't, and it isn't enough to see the jig-saw oneself, one wants other people to see it, after a fashion, anyhow. There are a few people who do jig-saws for their own private satisfaction, but most of us like a witness to our cleverness.'

'I've never seen you do a jig-saw puzzle,' Denys said.

'No, I haven't the patience, and visually I haven't much sense of shape. But novels are a sort of jig-saw puzzle.'

'And memoirs, too, it seems.'

'Well, mine would be. Without the clue it wouldn't

make sense, it would be the picture of a quiet, very quiet life, but it would be misleading.'

'And you don't want to mislead people?'

'I'd rather not,' said Richard, fretful at his thoughts. 'If they want to know about me, I'd rather they knew the truth. They mustn't know it, that's the difficulty.'

'They mustn't know it?'

'On no account. If I tell you, I won't bind you to secrecy, it isn't necessary, but nobody must ever, ever know.'

'Then why tell me, if I'm not to put it in the book?'

'For two reasons. One is that I don't like the idea of dying with a secret. And the other is that though you can't put it recognizably into the memoir, you can make its presence felt, just as you can describe the results of an accident without describing the accident itself. You can show me as the product of the experience.'

'That's how I should show you, because that's how I know you.'

'Yes, but you don't know the context.'

'When am I going to know?'

The older man stirred uneasily in his chair and his troubled gaze travelled round the cornice until it fell on Denys.

'It's now or never, I suppose,' he said.

'Why do you hesitate?'

'Partly because I'm afraid of boring you.'

'If I'm bored, I'll put my hand up.'

'And partly because I don't want to burden you with

my private affairs. For they are a burden. They are like parasites that batten on their host and then try to gnaw their way out.'

'What unpleasant images you use. Shall I be harbouring a sort of tape-worm?'

'A very long one. And another thing is, I don't want to appear to you in a bad light. You've always looked up to me till now – not in the physical sense of course—'

'Or in the moral sense.'

'Perhaps not,' said the older man. 'But in a general way you respect me, don't you?'

'Of course I do,' said Denys.

'Well, after this you may find you can't. That would be a blow for me and might upset our friendship. I should hate you to despise me.'

'Should you mind despising *me*?' said Denys.

Richard opened his eyes wide.

'Well, that would be a new experience.'

'And you don't expect to have any new experiences?'

'No,' said his employer. 'I shall be on the retired list in every sense.'

'Then will you still need a secretary? That's what I want to know.'

Richard smiled at him fondly.

'Yes, all the more.'

'Why all the more?'

'Because I shan't have the companionship of my work.'

Did a faint cloud cross the young man's brow? If so, Richard didn't notice it. He was absorbed in visions of the future, when, exercise-book and note-book laid aside, he would enjoy a series of intimate occasions like this one, but without the ordeal of confession hanging over him.

'We could travel,' he said.

'But will you be well enough?'

'I shall be well enough if you are there.'

Again Richard failed to notice the look of unease on the young man's face.

'It will be nice to know,' he went on, 'that we shan't have to *break off* for any reason at all, except, except . . .'

He didn't finish the sentence, nor did Denys finish it for him. Instead, Denys said, 'You won't find it too much of a strain, saying whatever you are going to say?'

'Well, if it proves to be, we've got the remedies ready. You know where they are, don't you?'

'On your dressing-table.'

'Yes, but if anything happens, you'll have to get a move on, as we used to say, none of that slow motion stuff, as though tomorrow would do.'

He glanced affectionately at his protégé.

'You aren't exactly in a hurry yourself,' retorted the young man. 'If you're so anxious to get this off your chest – cleanse the stuffed bosom of that perilous stuff—. Do you know, it's half an hour by the clock since you began to tease me with it? If you were an R.C. as no doubt you ought to be—'

'Why?'

'Because then you would have confessed this sin, whatever it is, long ago, and you wouldn't have kept your father confessor waiting either. He would have said, "Hurry up, my son, spit it out. I haven't got all day".'

'Very well then. But where shall I begin?'

'You are a novelist. You ought to know.'

Richard took one or two quick breaths, looked at the young man, looked away again, stretched his arms out in an ineffectual gesture, and then said, 'You can have another whisky if you like.'

'Not till you're under way,' Denys said inexorably.

'All right, here goes.' But several seconds passed before Richard began to speak, and then his voice was quite different from his usual voice. It sounded de-personalized, as if he was broadcasting to many people – or perhaps to none.

II

I was brought up to be a farmer – I'll tell you how it was.
My father was a Bank Manager at Fosdyke, a small
town in the Fens near Medehamstead, and besides being
a Bank Manager, he had an interest in a brick-works,
quite a small affair it was, and he regarded it at first, I
seem to remember, more as a hobby than as a source of
income. It just paid its way. Later, when I was of an age
to understand such things, he told me it brought in on
an average £500 a year which, with his salary, gave him
an income of nearly a thousand, which seemed to me a
great deal, and was a good deal, in those days. But the
brick-trade was extremely speculative – you could expect
one bad year in every three years, people said – and in
the bad years it brought in nothing at all and sometimes
made a loss. My father was anything but a gambler,
indeed he disapproved of it, being a Nonconformist and
a rationalist; but he had great confidence in his own
judgment, and though he wasn't by instinct a business
man, he brought to business the same steady enthusiasm
he had for games. He wasn't a natural games-player, but
he played cricket, tennis, golf and billiards better than
most men because he applied his mind to them, and it
was the same with business; he took it as seriously as he

took games. He took most things seriously, even humour to which, both in literature and life, he was much addicted. Edward Lear and Lewis Carroll were two of his favourites. It was odd that a man who had so little nonsense in his make-up, should take so much delight in nonsense; but, it explains, perhaps, his unswerving belief in the brick-works, which to some of his business friends, and to my mother's relations, seemed a very questionable aid to making a living. But he paid no attention to them; he was one of the most self-reliant, self-confident and self-contained men I have ever known.

My mother was just the opposite. She was always seeking advice. She could hardly cross the street without asking if it would be wise. Anyone who was ever recommended to her, a doctor or a dentist, a carpenter or a plumber, immediately enjoyed her regard; she valued other people's opinions far above her own. Especially men's opinions, and above all, my father's. Almost any man, as long as he was not a conspicuous failure, enjoyed her esteem. Not that she was unaware of a man's weaknesses, indeed she was quick to spot them, especially the quality of conceit. But even while she was making fun of them, in her shy, diffident way, it was plain that she regarded men as superior beings, before whose innate wisdom she must bow. There was nothing affected about her humility; she genuinely had a poor opinion of herself. But this she combined with an intense sex-solidarity. Helpless and weak as women were, they were also potential if not actual objects of male adoration. Men might pass their working or even their playing hours in pursuits which were far above her head, but the real object of their existence was to be in love with women. Any romantic story appealed to her; if there was the element of self-sacrifice in it, the appeal was increased; and if the self-sacrifice took the form of some worthy man (worthy he had to be) laying his all at a woman's feet, she could hardly restrain her tears. More than one man had wanted to marry her, and though they fell short of her vision of an ideal love (the ultimate realization of which she took for granted) their abasement before her was a fact infinitely precious to her – precious because it was a compliment to her whole sex, as well as to her. She was practical in many ways, especially in small ways – economies too passionate to incur the charge of meanness, the preservation of objects which might one day come in useful carried to an extreme so absurd as to be almost noble – but what she lived for was a supreme emotional gratification.

How far my father supplied this I don't know. In public, at least, he wasn't at all demonstrative. He didn't suffer fools gladly, he had an irritable tongue, and when my mother was foolish, she came in for the rough side of it. Sometimes she would come to me crying and say, 'Daddy has been cross with me', and I would try to comfort her and sometimes mingle my tears with hers. But young as I was, I realized that reason was generally on my father's side and realized, too, that my mother was only being temporarily and superficially upset. Perhaps she half welcomed these proofs of his mas-culine independence as exemplifying the god-like and unpredictable quality in him, while he was too much of a man to be lastingly or even seriously provoked by a woman's moods. Too much of a theorist, too. He had theories about almost everything, and no doubt the conduct of married life was one. My mother might sulk for several hours with a closed face and tight lips; but in the end she would forgive him; while he, not feeling the need of forgiving or forgiveness, for episodes at such a low level of importance, would regard her spasm of irrationality as over and the incident as closed. The deeper reaches of their relationship were unshaken; never, so far as I know, did they stray, even in thought, from each other, though my father was sensitive to a pretty or, as he would have called it, a handsome face, and when he saw one, would call my mother's attention to it. Being pretty herself, perhaps she did not mind.

She was indulgent to him as well as he to her. In those days, at least in our circle, the men were apt to rule the conversation. If they wanted to talk shop or air some single topic in which only they were interested, they did not care whether or not it might interest the rest of the company. My father could talk well and dispassion-ately on any subject; but if politics or golf held the field, he could get as heated as the next man and what seemed like hours would pass while this or that hole was being replayed, or this or that political measure being debated. My father was a Liberal; most of his friends, and my mother's two brothers, were Conservatives. Feeling ran high; voices were raised; violent quarrels seemed immi-nent. Listening I was often too frightened to be bored and my mother's face wore an anxious look; it seemed that they would never speak to each other again. Sometimes she would utter a faint protest, but I don't think she really minded; she thought that was the way men ought to behave. But when the storm was over, they always parted friends or nearly friends.

But I was a man too, or going to be, and inevitably some of her solicitude for my father was transferred to me. Jealousy is the earliest of the emotions to show itself, as well as the last. I don't think that either my father or I was consciously jealous of the other, for jealousy was not in my father's nature – he was too self-sufficient – and I was too much in awe of him to be jealous of him. One might as well have been jealous of one's mother's devotion to God – though doubtless some sons have been. But where I was concerned, my mother soon began to display unexpected firmness. I was a delicate child, and rightly, perhaps, my mother thought that Fosdyke was not a healthy place. One of the few points in which she strove to get her own way with my father was in the matter of health. He was both chesty and throaty, and though he himself didn't pay much attention to either of these conditions, she worried on his behalf, and would have liked to make a molly-coddle of him. She did succeed, to some extent, in making him health-conscious, and at her entreaty he would take to his bed, even if he thought it silly. But with me she took a stronger line. Like many children in those days, I was subject to croup. It is a disease that has now disappeared, even from the Encyclopedia. But it existed then and was very alarming, for it came on almost from one minute to another, with a spasm in the throat that was like choking. Later I came to recognize warning symptoms, but in some ways this only made matters worse, for I knew what was coming, and the doctor could do nothing to ward it off. I suspect that a good deal of my hypochondria and neurasthenia dates from the nervous strain of those attacks of croup – the choking, the ipecacuanha, the waiting to vomit, the partial relief, never as complete as I had hoped, when I did vomit, and then the next stage, which was hardly less frightening and disagreeable – bronchitis, with linseed poultices, back and front, liberally laced with mustard and encased in a thin film of oil-skin which left one's chest and back sore and red for days; while for weeks I had to wear a thick flannel chest-protector, diminishing in thickness as time went on, to avoid the risk of chill. I still have some of these chest flannels stored away, folded by my mother's careful hand. Losing her, I never felt so safe in the world again. I took it for granted she would save my life whatever happened, even at the expense of her own, just as I took it for granted that my father would be too much in command of any situation that arose to make such a sacrifice necessary. Her power came through him, ultimately. What a capacity for trust one had in those days!'

'And not now?' said Denys.

'No, now one trusts a few individuals, just as I trust you, because otherwise life would be impossible. But not humanity at large – how can one?'

'I don't come of a very trusting or trustworthy family,' said Denys. 'We were always out for what we could get, and expected other people to be too.'

'I know you were robber-barons, and ground the faces of the poor, but for me such people only existed in history books. No doubt my father came in contact with buccaneers of various sorts, but he kept them away from my mother and me, just as a breakwater keeps out the sea. I knew that behind the breakwater the waves foamed and heaved, just as they did in our picture of Grace Darling, but I knew they could never reach me. You can have no idea, Denys, of the feeling of security there was at that time; not only because I was a child and loved and protected, and lived among people to whom the worst thing that could happen was a spill in a dog-cart, or a neglected cold turning into bronchitis. And security was real to me despite the fact that my mother worried almost on principle, not only about my father and me, but about all her relations, of whom more anon. She thought that not to worry was the same as not to care. Not to care was the cardinal sin, a sin against love – the love which ruled her own life and – so she persuaded me – the life of the world outside. All my awareness of the outside world reached me coloured by her conviction that, thanks to love, nothing could go really wrong, or if it did, not wrong for long. Disaster, of which her own thoughts were full – indeed they cannoned from one anxiety to another – was something which could always be kept at bay provided one took sufficient trouble. And so with the world. The world of politics was much less real to her – and to me – than the world of personal relationships. But there, too, the rule of love was supreme. Happenings like the Boer War (my father was a Volunteer but he was also a pro-Boer, or nearly) were exceptions which had not much meaning for her, except the meaning that all would come right in time. But meanwhile one must be always on one's guard – and that was why she decided I must be a farmer.

Her father was a farmer in the Lincolnshire Fens – the Holland division of Lincolnshire – and we regularly went to his house for Christmas and for other visits too. St. Botolph's Lodge was fifteen miles or so from Fosdyke, a house by the roadside, larger, I came to realize, than our house and isolated – there were no houses of any size within a quarter of a mile. The nearest town, Rookland, was about two and a half miles away. When I was old enough I sometimes walked there, though we always drove back, sometimes in the light-cart (as the vehicle was called in which my grandfather went to visit his outlying farms), and on special occasions in the dogcart, a smarter equipage, and on more special occasions still in the wagonette, a black vehicle, horse-shoe shaped – with a door at the back, glass windows, and dark blue upholstery – it could hold seven, I think, at a pinch. Beside the driver was a box seat, which I was sometimes invited to occupy as a special treat. For me it was more a threat than a treat. I enjoyed it once I got there (I had to be helped up with the aid of two rather slippery footholds), but always had to overcome a certain reluctance, for in spite of the glory of the position, it brought the reality of danger nearer. In those days horses were constantly shying – with those of a nervous temperament, the mere sight of a strange gate-post was enough to set them off, then there might be violently accelerated motion or even a gallop, for a hundred yards or so, before the animal got back into its stride, and of course there was the remote risk that it might *run away*. This was one of the worst things that could happen, in my mother's view, just as stopping a runaway horse was the highest proof of courage that a man could show. Anyone who was known to have done it was a hero to her; I can still hear the awe in her voice when she said of someone, 'He once stopped a runaway horse'. Courage was a quality she rated very highly, believing she had none of it herself. 'I haven't the courage of a water-rat,' she would say, though why she singled out that creature for cowardice, I don't know. In fact she had plenty, even of physical courage, when it came to the point; but in prospect even the smallest ordeal, especially the ordeal of a public appearance, terrified her. She could never bring herself to mount a platform. Whereas my father was never happier than when on his feet, addressing an audience on almost any subject whatsoever. He was as naturally a public figure as she was a private one.

Driving in the Fens was, in fact, a more dangerous experience than driving in other parts of the country, for every road, or nearly every road, was bordered by a dyke – one of the myriad waterways that drain the Fens. Water-courses they were not, for perceptibly, at any rate, there was no more movement in the water than there was gradient on the road; the only hills the fenman knew were artificial slopes that led to bridges. Between the road and its attendant dykes the grass verges often narrowed, leaving little room for error on the driver's or the horse's part; and 'to get into the dyke' was an experience that was justly dreaded. It meant being overturned and perhaps drowned as well. Such an eventuality was never quite absent from my mind as I sat beside the coachman on the wagonette, whereas in the snug, stuffy interior, cushioned and padded, with windows which one needn't look out of if one didn't want to, the danger seemed negligible.

My grandfather had several farms besides the home farm around his house. The 'Meadows' was one, 'Griffin Fen' another, 'Black Bank' another, 'Jordan's Plot' another; they lay in different directions – the furthest about five miles away. We visited them almost daily, and as a child I enjoyed these expeditions very much. I sat like a parcel beside my grandfather, in a state of dreamy contentment. What we talked about I don't remember; he was a man of few words, as I am.'

'I shouldn't say that,' interrupted Denys.

'Why, when have you ever known me talk much?'

Denys brought his wrist-watch slowly up into his line of vision. 'You haven't drawn breath for about twenty minutes.'

'Really?' Richard knit his brows. 'Am I being a bore?' He didn't give Denys time to answer, and went on, 'But I shall draw breath presently, quite a lot of breath, and perhaps ask you to help me out . . . with verbal oxygen. You see, this is the easy part . . . where was I?'

'You had just said you were a man of few words, like your grandfather, and I challenged you.'

'Oh, yes. I suppose I get my taciturnity (don't laugh) from him. He didn't talk much, but if anything amused him he laughed uncontrollably. He had a beard, as people had in those days—'

'So they have now. I might grow one, if you'd let me.'

'Am I such a tyrant? Now, young men wear them to emphasize their youth. Then, they denoted age. Old age was almost a profession, men and women entered it as if it was a cloister. If I wore a beard—'

'Thank goodness, you don't.'

'– You might respect me more.'

'I couldn't.'

'You could, or you wouldn't interrupt me. What I was trying to say was that when my grandfather laughed, it was the only time he looked at all like Falstaff. He shook like a jelly. But he was a most abstemious man, and brought up a Nonconformist, as we all were.'

'I never knew that.'

'No, it's one of the things I haven't told you. You'll learn quite a lot, if you will only listen. My grandfather didn't have much to laugh at. He was a widower, at a time when that meant more than it does now—'

'Did it make people happier then than it does now?'

'No, idiot, it made them more unhappy. You wouldn't understand, because you have no feelings. I wish I could interest you in my grandfather.'

'Oh, but you do.'

'Well then, he had these farms, but he was anything but well off. Of course at that time, your ancestors had seventeen or eighteen servants.'

'I can't remember, but I dare say my ancestors were a shady lot, with warders to look after them, not servants.'

'Oh nonsense, you're like everybody today, you want to think you are capable of enormous crimes. "There but for the grace of God go I." Whereas the average person, little as he or she would like it to be known, is no more capable of an enormous crime than of an enormous virtue.'

'Speak for yourself, Richard.'

'I was speaking for myself.' A note of uncertainty crept into Richard's voice. 'When I said crime, I didn't mean sin. There is a difference, isn't there? No doubt we are all capable of sins. I'm not really a weak character, but my nerves aren't good, and sometimes I give in to them. But I got side-tracked by the servant-question, which wasn't acute then, as it is now. With my grandfather it wasn't a status-symbol, still less a sign of wealth, to have a certain number of dependants. For a man in his position they were necessities, not luxuries. The farm and the farm-house couldn't do without them. It was an inelastic, semi-feudal system; he *had* to live in that way, it didn't mean that he was well off. In those days farmers weren't. Even in South Lincolnshire they could only just make both ends meet. My grandfather had two sons, Uncle Austin and Uncle Hal, both brought up to be farmers, and they used to call on us at Medehamstead, on market-days when we had moved from Fosdyke—'

'Oh, so you moved from Fosdyke?'

'Yes, because my mother insisted. The place, she said, was an open drain and responsible for my father's sore throats. I think the sanitary arrangements at Fosdyke were very rudimentary. The refuse one saw in the streets – in the gutters, I mean, and even on the pavements! You could see diphtheria rising from them in a mist. But what I was trying to say—'

'Please, *please* go on.'

'– was that my grandfather didn't have an easy time. He had a groom, a shepherd, a carpenter, a gardener, two servants in the house, a charwoman called Mrs. Bywell, whose face I can still remember, turning up grinning and toothless from the floor she was scrubbing, a foreman at each farm, I suppose, farm labourers, horse-keepers and horses. It all suggests a large tied-up capital, but I can assure you, Denys, that he wasn't *well off*. If he, or anyone related to him, had been financially secure, my story would lose whatever point it has. What he, and Uncle Austin after him, did for me, and us, was done at great personal sacrifice, in every way. It was said that farmers paid no Income Tax because they didn't keep books – but what was Income Tax then? In my grandfather's district (don't flinch at the word grandfather, I shall often be using it) several farmers had *failed*, and if you knew what that meant, in those days, you would realize what the farmers were up against. *Failure*. It meant much more than the ordinary failure which each of us now dreads – not being able to fulfil ourselves, or our promise, or the hopes that well-wishers entertain for us. It meant, besides financial ruin, a stigma that you can't even conceive – it meant, for a great many people, *suicide*, literally. They couldn't face the shame of it, for themselves or their relations. My mother was nothing if not economical; when a visitor came, she had a card pinned to his or her table-napkin, with the name on it, so that if the visitor came again, it could be used without distaste. A friend of my father's, a frequent visitor and a clean feeder, declared he had counted thirty-two pinpricks in his card. But my father would sometimes say to her, "You'll have us in the bankruptcy court if you go on like this!" – referring to some other extravagance than the reckless washing of table-napkins. Of course I knew nothing of it, but during those early years when we paid periodic visits to my grandfather, the threat of "failure" was imminent. My father used to ask my farmer-uncles (he never asked my grandfather) "How's agriculture?" in a bantering tone. They didn't reply, as well they might have, "How's banking?" for they, like most people, were a little in awe of him. But even I could see they didn't like it. My mother was too much aware of other people's feelings; she couldn't bear to hurt them. She would say, "If you ask so and so *very nicely*" (to do something he or she could never want to do), "it will be all right". Whereas he, without wanting to hurt anyone's feelings, was too little aware of them; he thought that people should be told what they ought to know, whether it was the way to knock in a nail or to address a golf-ball, or to conduct their business, or their lives in general; and if they didn't take his advice, it was their look-out. But where had I got to?'

'You were still harping on your grandfather.'

'Oh yes, and my farming expeditions with him. Besides laughing himself, he liked to make *me* laugh. As I told you, the drains and dykes in the Fens moved in slow motion, if they moved at all. You could hardly see the water for the blanket of greenish-yellow scum that grew on it – cott, we called it. A strong wind would sometimes curdle it and pile it up in ridges. But there was one break in the water-torpor. On the road to Rookland from St. Botolph's Lodge, St. Botolph's Drain boasted a tributary. This tributary was nearly always dammed up by a sluice, or slacker as we called it; a black wooden obstruction, worked by a winch, and evil-looking, like a guillotine, which held the water in. But sometimes in wet weather it was raised, letting the imprisoned water gush out into the drain – a foaming waterfall perhaps two feet high. This rare spectacle always excited me; and when my grandfather saw it he would laugh uncontrollably and say, "The mighty Niagara!" Without this comment, the experience would have been incomplete. I don't know why it stirred me so profoundly to look forward to, to feel, and to look back on; I suppose it was the proof that even in the Fens Nature could have its fling.'

A shadow darkened Richard's face. He shrugged his shoulders and went on, 'What I most enjoyed about those drives was the sense of absolute irresponsibility. At home in Fosdyke even at the age of five, I was aware of things I must and must not do. My life was confined by prohibitions and inhibitions like the water in a Fen drain; and if I flowed faster than it did, it wasn't so much with my own momentum, my nature finding its own level, as with the stimulus which, in their different ways, my father and my mother gave me. They were such strong characters and so full of aspirations for me, that from an early age I was much more aware of what they wanted than of what I wanted. Their wishes were my commands and my great wish was to please them, or at any rate not to displease them. I lived in dread of doing wrong and with no great hope of doing right. Even now I feel I ought to ask permission before I do the simplest thing, though there is no one left to ask. If I hadn't been an only child (I think it was my mother's supposedly delicate health that made me that) or if I had seen more of other children, I should have known better what sort of person I was, and felt the same desire to be myself that other children have. As it was, I took the line of least resistance, and found my satisfaction in being what they wanted me to be. I was a careful and a care-full child, precociously conscious of moral issues, of which to keep myself in health was the most pressing, for if I fell ill my mother worried terribly, and she held her worry over me like blackmail. She would have done so to my father, only he, having a life outside our home, and a man's view of such matters, didn't feel the same obligation to keep her from worrying.

So when I went out with my grandfather and saw him sometimes shake with laughter, as if no such thing as care existed, I was very happy – and happy too because, during those drives, nothing whatever was expected of me. Sometimes my grandfather would invite me to drive, and put the reins in my hand, with his hand over it; and though I would gladly have been excused this privilege, I didn't mind it, because nothing depended on it. He didn't mind if I drove it badly, nor was he specially pleased if I drove well – it was just a pastime. And when we reached Green Bank or the Hundreds, or wherever it might be, nothing was expected of me either. Sometimes I stayed in the light-cart (with the horse safely tied up), sometimes I accompanied my grandfather during his tour of inspection among the half derelict farm-buildings. I didn't pay much attention to what he said to the foreman or the horse-keeper, I followed my own thoughts, to which these surroundings made an agreeable setting.

We went to St. Botolph's Lodge two or three times a year, I think; but it is Christmas there that I remember best, just as I remember best the landscape frost-bound, with the tussocks of coarse grass that lined the dyke-sides, mop-heads white and stiff and bowed with their coating of rime, and the roads which normally had a muddy surface, brittle and crackling and striking sparks from horses' hoofs. Or under snow, or in a thaw, with pools of blue-black water cupped in the whiteness. And at Christmas there was always a chance that my Aunt Carrie would be there.

III

My mother had three sisters, my pretty, capable,
affectionate, society-loving Aunt Ettie, my crabbed,
unpredictable Aunt Ada, who was sometimes great fun
and sometimes just the reverse, and my Aunt Carrie.
Aunt Carrie was the youngest; she was, I think, fifteen
years younger than my mother, and only about eight
years older than me though I was hazy about ages in
those days, and only certain of my own, because strangers so often asked me what it was. When I first became
aware of her, she was still at school – the same school
they had all been at, somewhere in the West of England. She was diffident and shy and didn't talk much;
she was tall and slim, with a small, thin face, a complexion more brown than pink, a nose that turned up a
little, hazel eyes and soft, fine dark hair that was fluffed
out, I seem to remember, over her forehead. Perhaps
I mix up her earlier with her later appearance, for I
wasn't an observant child, being absorbed in my own
thoughts. But I remember her movements, which were
the lightest that the action required. When her arms
came into play she pressed her elbows against her sides,
as if she was covering her chest up, almost as a boxer
might – though she was less like a boxer than any

34

human being I have ever known. She rarely stretched her arms out, she would rather get up and fetch anything she wanted. All her movements were soft and gentle, they seemed scarcely to displace the air; and she herself seemed to take up even less room than her physical envelope required.

Gradually and almost insensibly I learned that my Aunt Carrie was the apple of my mother's eye, that there never had been and never again could be such a paragon – so gifted, so full of feeling, so precious and so unselfish. Above all, so unselfish. Boys are dreamier than girls and I was dreamy, even for a boy; in the cloud of unknowing in which I lived I can't remember how this legend of my aunt's perfection grew up. It seemed to have been always there. My mother was the chief author of it, but it was accepted by all the members of the family and even by my father, who always addressed Aunt Carrie with a kind of deference, even when she was little more than a girl. The beauty of her nature (not her physical beauty, for no one, not even my mother, pretended she was beautiful) was an article of faith with us. I remember how shocked, almost stupefied I was when Aunt Ada, in one of her vinegary moods (she often liked to say something to hurt me) declared that everybody was selfish, more or less; and when I said 'But Aunt Carrie isn't!' she replied, 'Oh yes, she is!' It seemed like blasphemy, but it didn't shake my faith.

If my Aunt Carrie was aware of the esteem in which we held her, she never showed it, but she must have been, for intelligence was not the least of her qualities. But either her knowledge of it, or the thing itself, gave her a kind of apartness, which affected one even physically, as if it was a numinous exhalation, an almost visible coating of specially purified air, that surrounded her and made her a little unapproachable. You couldn't speak to her without first asking yourself whether the remark would be *all right* – whether it would reflect the proper degree of sensibility, whether it would be in tune with her feeling of the moment, whether it would come up to standard – the standard she set herself, for we never thought of her as setting a standard for anyone else. Even her name had to be spoken in a special way, with something of reverence and awe, to hallow the affection. 'Why do we wrap this gentlewoman in our more rawer breath?'

More than anyone, more, I suspect, than I or my father, did my Aunt Carrie incarnate for my mother the doctrine of love – and if she had had to sacrifice any two of us, it was we who would have gone first. And with love, as always in my mother's case, went anxiety. Was Carrie all right, was she working too hard, was she getting the proper kind of food? Was she looking thinner, paler? None of this worry did my mother try to conceal; it puckered her pretty face into a score of wrinkles – and that, I now think, was one reason why Aunt Carrie's visits were so infrequent, why at times she stayed on at school during the holidays (for she was as beloved by the headmistress and her sister as she was by us), on the pretext of having to practise –

for among her many accomplishments, the piano was her chief study. The burden of affection which she was fated to bear was too much for her. Once or twice she came to stay with us in Fosdyke, and I can still remember the fuss and strain that preceded her visits – how everything had to be just so, every eventuality prepared for – not only such possible disasters as that she or my father or I might fall ill, or that we might all fall ill together, but more unlikely and imponderable calamities, affecting the 'atmosphere'. The wrong people might be asked, the right people not come, and there was always the lurking dread (to which my mother sometimes gave voice) that my father's controversial manner might be too forcible for Aunt Carrie. 'You know, my darling, you don't always realize how blunt you are. You're so *Yorkshire*! In Yorkshire people do talk to each other in that way – it isn't that they don't respect each other's feelings, but they are much more outspoken, they say whatever comes into their heads! But here we're *not* like that. People's feelings are hurt, perhaps too easily hurt, when you tell them what you think of them – or not of *them*, but of their views. And you see, Carrie is so *delicate*, the slightest disagreement upsets her – she feels so much for other people and so much more *than* other people, that she can't help feeling for herself. She would *hate* you to think she did, for that would hurt *your* feelings – but do *try*, my darling, when you are talking to her, *not* to give her the idea that *her* ideas are silly, just because they don't happen to agree with yours!'

My father would promise, and add, irritably, 'You don't do Carrie justice, Chick,' (he sometimes called my mother Chick, or Chicken, though her real name was Mary). 'She isn't such a fool as to take offence just because one differs from her. How is she, or anyone else, to *learn* if they do that?' My father thought one should always be learning.

But he didn't always keep his promise, because my aunt would not let some of his statements go unchallenged. She was much better able to look after herself in argument than my mother, who thought that everyone must go down before my father like a nine-pin, believed; but she did get excited and worked up. A spot of red appeared on her cheek bones, the fingers that twitched and smoothed the sleeve at her wrist showed increasing agitation; under the black lace of her lilac bodice (I think of her as wearing those colours) her breath came quickly. My father was a Radical; my aunt was a Conservative. Most farmers were Conservatives in those days, and being very loyal to her relations, she felt, I think, that my father's remarks were somehow aimed at them (as perhaps they were), whereas he, being a theorist in all things – even the clothes he wore so successfully and so long were designed to fit a sartorial theory as well as himself – he had no personal stake in the discussion and didn't see how anybody could have.

My mother cared nothing about politics and regarded them simply as an obstacle to harmonious personal relationships, as I think I did, too, in those days, for I can't remember what my father and my aunt disagreed about – only that every now and then they disagreed, a fact which made me as uneasy as it made my mother. Together we would watch the contestants with anxious eyes, as the tide of battle flowed this way and that, my father enjoying it all greatly, and my aunt half enjoying it too – the excitement of it. 'I will say this for Carrie,' he would say afterwards, 'she argues just like a man, and better than a great many men.' 'But she isn't a man, my darling, she's a woman, or soon will be.' 'What difference on earth does that make?' 'You can't treat a woman the same way as you would a man.' 'I don't see why not.' 'Besides, she's so *delicate* . . .'

But I'm going too far ahead. Aunt Carrie wasn't a woman yet at the time I was telling you about. She was still a girl, I suppose, but the peculiar quality she had – of goodness, you might call it – was always hers, and transcended age – it was a mark of personality. If she didn't often come to us at Fosdyke, it may have been as I told you, because of my mother's anxiety for her, and my father's argumentativeness – such a pity, for they both meant well, and looking back, I feel that every moment not spent with her, if she was there to spend it with, was a moment wasted . . . But it was at St. Botolph's at Christmas, that one had the best chance of seeing her . . . I hope I haven't made her sound a bore?'

'Good gracious, Richard, no! More bored against than boring, I should say.'

Richard frowned.

'No, I don't think she was bored – not then, at any rate. She used to write all of us the most wonderful

39

letters – even me, when I was of an age to read her rather difficult handwriting. The speed it travelled at! She didn't write to us in rotation, for safety's sake, to keep away the green-eyed monster, but when a letter seemed to be due, a letter came. The letters she wrote at Christmas, as substitutes for her presence, if she didn't come, were the best of all. Each of us was made to feel that he or she was the reason why Aunt Carrie was so sad to miss the family reunion; not a detail of our activities escaped her, or was not transcended by her interest in it. In a way she was more present in her letters than she was in the flesh; she could say to one person things she was shy of saying in the family circle. "Carrie writes a very good letter," my father would concede. "Not a very good hand, though. She doesn't distinguish enough between the up-strokes and the down-strokes. She hasn't been properly taught." This was rather much coming from my father who could, for business purposes, write copper-plate, but whose ordinary handwriting, though pretty, was notoriously illegible. But it was part of his character not to notice in himself the faults he imputed to others. His impersonality was his strength and his limitation. He did most things well (except, as my mother's relations sometimes said, driving a horse), but it was the theory, the way to do it, that really interested him, and he didn't mind much if his own performance fell short of his ideal standard. Nor, if he was playing golf or billiards and his opponent beat him, did he hesitate to point out to the victor his mistakes of style and method.

I never knew anyone, as dedicated to games as he was, who minded so little whether he won or lost. As for luck, he neither rejoiced when it favoured him nor complained when it was against him, though in both cases he slightly resented it as an intrusion of the unpredictable and incalculable on scientific certainty. But to return to Aunt Carrie—'

'That paragon!' interrupted Denys.

'Well, in a way she was.'

'That holy one, that saint!'

'Now please don't take against her,' Richard said, 'just because I may have presented her in the wrong way. I shouldn't like the cause of truth to suffer by my patronage, as Sir Thomas Browne said. We were Nonconformists then and would never have dreamed of calling her holy, or a saint – such words were outside our vocabulary, though Uncle Austin called us, ironically, "The Holy Family". "Unselfish" was the operative word. "Aunt Carrie is so *unselfish*!" – but I won't repeat it if it offends you. Anyhow, to go back to her letters – do you mind the Tristram Shandy technique?'

'Not with you, of course, but I confess that in Sterne's case I find it intolerably tedious.'

'What a flatterer you are! I can assure you that before long I shall simply race ahead, you won't be able to follow me for all the elisions, gaps, fore-shortenings, and so on. Fade-out after fade-out. If I get as far as that.'

'You won't at this rate.'

'No,' Richard sighed. 'I keep forgetting the object of the exercise, trying to forget it, as one does on the way to the dentist . . . or a funeral. I'm giving you this build-up of Aunt Carrie partly because if I'd listened to her, I shouldn't have . . .'

Richard stopped again. If it's difficult at this distance, he thought, what will it be like when it gets nearer? He went on:

'I still have a great many of her letters – all, I think, that she wrote me. When she didn't come for Christmas at St. Botolph's, we all got one, as I told you, seldom on the same day, she spaced them out over the week we stayed there. At breakfast round the dumb-waiter we were all, except perhaps my father, who was too rationalistic to have much Christmas spirit, secretly expecting one. Whoever was favoured would, on leaving the table, say with a rather self-conscious, smug expression, "I've had a letter from Carrie." "Well, I had one yesterday. What did she say in yours?" "Well," said I, supposing I had been the fortunate recipient, "I couldn't tell you *everything* she said, of course. Some of it was private. She asked me how I was getting on." "And how are you getting on?" my Aunt Ada would ask with a little laugh. "Very well, thank you. And if I had won any prizes." "And have you?" "Yes, two, Aunt Ada. And what books I was reading, and could I play the Spring Song yet – by Mendelssohn, you know." "Well, that isn't very difficult." "She seemed to think it was, because of the grace-notes. She said she looked forward to hearing me play it." "You must play it to us." "Oh, I don't think I could. Besides, I didn't bring my music. I might play it to her." "Did she say anything about herself?"

42

At this I had to consult the letter, reddening as I did so, for even at this tender age I realized that it was not unselfish, not Aunt Carrie-like, to remember the part about me and forget the part about her.

'Never mind, Richard,' said Aunt Ada, enjoying my discomfiture. 'I don't suppose she said anything very special to you. I had a letter from her yesterday, and I dare say your mother will have one tomorrow. Nothing much will have happened to her in the meanwhile that she could tell to you but not to us.'

'I've finished breakfast now, Grandpa. Can I get down?'

'If you're going out, Richard,' my mother called out after me, 'don't forget to wrap up *very* well.'

And I escaped on to the crisp, crunching gravel in front of the house, and out through the white gate between the two sycamores, on to the ice-bound road, where I could see, across the fields, the distant shape of Rookland Abbey, its massive square tower and pepper-pot steeple, its great empty west window, which reminded me of a beggar holding on a stiff arm a coat with a hole in it – and, if the day was clear, the sublime half-circle of the dog-tooth arch.

IV

I wonder if Aunt Carrie had any inkling of the mild heart-burning that her letters, no less than her presence, caused her many devotees (for, as I told you, she had them outside the charmed circle of her family). Was the effort of apportioning equal parts, fair shares of herself, to each of us, too much for her? Was all that solicitude and admiration and love easier to cope with from afar than by an *acte de présence*, which demanded not only the right words, but the right look, the right voice, the right smile, the right adjustment of interest as she turned her small, eager, attentive face from one of us to the other? Not to seem to favour one at the expense of the rest – not even my mother, the most fervent and exacting of her vocal adorers. And having to be our scape-goat in reverse, so to speak – bearing the burden not of our sins, for the 'holy family' was not specially conscious of having any – but of our ambitions and aspirations – the longing, which my mother and all her family possessed (my father's didn't) to shine in *some* sphere, to make itself known, to excel, to leave a mark! She must have felt that they had each staked a great deal in her, and what if she disappointed them? What if she disappointed their love for her, expressed (for they so outnumbered her) in more ways than she could count? And not least Aunt Ada's love, which, from her manner of showing it, might easily have been mistaken for another feeling? Have you ever fled from any one's affection, Denys?'

'No, sir, or I shouldn't still be with you.'

'Oh, come! You're twenty-eight now, and you have only been with me three years. Many people must have liked you – did no one ever like you too much?'

'I must have notice of that question,' said Denys, blowing a smoke ring.

'Well, I give you notice now, for in a few minutes we shall have dinner, and then you must do all the talking. I've been very selfish. My Aunt Carrie—'

'Oh do tell me more about her. I can never hear enough.'

'Nasty, sarcastic fellow, all I meant was that she would not have held the floor as I have. She let other people talk. She wasn't present, I'm glad to say, that last Christmas at St. Botolph's. All the rest of us were – my father, my mother, my uncle Austin with the wife he had just married, my uncle Hal, my aunts Ada and Ettie, and of course my grandfather. Well, we had just finished our Christmas dinner, or supper, or whatever we called it, and were still sitting round the table, when Grandpa had one of those laughing fits I told you about (I can't remember what the joke was). As usual, he was convulsed and as usual we joined in, for his mirth was most infectious, and we waited for the paroxysm to pass. But it didn't. He had swallowed a crumb or something, that

45

went the wrong way, and he began to choke. I remember seeing him get up from his chair and stagger towards the fireplace and then there was a heavy thud, and he had disappeared. I think I pushed my chair back, but I didn't get up. My father and my uncles did and they bent over him: I couldn't see him, the table was between us, but I could see their arched backs and groping arms and hear a heavy snoring sound which must have been his breathing. The room was lit only by a copper oil-lamp that hung above the table, and by the flickering fire-light: it was half dark, by today's standards. "We'd better go into the drawing-room," said my new aunt Esther, Uncle Austin's wife. "You lead the way, Richard." I remember being surprised that she asked me to go first, but I went and held the door open for the ladies, as I had been taught to do. "We'll follow you," Aunt Esther said, and for a minute or two I stood in the drawing-room, quite alone, except for my reflection in the convex mirror with the eagle over it, in the opposite left-hand corner; there was a green-shaded reading lamp by the piano, for we were going to have songs afterwards. I was more excited than frightened, and half enjoyed my ignorance of what had happened and didn't want my imaginings disproved or confirmed. Crisis – what a stimulus it is! And then my mother and my aunts came in, with grave, controlled faces, such as I had never seen before on grown-ups; they didn't notice me much, but I heard Aunt Ada say, "Hal is going for the doctor." "Oh, isn't Hardy there?" my mother asked. Hardy was the groom. "No, he's with his family." "But Hal?" said my mother. Of her two brothers, Hal, the younger, was her favourite: she always liked people to be *young*. "Can he harness the horse, all by himself, in the *dark*?" she asked anxiously. Aunt Ada gave her teasing laugh. "If he can't, it's time he could," she said. "He's got the stable-lantern, and it's not the first time he's put the horse to, in the dark, by any means. And Minnie" (that was the mare's name) "knows her way into the shafts, even if he can't show her." "But will Dr. Butcher be *there*? He may have gone out for the evening, just as Hardy has." "Oh, Mary, you won't make things any better by worrying." "Someone has to worry, Ada," said my mother. The implied reproach silenced Aunt Ada for the moment; then we all noticed that Aunt Ettie was crying. "Dear Father! poor Father!" she kept whimpering, between her sobs. "Do you think he'll ever get well?" "Of course he will, of course he will," said Aunt Esther. "But isn't it Richard's bed-time now, Mary?" "I suppose it is," my mother said, looking at me doubtfully, "I suppose it is." Then her mind switched to another anxiety. "What will Carrie feel like when *she* knows?" "Perhaps there won't be anything for her to know," Aunt Esther said. "We shan't know anything until the doctor comes." There was a light scrunch of wheels on the gravel and the familiar sound of Minnie's hooves, clip-clopping to the gate. "Poor Minnie!" I thought, but didn't say, "having to turn out on Christmas night." "That's Hal!" said my mother, tragically. "I do hope he won't drive into the dyke." "Of course he won't, Mary," Aunt Ada said impatiently. "If it was Walter, now, you *might*

47

feel worried." (This allusion to my father's indifferent driving slightly stung me.) Aunt Ettie was still sobbing and scarcely raised her head when the latch of the gate clicked. "Will Hal have remembered to shut the gate?" my mother said. And then she, too, broke down. "What will Carrie say?" she sobbed. "What will Carrie say?" "Don't think me interfering," said my Aunt Esther who, like Aunt Ada, had remained dry-eyed, "but I'm sure it's time this young man went to bed."

Obediently I went to the door, but when I opened it, I couldn't go any further, for opposite was the closed door of the dining-room, through which I could still hear that dreadful laboured breathing . . . I felt I couldn't pass it and looked back for help. My mother came running. 'Of course, my darling,' she said, 'I'll go upstairs with you.' She took my hand and went with me down the tiled hall to the old, gate-legged table, on whose ample outward curve our brass bedroom-candle-sticks were arrayed, each with a match-box at its base, a tall glass cylinder to shield the flame, and flanking that, hooked to the ring which held it, an extinguisher with a long thin handle. The candles were all of different heights – my mother chose a medium one, took off the shade and lit it for me. I had done it countless times and could have lit it for myself, for I was twelve; but at that moment, I seemed to have forgotten all my acquired accomplishments.

I lay awake for what seemed hours, listening to the noises downstairs and trying to interpret what they meant – the voices, the footsteps, the doors opening and closing, and it was only when I heard the garden gate click, and the sound of hooves and wheels, announcing the arrival of Uncle Hal with the doctor, that I fell asleep.

My grandfather had had a stroke; that laugh was the last sound I ever heard him make. He lingered on for several years but there were no more Christmases at St. Botolph's. We went there sometimes, and my parents saw him, but I never did. I used to wish I had, for nothing is so terrible as one's imagination pictures it – every reality has an antiseptic touch, however much it smarts. I didn't realize how happy I had been at St. Botolph's until I was cut off from it – for I was cut off. Even when I went with my parents, it didn't seem the same. There was a door upstairs, my grandfather's door, which I hated passing, and this one door seemed to close the whole house against me.

V

'And now, my dear Denys, where shall we dine – here,
or downstairs in the restaurant, or shall we go out
somewhere?'

'Here, I think,' said Denys. 'It's so snug. Besides stone
walls have ears, but down below they have longer ears, and
outside in the great city their ears are quite gigantic. Not
that you've said anything that could offend the chastest
ear, but I think I know what's coming, and if I'm right—'

Richard gave him a quick look.

'I'd better order dinner,' he said, and went to the
telephone. 'Whitebait, Denys?'

'Whitebait is always nice.'

'And afterwards?'

'I think I could do with a steak – the reddest, juiciest
steak. Listening is such hard work – it takes it out of
you, specially when the narrator tries to induce sus-
pense by not coming to the point – even when one
knows what the point is going to be—'

'Steak is too heavy for me,' said Richard. 'You have
it, Denys, you have the constitution of an ox.'

'I beg your pardon?'

'I meant you're young and healthy, whereas I'm a
poor old creature, whom the doctors have given up.'

'They haven't give you up – they're always buzzing round you.'

'It comes to the same thing. I shall have chicken, boiled chicken with rice, not Maryland, which is what I should like. And then, Denys?'

'Oh, perhaps a pear flambée.'

'I'll watch you eating it. And then coffee, of course, but not for me.'

He telephoned the order and then said, 'If you've guessed what I'm going to say, there's no point in beating myself up to say it.'

'But isn't it obvious? You were in love with your Aunt Carrie, and then—'

'Oh no, you've got it all wrong. She had something to do with it, but—'

'Oh then, I'm quite at sea. Is it something very horrid, Richard? Ought I not to hear?'

'It will alter your opinion of me.'

'For the worse?'

'Yes, yes, for the worse. But am I still the same person I was then? Are we the products of our past? Are you, for instance?'

'I never knew it could be such fun,' said Denys, still cutting gobbets from his *saignant* steak, 'to talk about myself. Of course I had your example, but at school we weren't allowed to: the self was *quite* taboo. You never went to a proper school, did you, Richard? That's why you can talk about yourself so freely – I'm utterly inhibited.'

'It's true I only went to a grammar school, a day school,' Richard said. 'Even if we could have afforded a boarding-school, my mother didn't want me out of her sight. Yours didn't mind, I gather. Cast the bantling on the rocks . . . I never had a snobbish thought before I was sixteen; I've had a great many since. So you really are an Aspin of Aspin Castle? Why didn't you tell me so before?'

'I thought you knew. No, Emily Brontë didn't invent us; we were Border chieftains and have been in and out of the peerage for hundreds of years. Aspin Castle is a ruin, but it still belongs to us, as it did to "the first chief of Aspin grey, that haunts his feudal home". I've sat within that Norman door, just as Emily Brontë did.'

With mock-heroic feeling, Denys intoned the lines:

> ' "How do I love to hear the flow
> "Of Aspin's water murmuring low;
> "And hours long listen to the breeze
> "That sighs in Rockden's waving trees."

A very different kind of water from those Fen drains of yours.'

'Yes,' said Richard, suddenly putting down his knife and fork. 'The only one of our drains that ever murmured was the mighty Niagara . . . But Aspin Castle – that *does* take us back.'

'I wish it had been Aspirin Castle,' Denys said, 'it might have taken us forward. Don't idealize the Aspins, Richard. I've told you they were a terrible crew,

52

robber-barons, horse-thieves and cattle-rustlers. I'm only warning you. Genealogically they may have been interesting, but in no other way.'

'Is there a Lord Aspin now?'

'I believe the title is dormant between two co-heiresses. Sleeping between two heiresses! It sounds such an enviable position.'

'But it entitles you to be called Honourable.'

Denys laughed.

'Well, you address me as Honourable, and some of my other friends do, and no one has ever said I wasn't – in the genealogical sense, I mean. And it's useful in shops, for getting things on tick. But the position is so obscure that even the College of Heralds can't clarify it. Ours is one of those old baronies in which the title follows the female line and that always leads to trouble. Don't follow the female line, Richard, promise me you never will.'

Richard didn't answer.

'You never have, have you, Richard?' Denys persisted, 'except for that one youthful aberration, the Aunt Carrie red-herring. But that, you assure me, was only spiritual.'

Richard looked down at his plate, and clasped and unclasped his hands.

'Now eat up your chicken,' Denys admonished him, 'or else I shall think I've taken away your appetite. You see I'm nearly ready for my pear.'

'Tell me more about what happened to you,' Richard said, 'after you left Eton.'

'I didn't go to the University, as you know,' said Denys, 'there was no money and besides, I couldn't have got in, anyway. When my mother married again, she lost interest in my sisters and me, and my father never had much. When he married too, we were like orphans of the storm. But someone always came to our rescue and we were well dressed and used to go to parties. Miranda, my younger sister, got tired of loafing, as she called it, and got a job as a secretary – ultimately she married the man and isn't a bad wife to him, I believe. I couldn't do that.'

'You could and did become a secretary.'

'I meant I couldn't marry my employer. My elder sister continues to tread the primrose path – I never quite know where to find her. We don't see much of each other, and our parents, hardly ever. We understand each other, of course; we don't have to explain things, but there's a kind of restlessness in us; we haven't any defences against boredom, and action always seems the easiest way out. Some people put up with frustration, but there's always something one can do, I find, even in the Welfare State. You'd be surprised how much action there has been in my life. When people say they don't know which way to turn, I can't understand them, for I always know. It's people with an objective who get stuck. Life always offers you something, if you're adaptable. They say you can only get out of life what you put into it, but that's not true in my experience, and it's an insult to life. Life is outside you, not inside; it isn't your creation, and if you think it is, you may go mad. It offers something to you all the time. It offered me you, and if I'd said, "Oh, I'm not cut out to be a secretary, I should do better and earn more as a ship's steward" – I used to want to be – think what I should have missed!'

'And what I should have missed,' said Richard.

'Oh, I don't know. You advertised for a secretary and I turned up – I didn't want to be a secretary, and you turned up. I was part of the pattern of your life, a piece missing from your jig-saw. But I have no jig-saw, Richard; you are just something that life has offered me.'

'And supposing life takes me away?'

Denys had finished and put down his knife and fork.

'I'd rather not think about that.'

'But where is your pear?'

Richard went to the telephone and Denys heard him say:

'Could we have the pear, please?'

A moment later he put his hand over the mouthpiece and said to Denys:

'They say I never ordered it.'

'But you did – I heard you.'

Richard tried again, and again put his hand over the mouthpiece.

'They still swear I didn't.'

'Tell them they're liars – or let me, you don't want to get yourself worked up.'

Pink in the face and a little breathless, Richard handed the telephone to Denys. Words very different from his, uttered in a tone very different, scorched the mouthpiece.

'Really, Denys!'

'It's the only language they understand, Richard. You're much too considerate with them – you are with everyone.'

'But they *promised*.'

'Promises don't mean a thing nowadays.'

'Oh come, Denys! You keep yours.'

'Don't be too sure. Well,' he said to the incoming waiter, 'a nice time you've kept us.'

'A nice time, sir?' repeated the waiter, in a foreign accent, and obviously puzzled. 'I'm glad it was a nice time.'

Even Denys had no come-back to that.

The waiter put the pear on a saucepan, lit the methylated spirit in the ornate little stove, and bent over it lovingly. Presently he began to ladle a liqueur on the glistening, sizzling pear. For a time it resisted combustion, then all at once there was a soft explosion and a towering flame shot up, golden at the peak, violet where it licked and undulated round the base of the pear, as if longing to eat it. Their eyes drawn to the flame, Richard and Denys turned round to watch.

'Phoenix and the turtle fled
In a mutual flame from hence!'

said Richard. 'Such a beautiful idea, but it doesn't always work out like that. It didn't with me, and it won't again. The one shall be taken, and the other left.'

A moment of constraint fell on them, and Denys hesitated before attacking his pear.

'Which of us is the turtle?' he asked, casually.

'Oh I am, this time.'

'Was there another conflagration, when you were the phoenix?'

'Yes, I suppose so.'

'Are you going to tell me?'

'Yes, but first tell me more about yourself. You haven't been very forthcoming.'

'Oh, I've been a rolling stone, you know. Yours is the first job I've ever held down, or wanted to hold down.'

'You've never wanted to get married?'

'Oh no, I've had affairs, of course. I grew up very quickly after I left school. School tends to keep you back. I was always looking forward to the next thing, in love as well as in life. You've always lived intensively, burrowing into yourself. I'm just the opposite: try everything once. I might even have tried marriage, if I'd had the money. There was money in our family – money's easier to come by if there's a title or two knocking about – but it never came my way. In between times I sometimes behaved as if I was well-off – I knew the right places to go to, and how to dress and talk. People quite liked me – I used to be in this or that set, I can drink a good deal without showing it too much, and I have very good health, as you know. But friendship hasn't meant a lot to me – I never minded saying good-bye – I rather looked forward to it. Rootless, that's what I was.'

'And now?' asked Richard, who had been following his protégé's recital with mixed feelings.

'Oh, now I'm rooted here, and do you know, Richard, I quite like it. I don't only mean that I like *you*, but I like what I never thought I *could* like – belonging somewhere. I like it when the porters recognize me and so on. I couldn't stand it once – that feeling of being a perennial growth – always to be found in the same flower-bed – not that I ever was, but just the idea of it revolted me. Now I rather like being a tool of the Establishment, and eating *poire flambée*, like any other tool.'

During this speech, Richard's face brightened considerably.

'Well, you must tell me,' he said, 'if it should grow irksome, and then I'll arrange for you to have a completely different kind of life, *mouvementée, accidentée*, altogether unlike the kind of life we lead. Only I'm afraid I shan't be able to share it with you.'

'Oh, in that case,' said Denys, scooping up from his plate all that was left – the pear-juice, laced with brandy and Curaçao – 'I shouldn't consider it. Oh no, Richard, as long as you stay put, I shall stay. Unless what you are going to tell me horrifies me so much that I shall feel I ought not to be associated, even financially, with such a man.'

The waiter came in, this time without being summoned. All smiles and solicitude, he asked if the gentlemen would be taking coffee. 'Pistols for two and coffee for one,' said Richard, adding, 'and that one isn't me. You know where the brandy is, Denys. Get yourself some, and leave a little for me, just in case of – just in case of—'

'An emergency,' Denys finished for him. 'But we don't expect one, do we? And besides, we have three pills – where are they, by the way?'

'In the gold snuff-box on the chimney-piece.'

'Ought you to leave something as valuable as that lying about?'

'Oh I don't know. It gilds the pills.'

The waiter wheeled away the dinner-wagon, and the room, having little character of its own, quickly changed its function, became a sitting-room again, and then, as Richard's voice rose and fell with more urgency than before, into something between a consulting-room and a confessional.

VI

'Where had I got to, Denys?'

'Your grandfather had had a stroke, which forbade further Yuletide celebrations at St. Botolph's. You went there with your parents but were not allowed to see him. I can't think why not, because you wouldn't have over-excited him.'

'Thank you, Denys.'

'You deliberately misunderstand me, Richard.'

'It wasn't on his account that my mother didn't want me to see him,' said Richard patiently, 'it was on *mine*. She thought the shock—'

'Ah yes, you were already liable to shock, poor Richard. Your Aunt Carrie—'

'You speak of her as if she was an illness.'

'I can't help being jealous of her, can I?'

'Yes, you can. But what had happened to her, when I left off?'

'Nothing had happened to her. Nothing ever could happen. She was still being adored by your mother, yourself, and the rest of her family, by your father with reservations, and apparently by quite a number of other people. You weren't sure how far she reciprocated these attachments. It's clear to me that she was an escapist, she shirked the family reunions, and so wasn't present when your grandfather laughed himself into a stroke . . . go on from there.'

'Just because you had no family life of your own,' said Richard, 'doesn't entitle you to make fun of mine. Aunt Carrie never shirked anything . . . But from that time on, I didn't see much of her. She was working in London at the Royal College of Music, and I was working at the Grammar School at Medehamstead – I wore a dark red cap with a white crest on it, the cross-keys of St. Peter, of which I was very proud. I wasn't much good at games – not that I didn't like them, but my mother told me I must spare myself all unnecessary exertion, so I didn't go all out, if you see what I mean.'

'That can't have made you very popular.'

'In those days games weren't organized as they are now, certainly at a day school they were not. And the other boys didn't really mind you working; they just thought it eccentric. People were still allowed to be eccentric, even boys were. Mother didn't mind me working either, really; she thought there was less chance of catching cold indoors at a desk than outside in a field. She didn't like me to sit up doing my home-work: "You'll strain your eyes," she said. "You ought to be holding the book there," indicating a point about ten inches from my face, "not there." But I didn't take long over my home-work, because my father helped me with it. He didn't always approve of the way they taught me, but he was a reasonable man, and would say, "Oh well, if they like it that way – but it seems silly to me." He was good at most things, especially maths and drawing, the subjects I was weakest at. He couldn't play the piano, though, which all my mother's relations could, even Uncle Hal, and he couldn't sing in tune, at least she said so. She was convinced of his superiority in almost every accomplishment, but she liked to keep one or two things to tease him about, and singing was one. So I practised the piano without his supervision, and once a week I had special lessons from the organist of Medehamstead Cathedral – a very irritable man, who, when I played too many wrong notes, would fling the window up and lean out, breathing deeply . . . But why am I telling you all this? In most ways I was quite a normal boy, and had friends who came to the house and to whose houses I went, but I didn't see many girls, hardly any, in fact: I don't think boys did see so much of them in those days: I was far more frightened of going to a children's party than of going to school, or even to the dentist. Social entertaining didn't enter much into my mother's scheme of things. She was shy with strangers and acquaintances and saw everything in grades of obligation – as to some extent, my father did, but he was better than she was at making his sense of obligation coincide with what he wanted. Until the end of his life he felt an obligation towards games, whereas she gradually lost hers for hill-climbing and botany – though at the name of a flower, or a hill in the Lake District, her eyes would brighten and her voice tremble with excitement. Dear Mother.'

'I never heard you say that before,' said Denys.

'Perhaps not, but I mean it – and please remember that I mean it, Denys, in case I say anything that sounds critical of her. She wanted the best for everyone she loved, and she wanted what was best for them, too. She didn't distinguish between the two – just as she didn't ask herself what love consisted in. It was an emotion and an idea, and it was paramount with her. It was natural to her to feel pride in the beloved; she felt a mounting pride in my success at school. Scholastically, I did go from strength to strength, Denys – it wasn't a big school and I dare say the competition wasn't very keen, but I carried all before me – they even spoke of my getting a scholarship at Oxford – until that summer, when I was seventeen, and got a cough.'

Richard paused and, as though from association of ideas, gave a slight cough himself.

'It came on for no reason we could think of – not a neglected cold, for Mother never would have neglected a cold if I'd had one, or if my father had. No amount of post-mortems – wet feet, sitting in a draught, getting hot and failing to change – accounted for my cough. It was just there, and didn't go away – on the contrary, it got worse.

Whatever it was my mother worried over it – worried to the extent of trying to show me she wasn't worrying. When I coughed, she forced her face to look expressionless; she made no comment; she talked of something else. But her own mother had died of consumption; she knew my father and I were chesty; gradually the idea that I was going the way her mother went got hold of her, as I could tell by her shut face and lack of response to all the little things she used to respond to. So it didn't surprise me when, towards the end of term, my father took me aside and said, 'Richard, I'm afraid your mother is worrying about you.' 'I know, Daddy,' I said unhappily, 'but I can't help it. I've told her over and over again, I don't *feel* ill.'

Short of some great calamity, an illness, my mother's worrying was the worst thing that could happen.

'I know,' he said, 'and I don't believe it's anything – you've been working hard, and growing fast, and you're a bit run down, that's all. I often used to have a cough at your age, but I took more exercise than you do, and so I shook it off. Now would you be very disappointed if—'

My father seldom hesitated. With him to think was to speak – it was the Yorkshireman in him, that my mother sometimes complained of. So I dreaded what was coming.

'Would you be very disappointed if you left school for a time?'

'Left school, Daddy?' I said. 'But why?' 'Because your mother wants you to, for one thing.' 'Why does she want me to?' 'Because you've got this cough. She thinks you ought to lead an open-air life.'

An open-air life! I don't know what picture the phrase conjured up: ice and snow, and mountain-slopes, I fancy, with here and there a chalet perched among the pine trees. Something that was utterly alien to me, the very negation of the life I knew.

'Oh *no!*' I cried. 'Now don't say "no",' my father answered irritably, and though I knew his irritability was an expression of his own unease, his dislike of saying something he didn't want to – it always rattled me. 'Don't say no,' he repeated. 'It's silly to say "no" until you've heard what you're saying "no" to. It wouldn't mean going abroad or anything like that – or being separated from us – at least not very far. It would just mean going to St. Botolph's, with your Uncle Austin, and learning to be a farmer.' 'A *farmer*, Daddy?' 'Don't say it like that, as if you didn't know what farming was. You were half-brought up on a farm.' 'I know, but—' 'Don't raise difficulties,' my father said, his irritation mounting with his distaste for his mission. 'It may not be for long, and anyhow a farmer's life's a jolly good life. You know the song, "To be a Farmer's Boy!"' He hummed it, out of tune. 'I sometimes wish I'd been a farmer myself.' This I knew to be untrue: my father often spoke slightingly of agriculture. 'And,' he went on, 'you always liked being at St. Botolph's in the old days.'

'Yes, but that was in Grandpa's time. He's dead now, and Uncle Austin – well, he's not the same.' 'Your Uncle Austin is a very good business-man,' said my father sternly. 'He could tell you more about business than I could.'

I knew he was arguing against his convictions: he never boasted, but equally, self-depreciation was utterly foreign to him.

65

'You'll have to learn to be a business-man some day. You don't show much aptitude for it now.' Again the irritable tone, and though I knew it wasn't meant for me, it hurt. 'But I don't want to be a business-man,' I moaned. 'And you never wanted me to be one, Daddy, before today. You wanted me to be some kind of teacher . . . Like Aunt Carrie was.' And then I had an inspiration. 'They couldn't have me at St. Botolph's anyhow,' I said hopefully, 'because Aunt Carrie's there. They couldn't have me too, could they?' 'That's a point,' my father said. 'I wonder your mother hadn't thought of it. I don't see how they could, either."'

Richard paused.

'Aunt Carrie, *again*!' Denys exclaimed despairingly.

'Yes, and now I'm afraid I must again go back a bit. Aunt Carrie passed her exams with flying colours, she became L.R.C.M. She bathed us all in glory. I shall never forget the day the news came, and my mother's tearful transports. She had the gift of living in someone else's success. She didn't think of herself in terms of success – success was not for her. The most she hoped for was to dodge failure. But success for those she loved – and above all Aunt Carrie! For days she went about transformed; her face that was usually furrowed with anxiety, and often drawn with distress and even alarm, wore a simple child-like smile. Her whole being radiated happiness. Even my father's rather severe features relaxed, and he observed more than once, 'Carrie has done quite well.' More than that, she was earning her own living – a thing that in our day, even in our unexalted sphere of life, wasn't expected of any woman. Women just lived at home until they married, and if they didn't marry, they stayed at home just the same. My pretty, capable Aunt Ettie had married a neighbouring farmer who, apart from a keen eye for business, lived only for her, and had a son of six, a beautiful golden-haired child. My mother had rejoiced for her, too, but not as she rejoiced for Carrie. Aunt Carrie was now independent; she no longer needed the money that my grandfather had scraped together for her and that my Uncle Austin continued to provide her with, after my grandfather's death. She lived in London with a family of musicians, who were as devoted to her as we were: I think that sometimes my mother was a little jealous of them. She taught at the Royal College of Music and had once or twice given concerts on her own. On these occasions Mother had been beside herself with anxiety – if only she, or one of the family, could be present – my father, preferably, for he always knew what to do, and supposing Carrie broke down, supposing she fainted, supposing – 'My dear Chick,' my father would expostulate, in tones of exasperated reasonableness, 'what earthly use should *I* be? People don't break down or faint, for one thing, and if they did, someone on the spot would know how to deal with it. How *could* a mere member of the audience—' and he would wax increasingly irritable, though I think he was rather pleased that Mother thought him capable of administering First Aid. Well then, a telegram must be sent at once to say Carrie had survived the ordeal, and when this had been received, my mother's being would again expand – I have never known anyone, Denys, whose outward appearance fluctuated so much with their nervous state.

But Mother's misgivings weren't altogether unfounded. Aunt Carrie didn't break down or faint, she acquitted herself very well, and her beautiful touch (her touch on the piano was an article of faith in the family – 'Oh, Carrie's *touch*!') came in for praise. But it filtered through to us, via my Aunt Ettie (who, I suspect, was more in my Aunt Carrie's confidence than my mother was, perhaps because she was less prone to worry), that the concerts did take it out of her, and that she had to rest afterwards ('Carrie has had to *rest*!'), and there was much head-shaking.

Just when the blow fell I never knew, for my parents (which meant my mother) kept it from me. My mother kept from me everything she thought would frighten or distress me. I lived, as it were, in a doctor's waiting-room, while in his surgery my parents discussed my health with him. Anything important, I felt sure, would happen without my knowledge – especially if it was important to me. My mother, on the other hand, liked me to tell her everything, and if I put off telling her any symptom of ill-health, she would say, 'Oh, why didn't you tell me before?' So I was in a chronic state of incomplete confession and suffered from it as a Roman Catholic might. This feeling that I ought to *tell* some one has haunted me, it's partly why I'm telling you; perhaps if I had told her what I'm going to tell you I should have been a happier man.

But I digress, as usual. About my Aunt Carrie I didn't learn till afterwards – if I have ever really learned. First she dropped out of the conversation, too self-absorbed to notice this. Then I was told casually, and without explanation, that she was at St. Botolph's. Next that she was still at St. Botolph's, not very well, but nothing to be alarmed about. I was fifteen at that time, and I suppose Aunt Carrie was twenty-three. Then that my parents were going to see her but not taking me because—'

'It would over-excite her,' put in Denys.

'Yes, something like that. Several times they went to see her. After each visit my mother came back with a tear-stained face (women in those days didn't make up their faces and my mother never did) and my father looked grave and didn't talk much.

But one day they took me with them. Though it was only twelve miles to St. Botolph's, getting there was quite an expedition. First we had to take a cab to the smoky, draughty station at Medehamstead; then a train on the now extinct Midland & Great Northern Railway, with a rather exciting bright yellow engine, to a wayside station called Willow Green, where the wagonette met us; and then we had a good hour's drive to St. Botolph's past the windmill, which had sometimes lost one, or even two, of its six sails, along the straight flat road to Rookland until, about a mile from that ancient town, it slanted a few inches to the right, bringing the Abbey into view. At the thought of my reunion with the great building my excitement mounted. Even its rather absurd outline – as of some gigantic

69

pepperpot left over from Noah's Ark – did not, for me, diminish its grandeur. Bluish and misty and insubstantial it seemed to float in the air, blocking the end of the road. Presently it grew more solid and I could see the frost-eroded forms and haggard faces of the saints and kings whose effigies clung crazily to the wall of the West Front. We did not drive right up to it; we turned to the left, following the road that skirted its northern side, and it was then that my mother said, as she had often said before, 'Don't look, my darling.'

I had been staring, bemused, at the north face of the Abbey, with as much awe as if it had been the north face of the Eiger, but knowing what was coming, I hastily withdrew my gaze.

'It's the M, you know,' said Mother. 'It's so terribly ugly, you mustn't look at it.'

'The M' consisted of three buttresses, two long ones and a short one in between, which had been built on to the north wall of the tower to shore it up. Together, they made a pattern like the letter M. I didn't know that their function was to prevent the tower falling down, nor I think did Mother; whether she remembered the tower before they were put up, I don't know. But she hated them. She was anything but a highbrow (a term not used in those days) but her aesthetic perceptions meant a great deal to her, and 'The M' embodied all she most disliked. I took my opinions from my father, but my prejudices from my mother, and so, without knowing why, I felt that 'The M' was a desecration, an abomination. I had read somewhere that the north side of a church was under the personal supervision of the Devil, which seemed to bear out Mother's view; and I used to think up any number of words beginning with mal- and mis-, all of which implied the bad, in one shape or another. I was never very happy about our own name, Mardick. In fact, at times, the only redeeming 'M word' (for so I thought of them) was Mother; 'marvellous', 'magnificent', 'miraculous', were exceptions that proved the rule. I already distrusted 'modern'.

I didn't raise my eyes until the danger of an M infection was past, and when St. Botolph's began to take shape in the distance, sheltering behind its five sentinel straw-stacks, I felt another thrill, and another kind of fear. Yet what was there in Aunt Carrie to be afraid of? She was an emblem of love, not of fear. One could be afraid *for* her – my mother always had been – but not *of* her. But I *was* afraid.

I only saw her for a few minutes, just before lunch. The family were all there except Aunt Ettie – and they gave me a warm welcome, even Aunt Ada did – though she couldn't help sticking in a little pin. 'Is your cap too small for you, or can it be that your head has swollen? You never come to see us now, you're much too grand.' She must have known quite well the reason I didn't come to St. Botolph's. It was a cold March day – I could see the red glow of the oil stove on the tiles of the hall under the staircase and smell the oil and the musty scent of firewood in the skip beside it – and all my affection for St. Botolph's came back.

'Dr. Butcher's with Carrie, now,' said my Aunt Esther; I couldn't get used to the idea, nor could my mother, that St. Botolph's now belonged to her. 'Now what will you do, Richard? What would you like to do? Would you like to go into the fruit garden and see the crocuses? Or would you like to go into the stack-yard? Or would you like to go into the breakfast-room and read? I'm afraid there isn't very much to do.'

Aunt Esther was the first human being, the first relation anyhow, who ever consulted me about my wishes, or took pains to prevent me being bored. For my mother it was enough if I was well, and responsive to the love surrounding me; whilst my father would have been shocked and disgusted if he thought that someone could not amuse himself. Even Aunt Carrie expended her infinite resources of sympathy on matters that were above the amusement-line. To be asked what I should *like* to do made me feel guilty. Wishes had no relish of salvation in them; they must be fortified by something *useful*.

'Can I hold Dr. Butcher's horse while he gets in?' I asked. Horses were divided between those that would 'stand' and those that wouldn't. Dr. Butcher's horse was one that wouldn't. A mettlesome creature like its owner, it was tethered to the gatepost next to the conservatory. 'Of course you can,' Aunt Esther said, 'but I should have thought it was the last thing you would want to do.' She was right; it was; but usefulness apart, I thought it was my only chance of getting a private word with Dr. Butcher. 'Only don't get cold, will you?'

she added, 'waiting about. Your mother would never forgive me if you caught cold.' She smiled, she was an understanding woman; and although to me, brought up as I had been, the idea of treating a cold lightly was almost blasphemous, I managed to smile back. Conscientiously determined to avoid a chill, I walked smartly up and down the lawn. It had just been mown, for the first time that year; I still remember the sweet smell. In one place, where the grass had been thickest and longest, they had mown it with a scythe, and it lay about like tresses of hair, still green. They had brought out the croquet-hoops, I remember, round-headed like Norman arches, and so wide that two balls could lie in them abreast. In the middle was a double hoop, two arches from whose point of intersection hung a brass bell – a pretty object but one that was already many years out of date, and the subject of much laughter from my Uncle Hal, who in his negligent way was good at croquet, as he was, or had been, at most games. My father, while admitting his skill, was rather shocked by his casual attitude towards them.

Two posts there were, painted in descending segments of blue, red, black and yellow, and each furnished with a cross-piece against which you could lean your mallet when your ball was not in play.

Against the cross-piece of the winning-post someone, probably my Aunt Esther, always anxious to provide for somebody's need to do something, had propped up all four mallets, inclining towards each other like piled arms. Very light to hold they were.

Uncle Hal often took only one hand to his. Round them were ranged the balls of shiny polished wood, also wondrously light and not painted one colour, as they are now, but in concentric stripes.

Tired of walking I planted the balls in strategic positions according to a system invented by my father, which, if you adhered to it and made no mistakes, would make it possible to do the whole tournée with one ball. The system never worked with me, but I always hoped. When it failed I could play two balls against the other two: I soon discarded scientific impartiality and backed one side – usually blue and black, on which I lavished such skill as I had, treating red and yellows as enemies – it's always been easy for me to take sides against myself. I had just passed through the second hoop when I heard the front door open, with a kind of volcanic disturbance out of all proportion to that simple operation, and Dr. Butcher's burly tweed-clad back appeared, framed by a host of faces, indistinct in the darkness of the hall.

As he was disengaging himself, I ran towards him, mallet in hand.

'Dr. Butcher!'

He waved goodbye to them and turned to me, a huge figure bursting from his clothes. 'Well, Richard! Are you going to brain me with that mallet?'

Dr. Butcher had always been a favourite of mine, and I think I was a favourite of his. He had once saved me from death, so my nurse told me. Mother didn't tell me, for anxious as she was for those she loved, and always dreading some fatal issue for them, she never mentioned the word 'death' in my presence. But apparently when I was two-and-a-half or so, we happened to be staying at St. Botolph's and some member of the family – I'm too much of an egoist to remember which – was ill, and Dr. Butcher who never grudged his time by day or night had come to see him or her towards bed-time. He was driving away when my mother, who was going to bed (I slept in a cot in my parents' room), heard the strangled crow that used to herald croup. She rushed downstairs, the front door was still ajar, for in those days no one bothered much with locks or bolts, and caught Dr. Butcher just as he was opening the garden gate. He ran back with her, leaving the horse to its own devices. I was blue in the face from the spasm, so my nurse told me, – you've seen me rather like that, Denys, but never so bad – but I managed to gasp out, 'Shall I die? Am I dead?' 'No,' he replied, 'you're worth fifty dead ones.'

'I always knew you were a tough nut,' said Denys.

'Well, that time I survived, and I suppose it made a bond between me and Dr. Butcher, though he never spoke of it. I had more self-confidence with him than I had with most people, so when I had shaken hands with him, I said, "Are you in a great hurry, Dr. Butcher?" "I'm never in a hurry," said he, "where patients are concerned." "But I'm not your patient," I said. "Not at the moment," he said, digging me in the ribs, "but you have been, and you may be again."

I was feeling so well that I didn't think it likely.

'Don't you ever get impatient with your patients?' I asked him.

I shall never forget how he laughed at this – it was a laugh that reminded me of Grandpa's.

'Only with scrimshankers like you,' he said. 'Not with Aunt Carrie?' I asked, surprised at my own boldness. He shot a look at me and said, 'No, less with her than anyone.' 'Dr. Butcher,' I asked, 'what *is* the matter with Aunt Carrie?'

At that I lost my nerve and said, 'Oh no, Dr. Butcher, I wasn't being serious. I just wanted to hold Princess while you got in.' Each successive horse, or rather mare, of Dr. Butcher's was named Princess.

'That was very thoughtful of you,' he said. 'Well, you go and fetch her and then I might tell you something.'

This was the part of the proceedings I least relished, Denys. To tell you the truth I was afraid of horses, and particularly afraid of Princess, whose impatience was a by-word. She simply would not 'stand'. She also made a great show of biting you when you held her bridle; you had to put your hand almost into her mouth, so that she couldn't twist it round and grab you. Not that she would have done, I think; but she liked teasing.

Gingerly I went up to her and unhooked the reins which Dr. Butcher had carelessly looped over the gate-post. Instantly she started her old tricks, pawing, stamping, head-tossing and so on, and turned so sharply in her tracks that if Dr. Butcher's smart dog-cart had been a four-wheeler, she might have over-turned it. I clung to her bridle, nearly lifted from the ground, but as soon as she saw Dr. Butcher she calmed down, and we reached the front door in comparatively good order.

'Well done!' he said. 'We shall make a horse-breaker of you yet.' Princess then bared her teeth showing the whitish underside of her thick lips, but I knew that theoretically she couldn't bite me, my hand was too near those yellow teeth.

Very nimbly for so heavy a man, Dr. Butcher climbed into his place, and was just taking up the reins when I reminded him.

'You promised to tell me something.' 'So I did, about Carrie, wasn't it? I can't tell you what's the matter with her, I only wish I could. She's had a disappointment, you know, a big disappointment, and it takes a lot out of you at any age. I hope you'll never have one. But it'll come right, you'll see it'll come right.'

Still holding on to Princess, whose wet lips were nuzzling my fingers, I said, 'I'm going to see her now. She asked me to. *What shall I say to her?*'

Dr. Butcher never failed to give one his consideration. 'Say to her?' he repeated. 'Say to her? Well, don't say too much – say you're all right, we're all all right, we're thinking of her, and we like thinking of her, er, er – you're doing very well at school, everyone's doing well, farming is looking up – nothing to worry about, nothing in the world. Does that help? Now I must be off. Open the gate for me, there's a good fellow.'

Glad to relinquish Princess, I ran and opened the gate into the road. Princess had already got into her stride and narrowly missed the near gate-post. 'Don't knock down both gate-posts at once' was a well-worn gibe directed at indifferent drivers, like my father. Shutting the gate, I turned to the house and saw Aunt Esther standing in the doorway.

'Carrie is ready for you now,' she said, 'unless you'd like to wash your hands first.' I said I would – (partly to gain time and partly because I loved the little wash-room which my Uncle Austin had built on to the north side of St. Botolph's, next the old bathroom). We had a bathroom too, at home, but it was a converted bed-room, and looked like it; the bath, though cased in mahogany and with a let-down lid, was an intruder, whereas the three little apartments at St. Botolph's were designed for sanitation, and, though I didn't know it, heralded another age.

VII

'If I seem a little agitated now,' said Richard, 'it's only the memory of my agitation then – I thought I was in for some queer experience. I had expected to see Aunt Carrie in her bedroom and had put on what I thought was a sick-room expression – but she wasn't there, which rather foxed me. Aunt Esther left me at the drawing-room door, saying, 'I shouldn't stay too long – you'll hear the gong for lunch,' and there I was in the so familiar room with Aunt Carrie sitting in the cosy corner, facing me. She got up as soon as I came in and I decided that I ought to kiss her. I wasn't much given to kissing and usually waited for other people to kiss me; I couldn't see the sense of it but knew it must be done. My mother kissed me, of course, and so did my other aunts, each with a very different technique – Aunt Ettie's was much the warmest, she really did *enfold* one. I didn't remember ever having exchanged kisses with Aunt Carrie, I didn't associate her with them. I even thought vaguely they might do her harm. But this was a special occasion and I wanted to behave in a special way. Don't hesitate, I told myself, just do it. So I advanced and kissed her – the first unsolicited kiss I had ever given. Would she respond, or would she shrink away? She did respond – and perhaps it was the emotion of the moment, but as her lips touched my cheek, I suddenly had a glimmering of what this foolish and (my father said) insanitary practice might entail and I drew back a little breathless, half inclined to repeat the experiment, but I didn't – the legend of Aunt Carrie came between us, as it came between her and so many people. Don't laugh, Denys, there was no question of incest.

Then, as we sat down in the cosy corner, whose cushions she hadn't even rumpled, under those white wooden niches, tunnels, buttresses, a fantasy of curves, that supported shelves and ornaments – Moorish they were in inspiration – I saw that she had put on her best dress, or what used to be her best dress – the lilac silk with black lace over it and the high collar she always wore to hide the scar on her neck – for she had had tuberculous glands, as many people had in those days.

'And now,' I reminded myself, 'you must think of something to say, you mustn't leave it all to her – it's very bad for invalids to talk.' (Mother had told me this.) But what *could* I say, when the occasion was so momentous? So I said, 'Dear Aunt Carrie' (I had never called anyone 'dear' to their faces before), 'I am afraid you have been very ill, and we have all been most worried about you, especially Mother, but I hope you have now taken a turn for the better.' Then I glanced at her and away again, for even I could see how ill she looked. 'But,' I said, 'you mustn't talk to me unless you want to, please, until the gong goes for lunch. I was very glad

80

when they informed me that you would like to see me, because I know that ever since you have been ill you haven't wanted to see many people, because they are a strain on you – and indeed, dear Aunt Carrie, I know from my own experience at school what a strain other people can be – they simply don't realize that sometimes one is praying to be left alone. If you could just tell me – indicate to me – something you would like me to talk about, I could fill in the time quite easily, I really could. The only thing I can think of now to say is that when I was holding Dr. Butcher's horse, Princess, which is so bad at standing, he told me you would certainly get better, which is, of course, the most wonderful news and I shall lose no time in telling Mother, because I don't think she thinks you will.'

After this speech, one of the longest I had ever made, Denys, I sat back, half-expecting that my aunt would not answer. Perhaps I thought she had been struck dumb, like my grandfather. When one is a child, one accepts without question the most surprising situations. I will give her two minutes by the clock, I thought, and then, if she hasn't spoken, I will kiss her and go away. When she did begin to speak, I could scarcely believe it and indeed her voice had changed, it was of a lighter quality than it used to be, and the touch of throatiness was more marked. For a moment I didn't take in what she was saying and heard it retrospectively. 'My dear,' she said, 'I did want to see you for several reasons, and one was to tell you how pleased and proud I am you are doing so well at school. It must

81

be a great satisfaction to your dear parents. Only you mustn't work too hard.' She stopped a moment and smoothed her sleeves at the wrist – the old gesture, but accentuated.

'Oh,' I said smugly, 'hard work never hurt anyone,' and then I remembered that it had hurt her, or was said to have, and blushed.

She was silent for a moment, considering. Her face always foreshadowed her thoughts without revealing them, otherwise I should have been even more surprised than I was when she said, 'Do you know why I have been ill?' 'No,' I said and suddenly I realized so acutely the magnitude of the question-mark that hung over Aunt Carrie's illness, that my heart began to pound. 'I thought your mother might have told you.' 'Oh no,' I said. 'Mother hardly ever talks about you now.'

I meant this remark to be reassuring as well as truthful but I could see it had the opposite effect.

'I wish she had,' she said, 'I wish she had – because, Richard, you are the only person I should like to know, who doesn't know already. Do I sound as if I took myself too seriously? I hope you'll never be ill, but if you are, you'll find yourself taking on an importance that you never wanted. You become a nuisance, for one thing.'

'Oh, Aunt Carrie,' I cried fervently, 'you could never be a nuisance.' She smiled. 'But I am. Austin and Esther are the kindest people in the world, but they have a struggle to make both ends meet. They have only one maid, Esther does most of the cooking herself, and here am I, and Ada – all of us a burden on them – at least, I am, I know that. I have to have my meals brought up to me, and so on. I'd saved up a little money, but not enough, you need a lot of money for an illness. There were other people who would have taken care of me—'

'We would have taken care of you, Aunt Carrie,' I said eagerly. 'Mother wanted to, you know.' A shadow crossed Aunt Carrie's face. 'Yes, yes,' she said, 'your darling mother . . . too kind, Richard, too anxious, too . . . too . . .' she couldn't define, and I only dimly apprehended, wherein lay my mother's quality of excess. 'It wouldn't have done,' she went on, 'it wouldn't have done if I hadn't come here. Austin . . . well . . . he wouldn't have liked it; and after all this is my home, as the baby cuckoo might have said.'

'You a cuckoo, Aunt Carrie!' I cried, horrified. 'Why you haven't turned out anyone!' She smiled again. 'Not yet, perhaps. But how it all began, how I came into the position of being, well, a burden . . . that's what I wanted you to know. Not because I want you to feel sorry for me,' she said, in growing agitation, 'or at any rate not ashamed of me, but because . . . Oh, how difficult it is to explain.' 'Can't you tell me, Aunt Carrie?' I urged her. 'I'm quite old, I'm fifteen, and I wouldn't breathe a word, not even to . . . not even to . . .' Lack of imagination saved me from possible blasphemy.

'Could I tell you, Richard?' she said, searching my face, 'could I tell you? I would much rather tell you, not only for my own sake, but for yours. I *don't* want you to think that what has happened to me – after all, I'm only one in millions – might also happen to *you*. You see, it's just a fluke that it happened, and because I'm not very strong. What I did was right, I'm sure it was right, and I'd do it again.' She began to tremble; the red rushed to her cheek-bones; I knew I ought to stop her, but I couldn't think how. 'The opportunity, the *opportunity*, my dear Richard,' she almost gasped, 'may not come twice – and you mustn't refuse it, you mustn't refuse *love*,' and I still remember how her voice dropped on the word, 'just because it hasn't turned out well for me. I am a warning, I know, but I don't *want* to be a warning, to you of all people. It was just bad luck.' She stopped and made a great effort, which seemed to run through her whole frame, and hold her clamped and rigid. 'When I first met Arthur,' she began, but the rest was lost in the booming of the gong which soon reached a pitch of resonance that made the room vibrate. With a gesture half comic, half despairing, my aunt signified that our interview was over. When I kissed her, she found no words to say, but as I was tiptoeing out, she called after me, 'I shall ask your mother to tell you.'

VIII

When Mother did tell me, it came as rather a disappointment and would have been more of a disappointment if she herself had not been so moved by it. Mother's devotion to Aunt Carrie was utterly unswerving. She never spoke casually of her, as one often speaks of a friend, however dear; all her references to Aunt Carrie were at the same level of seriousness. At first she wouldn't tell me, saying it was something I was too young to understand; and when I said that Aunt Carrie *wanted* me to know and had asked her to tell me, she even prevaricated – the only time I ever knew her do so – saying she didn't remember, was I sure, and so on.

What I expected to hear I didn't know. My father, who was in most ways so theoretical about my education – he didn't send me to school till I was twelve, saying that a tutor, a master at a nearby Council School – would teach me more – hadn't told me the facts of life, and what I picked up when I did go to school was so garbled and unlikely that I could hardly relate it to human beings, least of all to those I knew. Nor did I associate what my aunt had said about love with any experience of her own; I thought it was a general admonition such as my mother often made. She was always insisting on the importance of love, and persuaded me to learn the 13th chapter of Corinthians by heart, substituting 'love' for 'charity'. So it never occurred to me that Aunt Carrie had got into some sort of 'trouble' connected with love; I knew, by hearsay, that servant-girls and suchlike did, but never imagined that love could lead anyone of our sort into 'trouble'. Trouble! I had no idea what it implied. But I was eager to know about Aunt Carrie – not so much, I must admit, out of concern for her (though I *was* concerned), as because the mystery gnawed at me, and I wanted to hear some sensational and startling story.

My mother couldn't tell anything objectively; she had to satisfy a lot of preliminary requirements, the most urgent of which, in this case, was of course, that Aunt Carrie should be recognized as the heroine and the victim. No blame attached to her, nor to the man in the case – for there was a man. My mother, though a most generous-minded woman, was too much of a moralist to tell a story without imputing blame to someone, and I took after her and should have found the story savourless without a scapegoat.'

'I didn't know you were such a stern moralist,' said Denys.

'Oh, but I was – that was the worst of it, and I dare say I still am.' Richard looked round, avoiding Denys's eye, and the hand which he had raised to salute the word 'moralist', dropped to his side. 'Don't you want to fill your glass? I wish I could say "pass the bottle", like Marlow did in Conrad's novels.'

The allusion was lost on Denys, but not the invitation.

'Thanks, I will,' he said.

'And I gave an illustration of my moral outlook almost at once, for when she told me – we were sitting on the terra-cotta plush sofa in the dining-room, I remember, facing the long Regency side-board, that my father had bought so cheap – it was the place reserved for serious conversations – when she told me that Aunt Carrie had fallen in love, I said at once, – really shocked and feeling that the image of a life-time had been shattered – 'But wasn't that very *selfish* of her?' Mother explained that it wasn't selfish, first because Aunt Carrie couldn't do anything selfish, and secondly because it was natural for people to fall in love.

'But isn't it natural to be selfish?' I asked her.

My mother agreed that it was natural to be selfish, but love, she said, transcended self, or something to that effect. Oh, she wouldn't hear a word against love! This Arthur Brightwell was a school-master in a West Country school near the one where she and Aunt Carrie, in fact all four sisters, had been educated; my mother had known him when he was a boy. 'He was a nice boy, dear, and very good at botany, and Latin, and several other subjects, and very fond of music. But he wasn't *strong*, and that was why, when we heard that Carrie was interested in him, we couldn't help feeling a little *anxious*; it wasn't that we didn't think him *good* enough for Carrie—'

'Of course not,' I said, mechanically.

'But we were afraid of his health breaking down. You see his father had died of consumption. Well, when Carrie left Culver House and went to London to study at the Royal College of Music, Arthur gave up his post at Gretton School and went to London too – it was a great undertaking for both of them and there was very little money, though we all gave Carrie what we could, – but you must never tell anyone, Richard.' I promised solemnly. 'That was two – no, three years ago. Then Arthur got a job as a teacher in a school in North London, not far from where Carrie was living with the Claypoles, they were distant cousins of ours, and Agnes Claypole had been at school with Carrie. They were very kind to her, Richard, we must never forget that; and they were very musical; every member of the family, I think, played some instrument. But they were very strong themselves, and didn't realize how delicate Carrie was. They often stayed up playing late at night – a most unwise thing to do – and Arthur joined them, for he played the 'cello. He had to walk back – think of it – a mile and a half to his lodgings, for the buses had stopped and he couldn't afford to take a cab, and he had to get up early, to be in time for school. Oh, I think they were very much to blame, the Claypoles, though we must never say so; and I don't think that either he or Carrie got much really good, nourishing food. He was a clever man, Arthur was – what some people would call brilliant; he would certainly have gone to one of the Universities if he'd had the money. And he was so gentle, too, and sweet with children. I wish you could have known him, Richard.'

'But couldn't I, Mother?'

'No, my darling, you couldn't, because he died.' My mother stopped; her tears came easily and didn't choke her utterance, as some people's do. 'He got very ill with galloping consumption, you wouldn't know what that is, and the doctor didn't recognize it until too late. I blame him very much. If only Arthur would have gone to dear Dr. Snape!' (Dr. Snape was the doctor we sometimes consulted in London) – 'as I tried so hard to make him, but his doctor was the Claypoles' doctor – not that they needed one, as they were *never* ill.' My mother said this almost bitterly. 'I feel sure that it was walking home through those yellow fogs, without a respirator too, and getting *overtired*, that helped to do it. Only *very strong* people ought to live in London.

When it was too late, they got a nurse for him – a kind woman, I think she was, but too easy-going, which isn't a fault they often have, and, Richard, I believe she *drank*. She let Carrie go and see him every day – Daddy paid for her to have a cab – and she used to sit with Arthur in his little room, with only an oil-stove, so unhealthy for an invalid. Of course they shouldn't have let her do it, and if *I* had been there . . . But we didn't really know at the time, Carrie didn't tell us what was happening, she didn't want to worry us, and the Claypoles didn't think it mattered being ill, they were so strong. And then he suddenly became much worse and couldn't be moved, and Carrie used to sit up with him all night, five nights she sat up with him and on the fifth he died, with her hand in his. 'Carrie, hold my hand', he said, and it was the last thing he said. And when they came in the morning, they thought that she was dead, too, darling Carrie was dead, for she had fallen asleep out of exhaustion, and was lying beside him on the bed, with her cheek against his.'

Then my mother broke down and I cried too, partly to keep her company, partly because I was conscious for the first time of unconsolable sorrow and irreparable loss. Till then I had taken it for granted that everything would come right in the end.

'That was what happened,' said my mother, drying her eyes. 'I didn't mean to tell you, but you said Carrie wanted me to. They took her back to the Claypoles', where she was very ill and Dr. Snape – they called him in when it was too late – thought her *mind* might be affected. She had to give up everything, of course, learning, practising, teaching, playing – everything. All her *career*! Dr. Butcher lets her play accompaniments sometimes for Uncle Austin and Uncle Hal and Aunt Ada. People who really *know* have said there never was a better accompanist. If your voice hadn't been breaking, how she would have loved to play 'I know that my Redeemer liveth' for you! But she can't play much, not even accompaniments, because it upsets her if she plays a wrong note. Of course Aunt Esther plays accompaniments, too; but I never liked her playing, it's so showy. Dear Aunt Carrie always played with so much *feeling*, and somehow managed to keep Aunt Ada in *tune*. She has a sharp tongue, as you must have noticed, and she sings sharp, too. Daddy sometimes sings flat, but he is a man and it doesn't matter so much. Carrie's voice was never *strong*, but it was absolutely *true*.'

Some more my mother told me but I don't remember it; I do remember how strange and sad I felt, and the pain of hearing Aunt Carrie referred to in the past tense, as if everything she stood for – all the opening, flowering hope of the world – our world – had come to nothing; almost as if she was dead. And I remember, too, the feeling of relief, that mounted to excitement, as I gradually realized that all this had happened to someone else, and that I, Richard, was well and happy, – doing well at school, and free to pursue my life on the old terms, day by day moving towards an unknown fulfilment, unfettered by illness and the half-shame of other people feeling sorry for me.

And so it went on for two years or more, a rising curve for me, of accomplishment, congratulation and, I must admit, self-congratulation, as if life was a series of prize-winnings like the milestones on a Fen road – that didn't mark a change on the landscape but were all the time taking one nearer to one's goal. I had my set-backs, of course, times when I didn't do so well, when masters expressed disappointment, when I thought myself (and probably was) unpopular, when my parents weren't quite so pleased with me as I thought they ought to be. But apart from a few bronchial "attacks", as Mother called them, which didn't last unduly long, I couldn't have been better "in myself" – whatever that means.'

IX

Richard sighed and stole a glance at Denys' motionless figure.

'Denys, are you asleep?'

You never could surprise or startle Denys; he reared himself slowly in his chair, and languidly reached out for his glass.

'Of course not, Richard.'

'What was I just saying?'

'Please, sir, you were just saying what a wonderful success you were being at school, and how everyone liked you, and how proud your parents were of you, and you'd only had a few bronchial attacks, and you were on top of the world or had it at your feet, or anyhow under control—'

'Very good – ten out of ten. Now the question is, can you bear to hear any more?'

'If you can bear to tell me,' said Denys slyly. 'You keep saying how terrible it's going to be for you, when you come to the point . . . You haven't come to the point yet, have you? I mean, I haven't missed it?'

'No.'

'It was very sad about your aunt, but no one could blame you for that, not even your mother, not even you yourself.'

'No . . . What time is it, Denys? Your eyes are better than mine.'

Denys turned his head slowly towards the clock.

'Half past ten. You mustn't give yourself a bad night, you know.'

'No . . . But now that I've got started . . . Well, everything was going swimmingly until I got this cough – in the spring of I forget what year, but it was the summer that mattered. I had a cough and a temperature, too, in the evenings, – about a degree up, nothing much, but the doctor couldn't account for it. I kept catching my mother's eye fixed on me, and the feeling of being watched got on my nerves. I was already a hypochondriac, and a bad subject for that sort of anxious scrutiny. I was still working hard at school, and still winning prizes. I was always a pot-hunter, I'm afraid; I could only work with a carrot dangled in front of me. In case I've given you a wrong impression of her, Denys, I must tell you that my mother was a sweet, fluttering little creature, who loved pretty things, both to wear and look at; she noticed other women's clothes, and dressed with all the care her slender means and economical disposition allowed her to. The puritanical streak that in my father took the form of a stoical rationalism ('You must grin and bear it,' he used to say when anything went wrong) was in her case a half-emotional, half-religious conviction that in furthering the right course, no pains whatever must be spared by her or anyone else. For this she violated one side of her nature – the yielding side, the soft side, and sacrificed her temperament to her will.

One afternoon I came home earlier than usual and as I was passing the drawing-room door, I heard her and my father discussing something. My father always raised his voice in argument; my mother lowered hers. They were talking about me. I heard him say: 'You fuss about the boy too much, Mary. You'll make an old woman of him. He's all right – he's just growing rather fast. If you take him away from school now—'

I put my ear to the key-hole.

'There isn't any "if", my mother said in the low firm voice she used when she was determined to resist my father. 'We must take him away.' 'There's no must about it,' urged my father. 'I don't want him to leave and he won't want to leave – that's two against one. Aren't you going to consider his feelings at all?'

I pressed my ear harder to the key-hole. 'How can he know what's good for him at his age?' my mother said. 'In after-life he'll thank us (if we should still be here) for thinking more about his permanent health than his temporary happiness. Besides, how can he be happy if he isn't well? Health is the first consideration.'

'How do you know that Rookland is going to agree with him?' my father argued. 'Rookland is only twelve miles away – it's on clay, just as we are. Richard will never make a farmer – he hasn't the slightest aptitude for it – he knows no more about farming than a bull's foot.' 'You needn't be coarse, Walter.' 'I'm not being coarse – I'm only using an agricultural metaphor,' my father said. 'Richard will have to learn a lot of those things if he's going to be a farmer. Now do be ruled for once, Chick. It isn't his line at all. He'll be no good at it. It's not as if he had money like the queer couple at the Hollies, whom everybody laughs at, or would laugh at, if they weren't well off.'

'You mean the Soames's,' said Mother, who even when her feelings were most deeply engaged, could always be side-tracked by a proper name. 'I've always wondered about them and their daughter, who never sees anyone, poor girl.'

'Poor is just what they're not,' my father said, 'though I dare say they're not as well off as they're said to be. But that's not the point. The point is that Richard won't have the money to be a gentleman-farmer, or the ability to be a real one. Can you see him in the Corn Exchange on Saturday mornings, with a sample of wheat in his pocket? Why, he can't even drive a horse – he's worse at it than I am. And who is there at Rookland of his own age? He'll spend all his time with grown-ups. He won't have anyone to play with.'

'He's in his eighteenth year,' said Mother. I was just seventeen and for the first time I realized that as far as years went, I was no longer a child. 'He has his life's work before him. You stopped playing, Walter, before you were his age.'

'Yes, I had to put away childish things. But there were distractions at Fosdyke – cricket, tennis, billiards, and golf when I could get it – that Richard can't have at Rookland, even if he wanted them. Rookland is a desert.'

'Austin doesn't find it so,' said Mother.

'No, because he's keen on making money. Richard isn't. He needs a salaried job, and if he finishes his schooling, he might get one. He could do worse than go into the Bank, though I shan't press him. Or if he stays on a term or two longer, he might get a scholarship to Oxford or Cambridge.'

'What use would that be, Walter, if his health was ruined?'

'Oh, forget about his health. He'll only get into mischief at Rookland.' 'Why, what mischief can he get into?' 'Satan finds some mischief still for idle . . .' 'But he won't be idle. He'll be out all day on the farms, as busy as Austin is, and living an open-air life.' 'Oh, Mary, why must you keep harping on that? The doctors don't *know* that his lungs are affected. The specialist was almost sure they weren't. I know your mother died of it, and your Uncle James, but he wasn't a relation. Carrie is ill, poor girl, but not from that. My lungs are no great shakes, but they do their job all right – you see to that! You are wonderful in a crisis, Chick, but you tend to see one where there isn't one. In Richard's case—'

'A crisis is just what I am trying to avoid,' my mother said.

'There's more than one kind of crisis,' said my father. 'If you start monkeying about with the boy's life now—' 'Walter,' said my mother, speaking with such intensity that she almost hissed the words, '*Do you want to lose the child?*'

I turned and fled and that night in bed I had a double crisis – a *crise de conscience* for having listened to something that was not meant for me, and a nervous crisis too, the overwhelming fear of death.

I doubt if you can understand, Denys, at any rate I hope you can't, the strictness of the moral principles on which I was brought up. Any sort of disobedience to my parents' wishes – which to me meant doing wrong – worked on me, if it was deliberate, like a poison. I knew that I had done wrong by listening; and as I tossed on my bed, I felt I should never get to sleep until I had confessed to them my act of wickedness. I still went to bed an hour before they did, and a hundred times during that hour I decided to go downstairs, own up and make my peace with them and God. But somehow I couldn't; I couldn't let them think so badly of me. And there was something else. Precociously alive to nervous strain, I knew that if I got rid of this one, there was another one waiting for me. I felt its shadow creep across my mind, seeking an entrance, but I knew it couldn't get in so long as there was still an occupant. I tried to play them off against each other; and at last, long after I had heard my parents going to bed – I mean my father, whose tread was slow and heavy, you could hardly hear my mother's – I made a sort of compromise. I promised myself, and whatever gods I swore by, that in the morning I would make a full confession. My conscience accepted the bribe, but while the bliss of release from guilt was stealing over me and weighing down my eyelids, the other fear forced its way in. They were going to lose me! I was going to die! I tried to envisage the world without me, me, Richard Mardick, who had enjoyed life so much. I got out of bed to relieve nature, which during my agitations asserted its demands with increasing frequency. This time I lit the gas, not that I wanted it to find the article under the bed, but because I felt, as Goethe did, the need of light, light to see the world by, and make sure that it existed. My gas bracket had an inverted mantel – 'Veritas' it was called. Truth! And on my dressing-table I saw the clinical thermometer which my mother, perhaps forgetful after her altercation with my father, had failed to take away. Four times a day I took my temperature; in the morning, when I awoke; at school, where the matron kept the record; at six o'clock when it was highest; and at bed-time, when Mother came to say goodnight. I wasn't supposed to know how it varied, but I had a rough idea. At night it went down to normal, or nearly normal. I picked up the thermometer and looked, and to my horror it still said 99.6. I must be worse, much worse! I crept back into bed, left the light on, the dreadful light of truth, and when I closed my eyes it was still there, burning behind my eyelids. I made my farewells, I composed death-bed speeches; again I tried to make my peace with God. I sometimes try to now, Denys, when I have much more reason – and find it just as difficult.

Well, suddenly, these dark imaginings were pierced by a ray of light that wasn't the gas – it was the will to live, I suppose, that we all have. Had Mother forgotten, when she took my temperature at six o'clock, to shake down the thermometer? I shook it down, embraced it with my tongue in the approved fashion, for a full three minutes, and then consulted it. Behold, it had gone down to 98; I was not dying after all; and in the ecstasy of this reprieve I fell asleep with the light still on, almost before my head had touched the pillow.

X

Oh how bold I felt next day, when I was among my classmates! You remember how at school one had days when everything went wrong and even days when everything went right. Well, this was one of the good days – I remember it as the best day I ever spent at school. It was a Saturday; the May weather was glorious; everyone was nice to me. The lurking, lingering fear that for some reason I wasn't 'popular' seemed to be banished for ever. I talked with a new freedom, as though anything I said would go down with anyone I spoke to; I felt I had a passport to everyone's regard. All of them understood what I meant, and I understood what they meant. At school I always felt at least three years older than I did at home; I felt my age, in fact I felt older; for a good many of the boys, when they weren't teasing me for being a swot, respected me for being good at work; they looked up to me. Oh yes, I was not only seventeen; I was in my eighteenth year, as Mother said. Besides being older, I felt at least ten feet tall; and oddly enough when, during break, the matron took my temperature (I used to try to read its verdict in her face, but never could), she said, 'Do you know, I think you've grown?' 'What, since yesterday?' She looked at me again. 'Yes, since yesterday. You look a man now. You'll be having the girls after you,' she added with a giggle, 'perhaps you have already.' I felt myself turning red; it was the first time I had blushed at the thought of a girl. When I didn't answer, she gave me another look – a different look, and said, 'You're old enough, you know. You're quite nice-looking, too, or will be when you've filled out a bit.' Again I couldn't reply; a host of unknown feelings pressed upon me; I seemed to be standing upon the threshold of manhood, with a sweet, sunlit landscape spreading out before me. When I stood spell-bound, she gave me a little push and said, 'Now run along.'

It was all day the same, an enchanted day. When I went back into the class-room or whatever we called it, the master who took us in English literature said, 'You've done an excellent essay, Mardick.' I still remember the title of the essay, it was 'Which are the more interesting – persons or things?' – 'And I'm going to send it up to the Headmaster,' he went on. This was a great compliment that was very seldom given. Everyone in the class looked at me. In spite of anti-swot prejudice, they had enough solidarity to feel that each one shared in my success. 'You write like a man,' he went on, 'and better than some men. I'm not saying I agree with everything you say – speaking for myself, speaking personally, I am more interested in persons than in things.' Would you believe it, Denys, in those days I was more interested in things than in persons – or I thought I was. He went on, 'Now I shall read it to you, and as it's rather long (brevity isn't Mardick's strong point, but he may learn it later), you needn't answer any questions about Hamlet, you can just listen to Mardick for the rest of the hour.'

Imagine, Denys, how this set me up, and how popular it made me!

In the afternoon we had a cricket match. I had never been much good at cricket, in spite of Daddy's coaching on the lawn at home, and in any case this term I wasn't allowed to play. But I loved watching the game; it was the only time at school when one could really relax, and not feel responsible to anyone for one's behaviour. The *acte de présence* was enough, only if you shirked it could you get into trouble. This was an ideal afternoon; I felt utterly at one with myself and with all the hundred odd plum-coloured caps, embroidered with the crossed keys of St. Peter, who was our patron saint at Medehamstead. Nothing to distinguish me from any of the others except my thoughts, and how they glowed! – privately, for my own success and publicly for the school's success – St. Peter's school, for we were beating them, beating them hollow, but who has ever minded an easy victory? When the last wicket fell, and the applause broke out, for us and them, I felt almost disembodied, outside myself with joy – so much so that I didn't feel the light touch on my shoulder. It had become a thumping and a shaking, almost an act of violence that schoolboys are so fond of, by the time I realized I was being molested, and I looked up indignantly into the face of an older boy, who was looking down at me with the grim smile of authority.

'I thought you were dead,' he said, 'I've been looking for you everywhere. The Head wants to see you.'

'The Head?' I echoed. 'Yes, the Head, you blockhead.'
'What does he want me for?' 'I've no idea. A swishing,
I expect. What have you been up to?' I thought quickly.
'I think I know,' I said. 'I think I know.' 'Well, cut
along now, and I hope it won't hurt too much.'

I obeyed, and ran, as schoolboys so often do. I can't
remember when I last ran, Denys, it's quite a thing of
the past. I didn't stop until I got within those awesome
precincts called 'the Private Side', chilly with exhal-
ations of the Headmasterly occupation. But, after the
initial automatic access of guilt, I wasn't frightened. I
was excited but not frightened, because I guessed that
what the Head wanted to see me about was my essay.

The maid showed me into his study. It was a large,
square, rather bleak room, with photographs of Greek
statues on the walls, and on the floor a leather sofa and
armchairs, which had been drawn back from the fireplace, leaving an open space, for what? For swishing,
doubtless, and for a moment all my fears came back.
Like other over-law-abiding people I had a correspond-
ing sense of guilt. But I recovered, recovered to the
point of feeling rather annoyed that I had hurried to
keep an appointment when the Head wasn't there. I
didn't like to sit down without being asked, and the
shiny, slippery chairs seemed to repel the human frame.

At last he came – a tall thin sallow man with a black
moustache. Most men had moustaches then, they
hadn't long given up wearing whiskers. He shook
hands with me a little absently and apologized for
being late. 'I had to see the other team off,' he said,

waving me to a chair. 'I couldn't let them go without . . . er . . . condoling with them. We have a very strong side this summer, very strong.' His manner was more magisterial than that of most headmasters nowadays; yet he seemed embarrassed too, and remained standing, shifting his weight from one foot to the other.

'You've been a good boy, Mardick,' he began abruptly. 'Very good. Some might say *too* good' – he gave a laugh – 'but *I* shouldn't. I expect you know what I'm going to say to you?'

'Well, sir—' I began, and the opening sentence of my essay on the comparative interest of persons and things floated into my mind.

'It's a great pity in my opinion,' he went on, 'a very great pity. No doubt your parents know best, but we had hoped – well, never mind what we had hoped.'

I stared at him with a sinking heart.

'You're a good boy,' he said again. 'You've been a credit to yourself and the school, and we shall miss you – I personally shall, though I haven't seen a great deal of you, and in my opinion, for what it's worth – I think Dr. Manningham agrees with me – this little trouble of the cough and temperature is only a passing indisposition – growing pains, you might say. You've been growing fast, you're quite a man now.' He smiled. 'But your parents think differently, and it's for them to decide. I wouldn't go against them, even if I could; I shouldn't like to take the responsibility. But I'm sorry to lose you and I wish you luck in your . . . your new life.'

'Then am I leaving St. Peter's, sir?' I said.

'I'm afraid so, I'm very much afraid so. Your parents think that an open-air life on your uncle's farm will set your health up, and I sincerely hope they're right.'

I suppose I looked as stricken as I felt. The Headmaster moved over and stood by me.

'I'm afraid it comes as a bit of a shock to you. I thought your parents would have prepared you for it.'

'They did say something,' I mumbled.

'But you hoped it wouldn't happen? Well, it's no use prolonging the agony, is it? I've sometimes had to say good-bye in this room to boys I was glad to say good-bye to – in other words I've had to expel them.' The Headmaster screwed his face up, frowning so portentously that his moustache nearly met his eyebrows. 'You look sorrier than they did, which shows that St. Peter's still has something to offer its *alumni*.' He held his hand out, and I rose to take it. 'Well, good-bye, my dear boy,' he said. 'I shall follow your career with interest, and after your – er – agricultural training, I hope you'll live to write a Georgic. You never had to write one out, have you?'

Copying out a Georgic was one of the worst punishments one could get.

'No, sir,' I said.

'Never been set any lines, eh?'

'Well, sir, only a few.'

The Headmaster shook his head in mock dismay. 'Now, don't go blotting your copy-book just because you're out of my control. And come and pay us a visit sometimes, Mardick – Giles, I suppose I ought to call you now.'

XI

Not trusting myself to speak I nodded – the nod might
have passed for a bow – and somehow got out of the
room. My school-fellows had long ago dispersed – the
gateway was empty as I rode through it on my new
Humber bicycle – my father's present to me on my seven-
teenth birthday. It had taken me several weeks to learn
to ride it, with many spills on the lawn, narrowly missing the croquet-hoops – partly because my father had
such pronounced theories about the art of riding that I
couldn't combine them with the act. This was almost the
first time I wasn't conscious of my balance, of having to
lean over on the side the front wheel was turning, to put
on the brake, that scraped the tyre of the wheel, gently,
for fear of being thrown over the handle-bars, to make
sure before I mounted that it wasn't clogged with mud.
Never to use my foot as an extra brake when coasting
(not that there was any hill to coast down between
St. Peter's and our house). There were tram-lines to be
avoided, in case a wheel got caught in them and skidded.
These only went as far as the market-place, but afterwards came Narrow Street, where the Saturday traffic,
even in those horse-drawn days, was liable to pile up
and necessitate much mounting and dismounting.

'Always use the step,' my father would say; 'it looks slovenly to throw your leg over the saddle, and you might kick somebody.' His fears were always lest one should transgress some athletic or scientific canon; my mother's lest one should endanger life and limb.

But I didn't think about any of those things, I just rode on, down Broad Street, over the water-bridge until I came to the level-crossing, where perforce I had to get off, for the gates were closed, a goods train of the Midland Railway barred the way. This was the worst obstacle one could encounter, automatically I began to count the clanging, swaying trucks; fifty-six there were, not quite a record. At length appeared the guard's van, the signal of release. I put my foot on the step and waited for the man to open the gate; but he didn't come, and looking round, I saw why. Another goods train, Midland by the engine, was approaching from the opposite direction. The two trains met, they passed each other; a few hardy pedestrians hurried through the hand-gates. Then the new monster puffed its way across; fifty-eight trucks this time. I've seldom known such a sense of frustration as those two trains gave me; they seemed to hold up the current of my life, and destroy what little self-control I had left.

The gates opened grudgingly. On and on I rode, through the familiar landscape which soon became unfamiliar. I saw our house among the trees but I didn't take the turning down to it; I rode on towards London, eighty miles away, and it was only when it began to grow dark that my inward unrest gave way to physical exhaustion and I turned back.

My parents were waiting for me on the doorstep. 'You've given us a fright,' my father said. 'We didn't know what had become of you.' Mother didn't speak. 'It was such a fine evening,' I said, 'I thought I'd go for a ride.' 'You had no business to go frightening us,' my father said. 'It was very thoughtless of you – your mother has been terribly worried – she thought you might have been run over.' 'I'm seventeen now,' I said, 'surely I have the right to go for a bicycle ride? And anyhow I didn't want to come home.' 'Not want to come home?' my father said. 'Why not?'

And then it all came out. I shall never forget that evening – it was the most miserable of my life, up to then. I didn't recognize myself. My mind was doubly poisoned, to begin with by having to leave school, then by my act of rebellion against my parents – the first I had ever committed on a large scale. They had so brought me up and conditioned me, that I could only be happy if I was doing what they wanted.

While the food lay cooling on the side-board, I stormed and raved; I said everything I could think of – I said that they had spoilt my life and that I did not love them – but every word I said to wound them, wounded me far more. They were united to each other, convinced that they were right. I was disunited from myself, convinced that I was wrong. But were they united? They presented a united front, but I sensed their disaccord: I felt that my father, stern as his face was, and loyal as he was being to my mother, was really on my side; he had as good as said so, when they talked about taking me away from school. I couldn't bear the thought that I was leaving this last stone unturned, and I burst out, 'But *you* don't want me to go, Daddy, do you? You want me to stay here and finish my ... my ... education. You don't want me to be a farmer – you told me so!'

It was almost the first time I had seen my father taken aback. As many other fathers of that date would have done, he took refuge in severity.

'I may have said so,' he said, 'but I've changed my mind since then. We all change our minds, Richard, it's a sign of weakness not to, and that's one reason why you must change yours. And another is that your mother wishes it. She has convinced me, and Dr. Snape agrees with her, that an open-air life is ... er ... your best chance. You have done well at school, we freely admit, and we are proud of you, or we were, till you started making this fuss. You have upset your mother very much.' This was true. Mother had been crying ever since the interview began. 'You're acting in the most childish way. You're seventeen now and you ought to know better.' He paused to let this sink in.

I didn't feel seventeen at that moment; I felt fourteen or thirteen or twelve.

'And what will your aunts and uncles think if they hear you don't want to live with them? They won't be very pleased, will they?'

'Do they know you want to send me to them?' I managed to ask.

'Not yet, my darling,' Mother said, in that tear-stained voice that set all my nerves jangling. 'But we have no doubt what they'll say. They'll all be glad to have you – even Ada will. I know she is a bit sharp with you at times, but it's only her way. And you will have Aunt Carrie to talk to—'

'But that's just it,' I cried, catching the infection of my mother's tears, and using an argument which I thought would weigh with her, as a housekeeper. 'How can they take me in, when she's there, and often has to have her meals sent up to her? They won't want two invalids in the house,' I argued, throwing myself about on the hard, unyielding upholstery of the terra-cotta sofa. 'You bet they won't!' I shouted, glaring at Mother, whose tear-filled eyes opened wide in alarm. 'They'll wish me further first – they'll wish I was . . .' Dead, I was going to say, but I didn't want to tempt Providence. 'And how can they pay for me? I must have something to eat.'

'You needn't worry about that,' my father said. 'You'll go as an apprentice – many farmers take apprentices – and we shall pay the same fees as we pay for you at school.'

The word school brought back all my sense of loss and disappointment.

'Oh *no*,' I sobbed, burying my face in the sofa-back, as I used to when a child. 'You *can't* send me away, you *mustn't*! If you do, I shall do something quite awful, I know I shall! Something you will be ashamed of! I shall . . . I shall—' I stopped, appalled by a dark shadow which came racing towards me, as if I had invited it. My father rose.

'That's quite enough,' he said. 'We've listened patiently to you, Richard, but we don't want to hear any more. Now go away and tidy yourself, and when you're in a better frame of mind, come down to supper. You've made us over an hour late, as it is.' He stood up dismissively.

Being late for meals was a cardinal sin in my father's eyes, though he was quite often late for them himself.

I rose too, shakily, without looking at either of them, and began to leave the room.

'Oh, Richard, stop!' my mother called out after me. 'Don't go off like that, as if you were angry with us and didn't love us! We're only acting for your good and in after-life you'll thank us! Don't go away looking so proud and stubborn! Say you forgive us!'

I stopped at the door, just by the place where my father, practising a golf-swing, had made a nick in it. I was trying to change my feelings and my face into a pattern of contrition, when my mother said, 'And you haven't taken your temperature, my darling. Just stop and take it, and then you'll feel so much better.'

The habit of obedience was fast gaining on me, but the fires of rebellion still smouldered, and making one last throw, I said, 'I *know* it will be normal!'

I put the thermometer under my tongue and confronted Mother's tear-stained face with a devil-may-care expression. Defiance was no easy matter especially when its central point was a thermometer.

After the regulation two minutes, she took the thermometer from my pursed-up lips and for the first and
only time revealed its verdict. Her face had gone quite
pale. 'You're wrong, my darling,' she said. 'I'm afraid
you're very wrong. It's over 101.'

At that my resistance crumbled. So my parents were
right after all; I was ill, very ill. It didn't occur to me,
any more than it occurred to them, that they were to
blame for the rise in my temperature.

XII

'What's the time now, Denys?'

Denys' thin wrist turned slowly over.

'It depends how much you want to go on.'

'Time isn't as subjective as all that, my dear boy.'

'But isn't it? What you mean is, Richard, "Is there time for me to finish without getting over-tired?"'

'And without over-tiring you.'

'I was too polite to say that. Besides, isn't it my rôle to be a listener? All I have to do is stay awake. And should you need me in the night, I'm within call.'

'Yes,' said Richard. 'Did they ever put in that electric bell?'

'The bell to summon me – the bell from your room to mine – the passing bell? No, they haven't. They promised it for every day last week. Every day I telephoned; every day the man said he was coming. Every afternoon I stopped in to see it was done properly. They have no conscience nowadays, none at all.'

'And the window cord – have they mended that?'

'It's the same story,' Denys said. 'The man has been coming every day for I don't know how long. The jobs aren't big enough, Richard, that's the trouble. They're worth a promise, and that's all. If you were going to have every window in the flat replaced, and the rooms riddled with electric bells, they might think it worth while to come as well as promise.'

Richard looked round the room with a hunted expression.

'When I was young, a promise was a promise.'

'You only imagine that. Did you never suffer from diminished responsibility?'

Richard hesitated.

'Yes, I suppose so. But I didn't make a habit of it. Can you think of anyone – anyone we've asked to do a job – who's kept his promise?'

'Yes,' said Denys promptly. '*I* have.'

'Oh, my dear boy, I wasn't counting you.'

'No, but I count myself. I'm an abnormally good promise-keeper.'

'Why, what promises have you kept?' asked Richard fondly.

'To come and live with you, for one. Think what I gave up when I came here.'

'Your life of debauchery, you mean.'

'You may call it what you like, but I gave it up for you, as I promised I would.'

'You must find it dull here, without any debauchery to speak of.'

'That's as it may be. My point is, I promised to come to you and I did.'

'You make me feel I have a lot to answer for,' said Richard.

114

'Well, perhaps you have – and just because I kept my promise. And that's not the only one.'

'What other promises have you kept?'

'Well, not to marry, for one.'

'I don't believe you ever wanted to.'

'Oh, Richard, I *did*. I wanted to marry Celia, I wanted to marry Mary, I wanted to marry—'

'But you've always said you were in no position to marry – financially, I mean.'

'In a sense that's true – I haven't a bean, except what you give me. But Celia had something, and Mary had something, and I'm still able-bodied. Together we could have managed.'

'No doubt you could – but surely not with both of them? And you suggested a third. Who was she?'

'I'd rather not tell you. And talking of promises, I never promised to tell you *everything*.'

'No, that was *my* promise to you. But I'm not sure I'm going to keep it.'

'Oh, but you must, now that you've gone so far. And there was something else you promised me.'

'What was that?'

'I'm not sure it would be tactful to remind you,' Denys said.

'Do you think I may have forgotten it, whatever it was?'

'Well, you do forget things sometimes.'

'Remind me, then.'

'Oh, no, it wouldn't do. Besides you may have kept it – the promise, I mean.'

Richard knit his brows.

'Am I being very stupid, Denys?'

'No, very wise, I think.'

'When did I make this promise? In what circumstances?'

'We were sitting in this room – when was it? It must have been in the spring, because the plane-tree was just coming out – with those grey-green velvet pom-poms, as you called them, that looked so new and fresh beside the black, withering old seed-pods, or whatever they are. You've never been able to teach me botany! But you could see through them to the other side of the Square, as through a sort of trellis, so they can't have been very far advanced. Yes, it must have been April, late April, in a very early spring – and now I remember, we went into your bedroom, for some reason, that looks out on the other side—'

'You don't have to remind me of *that*,' said Richard, almost tartly. 'I know which way it faces.'

'No, but I was trying to remind you of the promise. We looked out of the window, on all those domes and towers – Oxford in South Kensington, you used to say – and flags were flying everywhere, and you said "Why?" and I said, "Because it's the Queen's birthday, you disloyal traitor," so that fixes the date, doesn't it, April 21st. And when did we first meet?'

'I never burden my mind with unimportant dates, but I think it was sometime in 1960.'

'Well, this was in the following year, which makes it April 21st, 1961, a Monday.'

'What a memory you have! Only just now you seemed so vague about it.'

'Things keep coming back to me. You had just got that little buhl clock on the chimney-piece back from being cleaned, and you were disappointed because it was losing, and we checked it with the time-signal—'

'What time did it say?'

'Twelve twenty-five, and it should have been twelve-thirty.'

'Denys, are you making all this up?'

'No, it's gradually coming back to me. And you said, "That reminds me of something." – Well, the promise.'

'Did the promise have anything to do with the time?'

Denys hesitated.

'You said something to the effect that time was getting on.'

'Ah,' said Richard, drawing a long breath. 'Now I know what you mean. Yes, I kept that promise. It'll be easier for you in more ways than one after I'm gone.'

It was hard for Denys to show relaxation, he was naturally so relaxed. But the hand he was stretching out towards his glass returned to him empty, and the cigarette-case he had taken from his pocket went back unopened.

'You're very abstemious tonight,' Richard remarked. 'No drink, no cigarette.'

'I'm saving myself up for your next instalment,' Denys said. 'Then I shall need every tranquillizer I can lay my hands on. Have you taken one, by the way?'

'No, do you think I ought to?'

'You're the best judge of that.'

'Get one for me, will you? You know where they are.'

Denys rose and opened the door of the corner-cupboard.

'There's such an array in here. Which is it?'

'One of the heart-shaped ones.'

'In my fingers?'

'Yes, of course. And some water to wash it down with.'

'Water is a thing I never *can* find,' Denys said. 'You'll have to wait.'

He went out of the room. Richard heard the tap running in the kitchen. The deliberation of Denys' movements gave an impression of reluctance; he never jumped to it. But why should he, Richard thought. He isn't my slave.

Returning with the tablet on his palm, and a glass of water in the other hand, Denys said, 'You ought to keep them on the table within reach.'

'Oh no,' said Richard fretfully, 'they're too squalid. *Memento mori* is all very well, but I am in no danger of forgetting.' He swallowed the tablet. 'Thank you, my dear boy, all the same. You're very kind to me, very kind.'

He paused wondering whether 'kind' was the right word. Kindness included a great many qualities; it was at once more and less than love. Less – no need to explain why it was less. More, because it implied in whoever had it an unvarying disposition to a certain sort of behaviour. Kindness was disinterested to a degree that love could never be. It didn't imply the self-indulgence of a preference; it was an attitude of mind, a movement of the heart, towards all sentient beings. Perhaps kindness was all the elderly could expect. The elderly could love the young, Richard loved Denys; no doubt of that. But did Denys love Richard? How often had Richard asked himself that question – sometimes tormentingly, sometimes (as now), with the conviction, the mental conviction that can sometimes influence the feelings – that it didn't matter much whether he did or not. No further experience that touched the emotions – and what value had experience unless it touched the emotions? – was likely to come his way. It couldn't, in the nature of things, come his way. The one experience he had to look forward to was death, and it ruled out all the others. The match was over and he was playing the bye. How often, before he had an inkling of what it meant, had he heard his father use the phrase. Indeed he had sometimes heard him say, 'I lost the match but I won the bye,' as if winning the bye was some consolation. In point of fact, his father hadn't minded losing, or not as much as he minded playing well or badly. His real opponent was the standard he set himself, a standard – for he accepted his limitations – less exacting than that of Colonel Bogey.

When had the bye begun for him, Richard? When was the match over? With the doctor's sentence, not long ago? Or much, much earlier with his summer at St. Botolph's Lodge?

'My life closed twice before its close.' As for that, are we not all, always, under sentence of death? And it hadn't closed the first time, he couldn't honestly pretend it had. It had taken another course, that was all, and given him a new companion, the companion that he had had to live with ever since and make the best of – a secret. Had he been a Roman Catholic, he would have confessed the secret, as Denys said; he would have had to. Sometimes he had thought of becoming a Roman Catholic, simply in order to confess it. His nature demanded confession; there had been times when he thought the secret might burst inside him like a bomb, splitting his personality into a myriad fragments, never again to be pieced together. But he didn't like the idea of turning to religion for what he could get out of it: and then, supposing the expedient failed, and the confession brought him no relief? Then he would be done for; he would have lost his last line of defence.

So he had let himself grow round it, as if it was an extra organ. The body was so adaptable, it could accommodate so many tumours, and not all of them were deadly; why shouldn't the spirit, too? And even strengthen itself with the knowledge of its lost innocence? That was a policy for life, the after-life his mother so often spoke of. 'It will be useful to you in after-life,' she used to say. Any amount of self-discipline, any number of disagreeable and painful experiences, could be accepted, even welcomed, on that basis. But when there was no 'after-life', only a few months in which to prepare for death? Of what use was it then to try and build up a character? To eradicate defects, or come to terms with them? To form good habits, force one's nature out of its proper course? Why did one try to improve oneself? For one's own sake or for other people's? Whichever the motive, it no longer operated, for there was no after except the here-after, in which Richard didn't consciously believe.

But if he didn't believe in it, why this urge to unburden himself, to complete a portrait which otherwise would be incomplete? No, not to complete it, that was the last thing he wanted to do, the last thing Denys must do. To fill in the outline, then? No, not even that. To suggest a background – the background of the Fens, perhaps, on a dark day? No, a background was too definite: it would betray too much, imply a secret that others might try to find out. What was wanted was a colouring, a tone, a sepia-tint, a mood – Richard's mood of that moment – which would be at variance with the events described – a success-story told in a hollow voice.

Could Denys do it? Richard wouldn't be there to see, but what he dreaded at that moment was the effect on himself that the disclosure might have. Would it utterly disrupt the balance of feelings he had created for himself and make the remainder of his life not worth living? And if he didn't really believe in an absolute standard of values which his confession would uphold, why make it?

Unable to analyse his motives, he tried to imagine his state of mind as it would be if he kept his secret to himself, and was at once aware of a disappointment amounting to panic, as though a flash-light that he had provided himself with for a night journey had suddenly given out.

'Come on now,' Denys said, 'you're ratting.'

Thus admonished, Richard took up his tale.

XIII

'I must tell you at once that they were all most kind to me,' he began, 'and if at any time I sound as if I was complaining, it is Fate I am complaining of, not them. Even my Aunt Ada, who could be so waspish, and could be such fun, went out of her way to make me feel at home. It isn't easy to feel at home in a place where you have always been a visitor, with a fixed date for your return. As far as I could see, there was to be no return. I had to adjust myself to this idea, and it was difficult, for I had always lived in visions of the future as much as in the present. My keenest sense of actuality had been at school; school was a microcosm that I entered into fully, but a day-school can never be as enveloping as a boarding-school and when I came home my interior life re-asserted itself, made up a good deal from the ambitions my mother had entertained for me, for it was she, not my father, who influenced my imagination. She was practical in small ways, and troubled about many things, but the man's world in which my father moved was a closed book to her, she could not follow him to the Bank, or to the political platform or the golf-links, partly, no doubt, because though he was successful at most things he undertook, his interest in them was always more theoretical than personal, and she was the least theoretical of human beings. And I took after her. Home was one cocoon, school was another. The perfect insect, the imago, that I dreamed of becoming, would not be moulded, licked into shape by the outside world. It would emerge suddenly, with no intermediate evolutionary process, and in that I was right: it did.

A good deal was going on in my uncle's house, and much of it I only vaguely understood – but I understood that I was not the centre of it, as I had been at my own home. At school, too, I had found a circle for myself, a small solar system of planets which revolved around this central luminary or that: the focus kept changing, but latterly, because of my successes and the hopes that were entertained for me, it had been me. There were several boys with whom, as a person, I counted, and there was a free-masonry among us, expressed in badinage, that made the interchange of thoughts and feelings easy. To use a term that hadn't been invented then, they belonged to my age-group. At St. Botolph's there was no one of my age-group. I didn't think of my aunts and uncles in terms of their ages. Their ages ranged, I suppose, from Aunt Carrie, who was eight years older than me, to Uncle Austin, who was nineteen years older – three years less old than my mother. I didn't distinguish much between their ages: they were all old to me, that was the point. With Uncle Robert, the genial, bustling, go-ahead man who had married Aunt Ettie, they presented a phalanx of maturity – all, that is, except Aunt Carrie who, being something between a saint and an angel, and always isolated by the nimbus of illness, had neither youth nor age.

Where was I to fit in? I vaguely knew I was an object of sympathy because of my ill-health – which also meant I was a failure. I had regarded myself as a failure before, when first I went to school and didn't do well and hadn't been liked, or so I thought, by the other boys; but that was years ago, and since then I had grown to look on myself as a success. The change to regarding myself as a failure was painful and bewildering to me. No one suggested that I was a failure, but I knew I must be, and not a glorious failure, like my Aunt Carrie, for whom gods and mortals wept, but a minor failure, a pale shadow of her, my diminished head not surrounded by a halo, but by an anomalous cloud of question-marks that obscured me even from myself, and stung me like the gnats (a particularly poisonous tribe) that haunted the bedrooms of St. Botolph's.

Was I really ill, or was I shamming? I felt they must be asking themselves this question, just as I asked it of myself. Dr. Butcher, who sounded my chest so care-fully, wouldn't say yes or no. No doubt he discussed me with Uncle Austin and Aunt Esther, and wrote to my parents, but he didn't tell *me* anything. His manner to me, which was always jocose, implied that he didn't take my condition as seriously as some other doctors did, but out of respect for medical etiquette, he wouldn't let this be known.

'Well, how is the new farmer getting on?' he would ask, taking out his stethoscope. Sometimes he came in the evening and I used to try to calculate from the number of shakes he gave the thermometer how high my temperature was.

What was his procedure, I sometimes asked myself, with Aunt Carrie? Did he tell *her* how ill he thought she was? She had been five years at St. Botolph's now, a semi-invalid; and nothing was ever said, to me at any rate, to show how she was getting on. Sometimes she would stay upstairs for meals, sometimes she would join us in the dining-room, when an extra place would be laid; no one, except occasionally my Aunt Ada, commented on her presence or her absence. It was evidently a rule, and I tried to follow it. Some of the virtue, the uniqueness of spirit had gone out of her. She looked like a wounded bird that cannot sing or fly; her face seemed longer, and her expression, the diffidence which in old days vanished and turned to eagerness the moment she was interested, had become more set, she sometimes seemed to be looking through one to discern a shadowed and hopeless future. She was a prisoner, I felt. Was she my mother's prisoner, the prisoner of her concern for the health of everyone she loved – Aunt Carrie, father, me? – for Mother was not unduly anxious about the other members of her family. Nor, though she was morbidly sensitive about 'giving trouble' in other people's houses, and would sometimes herself give trouble in her determination to avoid giving trouble, did she seem to mind, or even think about, the trouble that my presence and Aunt Carrie's were giving at St. Botolph's – two useless mouths to feed. Aunt

Carrie certainly did mind and I, too, was uncomfortably aware of adding to the 'work' of the servants, the cook, the housemaid, and Mrs. Bywell, who scrubbed. There was a lot to scrub.

The London specialist had recommended that I should lie down for an hour before meals. He did not tell me that this was part of the treatment then prescribed for patients suspected of being tuberculous. Before my mid-day rest I was supposed to have a walk and take my temperature afterwards. But Dr. Butcher was against this regimen, my mother reported. He wanted me to lead a normal life. So I had breakfast with the others at half-past seven (Aunt Carrie, of course, had hers in bed, and Aunt Ada was constitutionally and proverbially late). Then I would drive round the farms with Uncle Austin, in the light-cart, just as I had with Grandpa as a child – but with this difference, that now I was supposed to be learning something – something that, as Mother said, would be useful to me in after-life. So instead of sitting dreamily in the trap watching the horse tossing its head to keep off the flies – an occupation or lack of occupation that I had always enjoyed – I followed him down into the farm-yard, muddy or dusty as the case might be – and tried to take an intelligent interest in the cows, the bullocks (beasts, we called them), and the crops. I didn't ask many questions, for at school I was more used to answering questions: besides, I liked to follow the train of my own thoughts, and always have. But I could tell, with the instinct of my age, that my uncle knew his job very well, just as I could tell, without having to be told, that I didn't know it and should never learn. Uncle Austin was by nature quick-tempered and impatient; he seldom showed this side of himself to me, but I was sometimes aware of a controlled exasperation of which I felt I was the cause.

Every now and then I went out with Uncle Hal, and to these excursions I looked forward as to a holiday – for Uncle Hal was a man who didn't take, or who pretended not to take, farming very seriously. Nor did he expect me to. He was a big strong fellow, with the geniality that sometimes, but not always, goes with men of that type. He sized me up and used to say, 'We'll make a farmer of you yet!' – as much as to say, 'We shan't, but it doesn't matter.' Alone of the family, he gave me the impression that things didn't matter. In this he was very different from my mother and father, and most of my relations, who, in their several ways, believed that things mattered a great deal; it was part of their religion. Uncle Hal used to say, 'I don't think we'll bother about Black Bank today – I'm sure it's getting on quite nicely.' Or, 'Let's give Griffin Fen a miss and take a look at the George at Rookland instead – only you mustn't let on about it.' I would sit in the trap and hold the reins till he came out and very glad I was when he did, for I still didn't like being left in charge of a horse.

Uncle Hal, as far as I can remember, didn't try to teach me anything, but of all the family it was he who had the most influence on me, certainly as regards my attitude towards my physical self. The others were just grown-ups, living in a world apart from mine. In those days, Denys, people weren't broken up into age-groups, as they are now, but the great divide between youth and age was much more definite. Uncle Hal was an adult male with some of the boy left in him; he could talk my language if he chose. The shades of the prison-house hadn't closed upon him. And yet the feeling, which I was only dimly aware of, that I was growing younger instead of older at the beginning of that long summer at St. Botolph's, came from him, more than from anyone, because by him I could measure my own stature, and the more I measured it, the less it grew.

This was partly due to his physical size, which I saw no hope of emulating. One couldn't think of him apart from it; he wore it like his clothes, I had every reason to be conscious of it because, when I came, he gener-ously gave up his bedroom to me, and went to another which looked east and was hardly large enough to hold him. His own room had a big window which gave me the fresh air I was supposed to need. It looked west-wards to Rookland Abbey, two-and-a-half miles away. You could see across the trees the massive tower with its squat spire, and stretching from it the straight line of wall, the arm, as I thought of it, which held up, like a torn garment, the empty frame of the great west window. In winter you could also see the Norman dog-tooth arch which many thought the crowning glory of the Abbey, but in summer the trees hid it.

The room itself was eloquent of my uncle's occupa-tion, for not only did it contain the cups and medals he had won in athletic events, but its walls were lined with groups of cricket elevens, rugger fifteens, gym eights, memorials of his schooldays, and after. In these photographs you could see him growing from boy to man – the unformed, childish features which I could sometimes hardly recognize, changing to my moustached Uncle Hal. In the earlier groups, he would be on the outside, standing, looking diffident; in the later ones he would be sitting in the middle, bat in hand or football on his knees, for always he seemed to end up captain, and as such he wore a captain's air of authority, not looking for trouble but quite prepared to meet it. And always radiating health.

It was his health I envied him, his health and the well-being that went with it, of which he seemed so utterly unconscious. Looking at him in his stages on the way to manhood made me feel small, undeveloped, juvenile, with the growth I had been putting on, checked and frustrated. And as the days passed, this conviction took hold of me and strengthened. The years dropped from me. I was the little boy who used to spend Christmas at St. Botolph's, to whom his elders were kind and forbearing, and who was deferential and polite to them. I could see no way of asserting or even expressing myself that wouldn't somehow be disrespectful. Angry young men were then unheard of, though I suppose not unknown; besides, whom had I to be angry with? Only with Fate, which had inflicted this dubious illness on me, in which I, and, as far as I could see, most other people, only half believed, though they were too tactful to say so. I could be, and sometimes was, angry with Mother. But resentment against her was an emotion so foreign to my thoughts and feelings, and so painful, if I allowed myself to indulge it, that I quickly gave it up.

The cough sometimes kept me, and perhaps others, awake at night; they would say they heard me coughing. But I didn't *feel* ill, even in the evening when my temperature was presumably up, indeed then least of all. Unless Dr. Butcher happened to be there, my Aunt Esther took it. As usual, she was most active on my behalf, suggesting things I might do to amuse myself; for she alone among my relations thought that amusement was an essential ingredient of life. But after a while her invention flagged and anyhow the amusements she suggested – walks, solitary croquet practice, exploring the garden, driving with her to Rookland to do some shopping – were not such as would engage my normal interests, which still harked back to the collective life of my contemporaries at school.

Moreover, just after I came, appeared a new inmate to take up Aunt Esther's and the household's already overburdened time – this was her widowed mother, a bearded, deaf old lady. I tried to be nice to her – Mother had told me I must always be nice to old people, because they were lonely and I myself should be old one day – but like someone on a bad telephone wire, I couldn't get through to her, and was never quite sure if she knew who I was or what I was supposed to be doing. In those days quite young women voluntarily relinquished youth, and put on caps that gave them the status of an old person, a caste apart, almost as if they had been nuns. Mrs. Wright generally had her breakfast upstairs, but she appeared at other meals, and added considerably to the difficulty of conversation, for she could not join in but must not be left out.

One result of her arrival was that Aunt Carrie insisted on giving up her bedroom (there were three bedrooms on the south side of the house, two large ones, and a small one in between, occupied by my Aunt Ada – from the glimpses I sometimes got, it was always very untidy). Aunt Carrie had had the left-hand one; the other, the Lilac Room, was reserved for guests. Aunt Carrie moved into the Pink Room, Aunt Ettie's room before she married, with an iron bed, an east aspect and not much light at that, for the heavy eaves that surrounded the house, and sheltered swallows' nests, took away much of the light there was. Just outside her door was a grandfather clock with the loudest, most startling and strident strike I ever heard. It gave a few wheezes of warning, and then! – I sometimes used to lie awake listening for it, in my room across the landing, and for Aunt Carrie the Pink Room must have seemed like a belfry or a smithy – but she would have it, and though Aunt Esther protested, Aunt Carrie's lightest word was law. Unselfishness was the only form of self-expression left her; but it was ingrained in her nature and never looked like self-denial.

I longed to confide in her. I felt that if only I could have one good talk with her, all my difficulties – the uncertainty and bewilderment I felt, the loneliness, the sense of guilt and failure – would be removed. She had been through all that I had, and much more: she must know about it. But I didn't like to waylay her, or ask for an appointment with her, the legend of her apartness that must on no account be intruded on, was much too strong. If St. Botolph's was an isolation hospital, it was we who were in quarantine, not she. And I felt diffident of approaching her with problems that could only remind her of her own – nor could I be sure, even with her, that my illness wasn't regarded as a figment of Mother's imagination.

Moreover, she too had changed, I felt. Five years of invalidism, distress and disappointment had left their mark on her. She had lost something. Instead of the shy, soft diffidence that was once so easily aroused to eagerness and an overflowing impulse to meet her friends on whatever ground they chose, there was a permanent preoccupation – not with herself, I suspected, but with the problems she was creating for her relations. Sometimes she would give me a swift, sad look, as if we shared a secret that was best not spoken of. We talked, of course, she always talked when she was sitting with us, but it was like talking for the sake of talking – so much that was vital had to be left out.

My parents came over when they could, perhaps once a fortnight, and sometimes stayed the night, but when they came they brought a feeling of constraint and disagreement – my mother having got her way, but not really happy about it, my father having yielded to her, but not happy about it either – at least that was the impression I got. The laughter and the animation – my father's jokes about agriculture – which were sometimes aimed at me and in which I joined half-heartedly – sounded hollow. I dreaded the coming of the significant lull that meant I was tacitly expected to withdraw, and leave the question of my health to be discussed by my elders. It was almost a relief when the time for parting came, and my mother with a strained face, sometimes tear-stained, and my father with a set face, mounted the dog-cart to be driven to the station. I would follow them through the gate on to the road, and wave till they were out of sight. In those days, on a Fen road, many minutes passed before the parting guest was lost to view. I waved as much from duty as affection, for though one part of me felt my parents could never be wrong, another part felt that they had let me down. Kindness is a difficult thing to live with—'

'You're telling *me*!' interrupted Denys.

For a moment Richard was taken aback.

'Oh, but it's different in *our* case,' he said, 'I'm not kind to you, I'm just self-indulgent.'

'But the effect is the same.'

'Surely not. Anything I can do for you, Denys, I enjoy doing. And you repay me – in a score of ways. With my relations, I lived on charity. Not in the literal sense, for, as I said, my father told me, in the rather irritable, unwilling way he always spoke of anything to do with my illness, that I needn't worry on that account: he was paying my uncle the amount normally paid to farmers who took pupils. 'It's a well-recognized thing,' he said, challengingly, 'and as much to your Uncle Austin's advantage as . . . as it is to yours. And don't forget that.' I didn't forget it, and in a way it made me easier in my mind; all the same, I couldn't help feeling that the disadvantages, for them, far outweighed the advantages. I was in their way, an alien ingredient. They wouldn't have *chosen* to have me, I felt sure, any more than I would have chosen to go. All I could repay their kindness with was gratitude, and gratitude isn't an inexhaustible spring, by any means. Sometimes I even wished they wouldn't be so kind, since I couldn't be kind in return, and rather welcomed the occasional criticisms and asperities of my Aunt Ada – 'Don't sit like that, Richard,' she would say, when I hung curved over my book, 'or you'll grow into a question-mark' – because they gave me a grievance, something to bite on and resent. There wasn't much kindness at school. Part of the zest of being there was the knowledge that any commendation you got you had earned for yourself. I had trained myself to expect all kinds of criticisms, and without them I felt I was in a vacuum with little or no personality, just somebody that people were kind to and sorry for. Failure irked me. I had been a success, but success is something that must be kept in constant repair; nothing is so stale as past success. Here, at St. Botolph's, I had no future, only a featureless prospect of ill-health as to the duration of which I was kept in the dark. Sometimes I thought I would ask Dr. Butcher straight out what he thought my chances of survival were, but I didn't partly because I dreaded what his answer might be, and partly because I still felt, and felt increasingly, that my future was in the hands of my elders, only they knew about it, only they could decide what it was to be. I could hardly have been more dependent on them if I had been an infant in arms.

Complete with luggage for a life-time, I arrived at St. Botolph's. It seemed to have shrunk from what I remembered – it was an ordinary farm-house, like a dozen others scattered about the district, pitifully small compared with our red-brick creeper-clad school building, small even compared with my own home at Medehamstead – the house many sizes too big for us that my mother had persuaded my father to buy when we left Fosdyke. St. Botolph's might be sacred as a shrine for Aunt Carrie, but I had outgrown it – I was used to more spacious surroundings and a larger and more exciting world. Yet as the days passed, it gradually resumed its hold on me, its imaginative hold, I mean, and as unconsciously I slipped back into being a child, my remembered childhood's sensations re-asserted themselves. Certain features of the house and garden began to have their old, half-mystical attraction for me. The crescent of trees beyond the lawn was one. It contained, besides a sturdy lime-tree, a tall tapering cedar of a rare kind, rarer, Aunt Ada said, than our cedar at Medehamstead, which I called Dear Dora. In the middle of the crescent was a space and a rusty little iron gate that led to the steps down the ha-ha, into a wide paddock, bounded by the belt of poplars, which housed the rookery. Fallen tree-trunks, barkless and bleached with age like stranded, fossilized monsters, littered the paddock. I had scrambled on them as a child, and as a child I scrambled on them again. And there were other places, too, around the house that exerted a pull on me – the courtyard at the back, flanked on two sides by the house itself, and on the other two by the wall of the fruit-garden opposite, and by a line of farm-buildings that ended in the coach-house, with the harness-room, above, to which I would sometimes repair and revel in the smell of leather.

Smells meant a great deal to me then – now they mean nothing – and the one that most delighted me was the smell surrounding the fruit-garden gate. Tucked away between a coal-shed and rather wispy yew-hedge, the gateway itself was a surprise; and blown outwards from it was the rich scent of the garden mingled with the hum of bees. It was a magic place, that doorway, and to go through it, a transforming experience – one wasn't the same person on the other side of the wall.

There were other smells as well. Built into the side of the house that faced the road were two earthen privies, survivals from pre-plumbing times, but the farm-workers must still have used them, for the stench within was indescribable. All the same I sometimes visited them, on my way to or from the fruit-garden, and the contrast between the two experiences was amazing.

A dog's life, you might say, Denys, nosing about at smells, and you would be right, it was: but thought had become unsatisfying and even painful to me, for what had I to think about? Much easier to travel backwards down the years, and identify myself with the small boy whose sensations were more developed than his mind and whose delight it was to gratify them.

There was a dog, too, Ranger was his name, a fox-terrier of an amiable disposition, beloved by all. Generally his behaviour was unexceptionable; he even got on well with the black cat, Smut, whose name suggests how innocent my aunts and uncles were. He would let Smut walk under him with tail erect, a gesture that the cat was fond of making, whether in affection or defiance I cannot say. Like most dogs, Ranger liked to lick one, and it was this habit of his that brought about if not a crisis, a definite worsening of my nervous state. Really it was a matter for a doctor, but I should have never dared to take Dr. Butcher into my confidence about it.

Most of the books in the house were in two tall bookcases in the breakfast-room, why so-called I don't know, for no one ever had breakfast there that I can remember, nor did any member of the family often use it. It had a window on the courtyard, and another on the crew-yard, a rectangle enclosed between two gates and often very muddy, where at times the cattle were penned for some purpose which I should have known, but didn't. To the breakfast-room I would retire and take a book out, generally the Encyclopedia rather than a novel, for novels dealt with grown-up people falling in love, and this, I felt, would never happen to me – couldn't, owing to the logic of my circumstances. Indeed, any region of thought relating to the future, and most of my thoughts pointed that way, I instinct-ively avoided – just as I do now, Denys, but with more reason now, for the doctors have all spoken with one voice, and I know what they say, whereas then I didn't know, except that whatever they said, they were not agreed on it.

But the knowledge contained in the Encyclopedia seemed to me timeless, static, and complete, as it seemed to many people in those days. It was the word of truth that never could be questioned. We didn't realize that knowledge could be progressive, imperfect, superseded. 'I know it is so, because I read it in the Encyclopedia.' Some of my reading, you won't be surprised to hear, was about diseases, especially chest-complaints. The article entitled 'Phthisis' came in for a good deal of study, for phthisis, I supposed, was what I had: I had the symptoms, or some of them, the evening temperatures, for instance, and one at least of the 'physical signs' – spatulate finger-tips. I found myself feeling sick when I read these details, and made a prudent resolve to give the article on phthisis a wide berth.

But my morbid interest in illness, which I inherited from Mother, didn't stop there. I looked about for other diseases, preferably those which had sensational symptoms but which I didn't think I was likely to get – lycanthropy, for instance: I couldn't see myself turn-ing into a wolf. How I hit on hydrophobia, I don't know, but it fascinated me beyond the rest. In describ-ing the symptoms of hydrophobia, the author of the article let himself go. The extreme thirst combined with hatred of the sight of water – the bouts of delirium in which the victim wanted to bite his friends, alternating with periods of sanity in which he recognized and loved them – all this was done from an artist's as well as from a medical standpoint, and they affected my solitary arrested imagination in a way they never could have when school was giving me other things to think of. But the obsession might have stayed passive, a subject for brooding but no more, if something hadn't occurred to activate it. Ranger fell ill, he was hot-nosed, restless and, which was utterly unlike him, irritable. The vet. was summoned, but before he came, Ranger, with whom I was playing in an attempt to cheer him up, snapped at me. His teeth grazed my skin – I don't think they broke it, but the Encyclopedia said that, to bring on rabies, a lick was enough. In a day or two Ranger was himself again, but I was not. The fact of his recovery did not reassure me; the germ of hydrophobia could lie dormant, so the Encyclopedia said, for six months in dog or man, before declaring itself. Six months to wait! and at any time the dread symptoms might assert themselves. I knew by heart what they were.

After the first panic, a thin mist of melancholy settled on me, a gauze curtain between me and reality. I functioned as usual. I spoke when I was spoken to, and sometimes volunteered a remark – but cutting me off from direct contact with experience was always this preoccupation. My spirit was heavy and overcast like the summer, which always promised rain or sunshine, but never brought them. How worrying this was to my uncle, as a farmer, I well knew; I could see for myself how dry the earth was, the black, clayey soil of the Fens, clotted in lumps, and blowing about, if there was a wind, which there seldom was, in the form of dust which came in through the windows – and especially through my big window, which looked westwards to the Abbey.

As a farmer in embryo, I, too, should have worried about this, just as Uncle Austin did, and all the farmers whom I came across. There were quite a number of them, all keen business-men. They welcomed me for the sake of my family who had been fen-farmers for several generations; they rallied me and playfully asked me ironic questions about my progress; but I could tell, or thought I could, that they didn't take my pretensions to be a farmer seriously – they didn't think I should make one. Nor could I take seriously their complaints about the drought. Justifiable though these were, that belonged to a different order of reality from the one that possessed my mind; they were too practical, and I consoled myself by remembering that farmers always had grumbled about the weather.

The weather did affect me, however, it affected my nervous system, for the dark, lowering days pressing down on me seemed to prefigure the plight of my parched, sunless spirit. It has always been easy for me to identify myself with the elements – too easy. I could discern no current in myself leading in any direction; I was as stagnant as a Fen dyke – or rather I was like one of those dykes that had dried up and had wide cracks along the bottom. And the family, so it seemed to me in my non-participating mood, were at heart the same. They talked and joked, but inwardly their lives were governed by routine. Nothing could ever happen to them, the pattern would never change. Uncle Austin would never have the child that, according to Mother, he was longing for; Aunt Carrie would never get better; Aunt Ada would be confirmed in her spinsterhood; Mrs. Wright would live to be a hundred; Uncle Hal would never pay his long-promised visit. I forgot to say that Uncle Hal, my hero, had given up farming and taken a job in London with some wine-merchants who were distant cousins of his. He said he preferred wine to wheat. I might have been under the enchantment that surrounded the Sleeping Beauty – except that I was no beauty, and plagued by a fretful wakefulness, not wrapped in a charmed sleep.

But I was wrong. The pattern of life at St. Botolph's was not nearly so static as I supposed. If I had had more curiosity, if I hadn't accepted as final that the vital facts about me and about Aunt Carrie, if known, would always be withheld, and concluded too readily that I should never know anything about what was going on, if anything was, I should have realized that the lantern-jawed young farmer – he didn't seem young to me, I suppose he was about thirty – who paid us occasional visits, was also paying court to my Aunt Ada. It didn't occur to me, partly because I wasn't interested in such matters, and partly because Aunt Ada didn't treat him in the way I should have expected people in love to treat each other. She was even sharper with him than she sometimes was with me. She teased him, she criticized him in a score of ways, for his clothes, his manners, his way of walking, his accent – he couldn't do anything right for her. I even thought she disliked him, and I was sorry for him, and wondered why he came again and again, to receive so many scratches. I noticed that between these bouts of teasing she looked at him in a special way, that she seemed to know all about him, and his relations and friends, and what he was doing, and how his prospects varied from day to day, and I saw his face light up when hers lit up – as it often did when her sense of fun replaced her acid moods. Then they would go off for a stroll together, before or after supper, and come back with the look of people who had a secret which they didn't mean to impart.

But probably I never should have found out what it was all about if Uncle Hal hadn't unexpectedly arrived on his long-promised visit. I thought he would want his room back, but he didn't. He liked to think of me, he said, keeping his bed aired, and didn't care where he slept. He was as aggressively healthy as he looked in his many photographs; but I didn't grudge him that – indeed I welcomed the irruption of his positive well-being into our semi-invalid community. Only on one subject was he restrained and that, as you can imagine, was the subject of Aunt Carrie; he spoke to her but he never spoke of her – he obeyed the iron law of silence as the others did. But about most subjects he was irrepressible, nor did he mind saying in public things which couldn't have been said tactfully in private. 'Ada,' he called across the table, the first time we were having supper together, 'how are you getting on with Stanley?' (Stanley was the farmer who had been paying visits to St. Botolph's.) 'How are you treating him? Have you been nice to him, or haven't you?' The trickle of conversation which my Aunt Esther seldom failed to keep alive, died away, and we all looked at Aunt Ada, as Uncle Hal had meant we should. She couldn't be angry with him, no one could, as I afterwards discovered; but embarrassed she was, and her rather sallow complexion slowly turned pink. I had seen a grown-up person blush before; my mother often changed colour, so did Aunt Carrie, but never for that reason; and for the first time, I think, I suddenly realized the power of love, and it made a chink in the armour of my self-absorption. 'You mustn't be too hard on him, you know,' my uncle went on, 'you'll scare him if you are.' 'I treat him just as I would any man,' my aunt said, trying to laugh. 'He isn't perfect, you know, we none of us are, not even you, Hal.' 'I know that quite well,' Uncle Hal said, 'but I don't want to be told so, nor I dare say does he. Is it true, Ada, that he hasn't been quite so attentive lately?' This outrageous remark somehow didn't cause offence, for Uncle Hal had a way with him, it was understood that there was no malice in him, the ebullience of his nature carried all before it. When she didn't answer, he looked at me and said, 'And you, Richard, our poor invalid farmer. What are you finding to amuse yourself with?'

Now I was the focus of attention. I mumbled something about being very happy and enjoying farm-work. 'I don't believe you do a stroke,' he said. At this Aunt Esther and Uncle Austin spoke up for me, she, perhaps, with more conviction than he. 'Richard is coming on splendidly!' she said. 'And he's such good company for Austin.' 'Yes,' said Uncle Austin, 'it's a nice change to have somebody to talk to who isn't only interested in crops and cattle.' I scented criticism in this remark, though I tried to think it was sincere, but Uncle Hal clearly thought it wasn't. 'I bet he doesn't talk about crops and cattle,' he observed, 'he has better things to talk about, and think about, too.' 'Well, what, Uncle Hal?' I asked, as pertly as I could. 'Need you ask?' said he. 'A fellow of your age – it wouldn't be natural if you didn't.' I saw what he meant, and blushed longer and more painfully than Aunt Ada had.

'There, you see!' said Uncle Hal triumphantly. 'The boy is in love, or if he isn't, he wants to be and ought to be.'

Aunt Esther came to my rescue. 'Nonsense, Hal,' she said. 'Don't take any notice of him, Richard, he loves to tease. Some day you'll go too far, Hal,' she added, giving him a quelling look. 'We try to find things to amuse Richard, of course; but this is a dull, lonely place. I shouldn't want to stay here if it wasn't for all of you. Some day—' she sighed and left the sentence unfinished. 'I only wish Richard had some one of his own age to talk to. But who is there?'

'Well, there is Lucy Soames,' said Uncle Hal. 'She is

just his age or I believe she is, and she's an heiress, she'd be just right for him.'

Before I could answer – if I could have answered – Aunt Ada broke in, glad to get her own back. 'Why do you say such silly things, Hal? You know quite well that Lucy Soames never speaks to anyone – she isn't allowed to. I expect there is a reason for that – I'm told she's deaf and has an impediment in her speech. That's why they don't want her to meet people, they are ashamed of her really, because she isn't quite normal.' 'Which of us is?' asked Uncle Hal. 'Are you quite normal, Ada? And looking round this table—' 'Now, Hal, that's quite enough,' Aunt Esther interrupted. 'I've heard, too, that Lucy Soames isn't quite normal. Something about her feet being an odd shape – but I don't believe a word of it. If they want to live their lives in their own way, it's their affair. I only wish that she and Richard *could* meet – it would be something to amuse him.'

'Not if she's deaf and dumb and hammer-toed,' laughed Aunt Ada.

'I'm sure she isn't.' Sometimes Aunt Esther lost patience with Aunt Ada. 'But there's nothing we can do, to make them meet. I don't suppose you've ever seen her, have you, Richard?'

As a matter of fact, I had seen her, several times. Being such a near neighbour, I couldn't have failed to see her, when their dog-cart met our light-cart (their use of the dog-cart for all occasions was what would now be called a status-symbol) on the Rookland Road. Uncle Austin would raise his hat, and so would Mr.

Soames; I took my cap off. But I don't think she ever looked in my direction, even when Mrs. Soames, heavily veiled, was sitting by her husband, and their daughter was on the back seat, that perilous position from which one was so easily shot out. She didn't even raise her eyes.

A legend had grown up round the three of them, a legend of solitariness, inaccessibility, misanthropy. In those days, Denys, at any rate in the Fens, there was no habit of sociability such as we have, and as no doubt they have, now. People didn't drop in on each other much, either casually or by arrangement: there was no telephone to make such meetings easy: besides, the horse had to be harnessed and put to, it was a *business*, not like jumping into a car. And so most of the Fen families were self-contained, and even a visit between relations (I had several great-aunts in the neighbourhood, my grandmothers' and grandfathers' sisters, widowed or complete with husbands, who always seemed to remain in the background) – even those visits were something of an event. All the same we *had* a social life, centring perhaps round Dr. Butcher, for doctors, then as now, were sociable – their profession makes them so – and Christian names were used, though sparingly. But from this society, which was quite real although it didn't function much – except when certain port-drinking farmers got together – a great deal of port-wine was drunk in the Fens, and the farmers were justly proud, and sometimes boastful of their cellars – from this society the Soames' were utterly cut off. By their own wish, of course. Whether they actually put it about, when they settled, before I can remember, at The Hollies, that they didn't want to know anyone, I can't say; but the legend of their unsociability grew, and they lived up to it. Nobody crossed their doorstep, and they crossed nobody's. With it grew the legend of their wealth. Mr. Soames was a gentleman-farmer; he farmed for the fun of it; he was, everyone agreed, a very indifferent farmer and a bad business man; but why not, when he had no need to make both ends meet? Most of the farmers we knew, including ourselves, were struggling to keep afloat; and the possession of independent means set the Soames' apart from us. It would now, but in a different way. There was no socialistic feeling that they had no right to their wealth, but it put them in another category. One thought of them as 'living upright' – that old Fosdyke expression for people who had private means.

How much money had they? Forty thousand pounds, eighty thousand pounds? I used to hear the figures bandied about – with speculation, affirmation and denial, but their practical bearing meant little to me. I knew about Simple and Compound Interest, of course, and could have told you what, at a given rate of interest, £40,000 or £80,000 would bring in. But what was the purchasing power of those figures, what they represented in terms of living expenses, and how it might affect one to be in possession of such wealth – of that I had no idea. I didn't even take a realistic view of my sixpence a week pocket-money, and in principle acted on my mother's advice to save it up for something I *really* wanted. At St. Botolph's Lodge there was nothing I *really* wanted – except, perhaps, to get away: and that, I knew, I couldn't.

But romantically the Soames' fortune meant a great deal to me. It was the focal point of their legend – everything that was fascinating about them, their exclusiveness, their strangeness, their sheer unlikeness to other people, came from that. We, too, my mother's family, regarded ourselves as 'different'; hence Uncle Austin's quip about the 'Holy Family'. It was acknowledged between us, and taken for granted by me, that we stood on a pinnacle of moral worth. We did not expect other people to behave as well as we did – even my mother didn't expect it, though, on the whole, she took such a poor view of herself. It may be that the high principles of her family (which, Quaker-like, not only allowed, but demanded, strict attention to business) did set us a little apart from local society, just as our respect for education and the arts may have, and the multiple prestige of Aunt Carrie, which even her illness hadn't quite effaced. No one in the district had taken so much trouble, or paid so much, to give his children a good education as my grandfather had. But we didn't regard ourselves as socially superior, rather the opposite. I myself remember thinking, at quite an early age, that those less moral than ourselves were socially smarter. We did not hold ourselves aloof from the scattered isolated society of the Fens, indeed Aunt Esther and Aunt Ettie went to some pains to cultivate it, making allowances for the difficulties of transport and the distance of each house from the others.

So we had a social background, apart from that provided by my great aunts and uncles, and gossiped about each other. But the Soames' had none; they were utterly cut off. People said that he drank or that she drank or that they both drank; or that she was mad, or he was mad, or that they were all three mad. (In our family circle only Aunt Ada, who was curiously well-informed about the doings and misdoings of her neighbours, made these allegations.) But on one thing everyone was agreed, even Aunt Carrie, who hardly ever criticized anyone: that they were heartily sorry for Lucy for having such unhelpful parents. She had no chance at all, poor child. She had never been sent to school. Governesses came and went, but never stayed for long: there must be some reason for that . . .

Aunt Carrie once remarked, charitably, that perhaps the Soames loved their daughter too much to want to share her with anyone; and I remember that though nearly all Aunt Carrie's observations were received with respect, this one wasn't, and Aunt Ada said sharply, 'Nonsense, Carrie, they are just queer and selfish and stuck-up, if nothing worse, and you do no one any good by defending them.' This caused a mild sensation, but I remember that Aunt Carrie stuck to her point.

XIV

One other thing Uncle Hal did when he was with us, though I wasn't meant to know about it, and ought not to have known. I was going through the hall into the garden, and stopped to examine the front door for blisters on the paint. As a child I had always been tempted to squash them, and I still was, which shows, Denys, how arrested if not actually retrograde my development had become. The drawing-room door was open and while I was looking for the blisters (as there was never any sun there weren't any) I heard Aunt Esther say, 'You're quite right of course, Hal, we ought to find someone for Richard to play with.' 'Well, not play with, Esther, he's too old for that, but somebody of his own age to talk to. He goes mooning about like a lost soul. And of course he'll never make a farmer – it's obvious to everyone except his mother—' Just what I had been telling myself; but somehow the words had more force coming from someone else. 'Oh I don't know,' said Aunt Esther in her placid way, 'it's early yet to tell. He's a good boy and does his best; but of course we are a bit old for him. He'd settle down better if he had some sort of companion.' 'Well, I've suggested one,' said Uncle Hal. 'My dear Hal, you must be joking.

Even if we could break through that barrier, they're such queer people, not our sort at all. Besides, we don't want him running after a girl – he's much too young.' 'Why not?' said Uncle Hal. 'At his age—' 'I don't want to hear about your sordid past,' Aunt Esther said. 'Perhaps not,' said Uncle Hal, 'but the boy must have some fun. All work and no play—' 'His mother wouldn't like to hear you talking in that way,' Aunt Esther said. 'And we have his health to think of – he's not to get excited.' Here she lowered her voice – not, I'm sure, because she feared an eavesdropper, but because in those days people lowered their voices when they spoke of illness. I couldn't hear what followed; it might have been my death-sentence, for all I knew. When their conversation became audible again, Uncle Hal was saying, 'Well, what about Charlie Wittold? He's a few years older than Richard, but so is Richard – I mean Richard's old for his age in some ways, but young in others. He might do.' 'Oh do you think so?' said Aunt Esther dubiously. 'I don't believe Austin cares much about Jack Wittold, and the boy—' 'Why, what's wrong with him?' 'Nothing that I know of, but I believe he's a bit wild.' ('Wild,' I thought, what does 'wild' mean? and I envisaged some sort of savage.) 'I don't think Mary would want Richard to make friends with him.' 'Oh, don't you?' Uncle Hal said. 'All this cotton-wool—' Again their voices dropped, and my conscience, which had all along been an uneasy listener-in, drove me out into the garden, where the geraniums and heliotropes and the Red Admiral butterflies calmed me down.

For at that moment I felt utterly miserable. My general melancholy, the sepia-tinted gauze-curtain that enclosed my spirits, darkened and became opaque. What future was there for me? I could see none; and if the lowered voices in which my aunt and uncle had discussed my state of health were anything to go by, there might well be none. I was worse than a failure, I was a nuisance; kindly as my aunt and uncle had spoken of me, their words confirmed it. I was an added burden on an overburdened household. I should never make a farmer; I had known it all along. But I should have to go on trying for the three years that Uncle Austin had promised my mother to keep me.

No doubt he had promised my grandfather to keep Aunt Ada and Aunt Carrie, as no doubt he had promised Aunt Esther to keep Mrs. Wright. He was bound by these promises; we were like mill-stones round his neck; St. Botolph's was a sort of hospital, and there was no escape for him unless we died. No wonder he was more peppery than usual.

Why had he and Aunt Esther no children? For the first time I asked myself this question; for the first time I connected children realistically with marriage. I had heard Mother say that Austin was very fond of children, and what a pity it was he had none. I supposed that children were the inevitable outcome of marriage; and conversely, that without marriage there would be no children. My mother was a passionate baby-lover and couldn't pass a pram without peering into it and trying to catch the attention of the occupant. I had an

152

idea that Aunt Esther wasn't so besotted by them; she had been used to town life and to little niceties of living, unconnected with child-bearing, which I greatly appreciated. But how could they have children, I asked myself, suddenly aware of the practical and economic side of the question, when the house was already full to bursting-point? I knew that children and their accessories took up a lot of room, and rooms; where would they *go*, how could they be fitted in? For I at once envisaged not one baby, but a crèche. But for me, I thought, and the others, they could have had as many as they wanted, and it was unfair of Mother to inflict me on them and at the same time lament their childlessness.

Heavy with these thoughts, I wandered along the sparse shrubbery, that shielded the west side of the house from the road, towards the two earthen privies that were built into the wall. Just this once more, I thought, just this once more, I will go in and enjoy the appalling but exciting stench. It provided the strongest sensation that I knew, no thought, however obsessive, could stand up to it. I knew I ought not to go, but all the same I did go. I went into the first privy, and then when its appeal had – I won't say evaporated but had reached its climax – I went into the second. Here the smell was, to the connoisseur, still more pungent, still more intoxicating. After a minute or two I reeled out, breathless. The air outside was almost unbelievably pure and sweet and fresh; I felt at once ashamed and remorseful, exhilarated and self-fulfilled. Through a gap in the flimsy barricade of yew I saw the humped shape of Rookland Abbey – the ruined nave, the square tower crowned by its squat pepper-pot, and the empty frame of the west window, the coat with a rent in it held out by a stiff arm.

You may wonder that I harp so much on Rookland Abbey, Denys, but it had been a reigning symbol of my childhood, and as, in my eighteenth year, under the influence of St. Botolph's, I found myself returning to the mentality and emotions of my childhood, so did the influence of the Abbey resume its sway. It was partly due to the veneration amounting to awe in which my mother held the ancient building; as it dominated the Fens for miles around, so it dominated her imagination. Mother always wanted to have something to be proud of, something local, just as she wanted someone local, her family, my father, my Aunt Carrie, me. She knew, of course, that there were many abbeys in England more famous than Rookland; but that didn't affect the prestige that Rookland had for her or that it had for me. To this day it astonishes me if someone hasn't heard of Rookland Abbey. I don't suppose you had, Denys, till I told you about it.'

'Had you heard of Aspin Castle till I told you about it?'

'Yes, I had, from Emily Brontë's poem.'

'Does it mean as much to you as Rookland Abbey did?'

'Well, I've never seen it, but I like to think of its association with you. I couldn't so easily associate you with a sacred building.'

'I wonder why not?'

'Well, you should know,' said Richard. 'No offence meant.'

He smiled, then his face clouded over.

'But to go back to Rookland Abbey. Besides being venerable, it introduced me to the aesthetic view of life. Within her limitations my mother passionately loved literature and art. She hadn't seen much or read much, but what she had seen and read remained with her and passed into her being. When she said the word "pretty", it sounded prettier than anything you can think of, and when she said "ugly", it conveyed the maximum of disgust and disapproval. She was so small and frail that any strong feeling seemed to possess her utterly. I've told you before about the "M", the pattern made by the three buttresses on the north side of the tower, and how, when we passed it, she would show signs of distress, and not only herself turn away from the offending object, but beg anyone who was with her not to look at it. Sometimes she would forget to make a demonstration of disgust; secretly I was disappointed by this failure of her wonted vigilance, but I always marvelled that a few bars of masonry could provoke such a violent reaction in her. 'But it's so *ugly*!' she would exclaim, her face puckered with distaste; and I would share her feeling without properly understanding what it was about.

Since then I have developed my own aesthetic responses, but never to the pitch hers reached. Ugly! To you and me it's a relative term, but to her it was absolute. Do you think of anything as being absolutely ugly, Denys?'

'What sort of thing? Abstract or concrete?'

'Concrete, I meant – something on the lines of Mother's "M". But could an act, a thought, a feeling, be morally completely ugly?'

'"M" for morals,' Denys said. 'Are you making a statement, or are you asking a question?'

'Both, I think,' said Richard. 'I just wanted your confirmation of the statement.'

'Doesn't it partly depend,' said Denys, with unusual animation, 'on whether you are thinking of the ugliness, abstract or concrete, without a context, existing by itself, or as contributing to some purpose, as a means to an end? A machine may be ugly in itself, but as soon as it begins to function, and you understand what it is *for*, and what it's up to, it ceases to be an object and becomes an instrument – and an instrument is seldom ugly when you see it at work.'

'You're right!' said Richard. 'Perhaps Mother's mistake was that she didn't see the buttresses functionally, as a necessary precaution to hold up the wall, she didn't see them straining at their task, if indeed they were; she saw them simply as making an ugly pattern – a blot on a beautiful building – that hurt her aesthetic sensibility.

Though I inherited her passion for the Abbey, I hadn't often been to service there because my grandfather was a Nonconformist, and a pillar – the main pillar – of the Chapel. My parents were Chapel-goers too, as was Aunt Ada, and most, though not all, of my great-aunts and uncles who were dotted about the district. So I suppose was Aunt Carrie, but I always thought of her as having a private relationship with God – anyhow she wasn't well enough to go to Church or Chapel. But Aunt Esther was an Anglican, and Uncle Austin became one when he married her. They went to service at the Abbey, the great north aisle of which had been the Parish Church of Rookland from pre-Reformation times. I, too, when I was at school, was confirmed into the Church of England, partly from snobbery, because it was more chic to be Church than Chapel, partly because St. Peter's School was closely associated with Medehamstead Cathedral: we didn't wear the crossed keys on our caps for nothing. I am still a Nonconformist in many ways, but in others I am almost timidly conventional, as you know, Denys.'

'Do I know?'

'Well, you ought to. My parents didn't object to my change of religious denomination. My mother was even in favour of it: she thought it would help me in after-life (not *the* after-life) to be C. of E. That was before I started having the evening temperatures which made my after-life almost as problematic as it is now.

Sometimes I went to the Abbey with Aunt Esther and Uncle Austin, and sometimes to Chapel to keep Aunt Ada company. When I went with her, I seldom got off without a scratch, for she didn't hesitate to attribute my apostasy to unworthy motives. 'Your mother never thought that Chapel was good enough for her,' she would sometimes say, for she liked to give Mother a dig, though she had the sense, as a rule, to keep her claws off Uncle Austin. He would have retaliated, for one thing, which Mother never did. For her, from Aunt Carrie downwards, family relationships were sacred. I rather enjoyed Aunt Ada's spiteful outbursts, when I was not their target; she was the one unholy member of the family – she hadn't been properly moralized. Uncle Hal was a law unto himself.

After Chapel we shook hands with everyone, in an access of pious good-will, and then repaired to my great-aunt Crosby's house in South Street. 'Poor sister,' Grandpa always called her – why, I never knew. Aunt Ada, Aunt Ettie and her husband, who were still true Nonconformists, brought me along. Here, too, would foregather Uncle Austin and Aunt Esther, and I, if I was with them. I used to have a bet with myself as to whether the Church-goers or the Chapel-goers would get there first. After service at the Abbey, there were no hand-shakes, the sermon was shorter and unless we had the Litany, we beat the Wesleyans to it. We were all muted and decorous on these Sabbath reunions; except Uncle Hal whose outrageous comments Aunt Crosby secretly adored.

XV

The day he left, which was the day on which I overheard his conversation with Aunt Esther, I had a sort of nervous crisis. While he was there a door – a door into the outer world – stood open; when he went, it was closed.

The crisis was physical as well as mental. I sweated, and knew my temperature was going up. If only I could have felt a rebel! – But who was there to rebel against? Only God, and I had been brought up in too God-fearing an atmosphere to make that thinkable. I had the sense to realize that everyone was doing their best for me. Uncle Austin and Aunt Esther weren't cut out for self-sacrifice. They wanted to live their own lives, like other people. Uncle Austin was passionately anxious to 'get on' – and he had four useless mouths to feed, with all the handicaps – social, financial, and the rest – that such a restricted way of life entailed. They both wanted, no doubt, to be by themselves; but they couldn't get away even for a night, much less take a holiday, so many responsibilities, not of their own choosing, weighed on them. Yet they shouldered them without a murmur. Uncle Austin was nothing if not critical, his tongue was as sharp as his eye, which I sometimes caught fixed on me, his wary, speculative eye, as if he was committing some peculiarity of mine to memory. He was an inspired and merciless mimic, and I was always half afraid of him and of falling short of what he expected of me; but never once had he wounded my rather morbid sensitiveness.

The only human being against whom I did cherish a slight grudge was my mother. She, I felt, was more concerned for my welfare than for me: it wasn't my life, but only my after-life, that she minded about. She was sacrificing me to her exaggerated dread of illness, as she would have sacrificed my father, if he would have let her. Yet she was the person in the world that I loved most; I couldn't think a hard thought of her without hurting myself. And who knew whether after all she might not be *right* about me, as she had been right about Aunt Carrie? Aunt Carrie, she always said, worked too hard and didn't pay enough attention to her health: and what had been the result? A breakdown that had wrecked her life and nearly extinguished her bright, hopeful spirit. Might not the same thing happen to me, unless I was patient and obeyed Mother's decree of exile?

But three years! They said it was to be three years, and I didn't feel that I could face it. In rising panic I tried to switch my idea of life from one in which security was the main – the only object – into one dominated utterly by *risk*, one in which no one would care whether I lived or died, least of all myself.

I must run away. But how should I support myself if I didn't tell my parents where I was? And clearly I couldn't tell them, or they would follow me and bring me back. The longer I thought about it, the less I liked the notion of the life of risk, but the more I felt committed to it. I have my mother's temperament, Denys – plenty of determination, but no courage. It doesn't make for happiness.

At supper I tried to take in what they were saying, but I couldn't even hear it. And I particularly wanted to – partly in order to distract my thoughts, but most because Aunt Carrie happened to be there. She sometimes lunched with us, but very seldom dined: I never knew whether her appearances depended on doctor's orders or whether she chose her own times to come. They were rather a strain on us, those visits, and on her too, I think. We tried to treat her and talk to her as she used to be, knowing that it didn't deceive us, or her; and she was nervous, a red flush mottled her thin cheeks, and she plucked and fidgeted with her sleeves even more than she used to. And yet her presence, as always, gave the sense of an occasion; she could still put us on our mettle, make us try to frame our remarks to suit some higher standard. And she, the last person in the world to want such a thing, was aware of it and embarrassed.

I, sitting next to her, heard the wheels of the conversation creaking, without understanding where it was leading. She addressed one or two remarks to me and I answered perfunctorily, almost at random. Then my wandering attention caught my own name in something Uncle Austin said and I listened, but too late.

'What's that?' said old Mrs. Wright, putting her hand to her ear. 'I said,' shouted Uncle Austin, 'that Hal said that Richard ought to make the acquaintance of the Soames' girl, Lucy Soames.' 'Hal is always saying silly things like that,' interposed Aunt Ada. 'Who is Lucy Soames?' asked Mrs. Wright. 'The daughter of our neighbour at The Hollies down the road,' said Uncle Austin, in stentorian tones. 'Odd fish, they don't see anyone or let their daughter either.' 'Then they won't let her see Richard,' Mrs. Wright remarked, in the quavering voice old people sometimes had in those days, but don't have now. 'I don't see why not,' Uncle Austin said. 'There are always ways and means. Their horse might be running away and Richard here might stop it.' 'I can't see Richard doing that, somehow,' remarked Aunt Ada, raising her voice to Mrs. Wright's pitch. 'I'm quite sure Richard could and would,' Aunt Carrie said, and I was grateful to her. 'But somehow I don't think ...' her voice trailed away: since her illness, the habit of not finishing her sentences had grown on her. 'Don't think what, Carrie?' Uncle Austin prompted in the special voice he kept for her. 'I think it might be a mistake,' Aunt Carrie said, with the effort it cost her now to get the words out, 'for Richard ... or for anyone ... to break through ... to try to break through a barrier for which there may be ... must be ... some cause that we don't know about.'

'But we do know about it, Carrie dear,' Aunt Esther said. 'At any rate we know what everybody else knows. His father was a brewer, a well-to-do man; hers had some property in the North of England, I think it was. Farming is his occupation, not his livelihood. They think themselves a cut above us, and perhaps they are.' 'I'm sure they're not,' Aunt Ada said. 'Mrs. Bywell's daughter, Peggy, sometimes works there. She says the place is filthy, absolutely filthy. They never even clean the curtains, so it seems. I can't imagine what you mean, Esther, by saying they're above us. We are farmers; they play at being farmers, that's the difference. Richard ought to take warning by them, not try to make friends with them.'

There was a pause for me to take in the implications of this.

'Esther didn't quite mean,' Aunt Carrie said in some agitation, the unbecoming red returning to her cheeks, 'that they were above us socially. They may be or may not be . . . But when people behave in an unusual fashion, as Mr. and Mrs. Soames do . . . there is often a reason for it that isn't at first apparent . . .' 'Well, some say that they drink, and some say that they're mad,' said Uncle Austin. 'Those are reasons, aren't they?' 'They say that to explain the barrier,' Aunt Carrie said, 'in a way that's flattering to themselves. I don't know the Soames', of course – I've never met them. When did they come to The Hollies, Austin?' 'About sixteen years ago, when the girl was still a baby.' 'And have they never spoken to you?' 'He has, in the way of business, but she hasn't, or the girl.' 'How strange, how sad,' Aunt Carrie said, in a voice from which the rasp of moral indignation was noticeably absent.

But Aunt Ada supplied it. 'I don't know why you say "sad", Carrie,' she remarked. 'To me it seems plain bad manners. Why should they think themselves better than their neighbours?' 'We don't know that they do,' Aunt Carrie said. Her thin hands, which the non-existent sun had somehow printed with dark freckles, played with her sleeves. 'They may think themselves worse, not better . . . There are other reasons for not wanting to see people besides thinking oneself better than they are. Illness is one.' 'Of course, Carrie,' put in Aunt Esther, 'if you're not well it's another matter. But as far as we know, the Soames' enjoy perfect health.'

Aunt Carrie shook her head. 'If it was just *us* they avoided, I might feel as Ada does. But it's *everybody*! I don't know . . .' Her voice trailed away. 'Perhaps they're under a spell.' She turned to me. 'Would you like to break the spell, Richard?'

I heard, but I was still in a stupor of non-comprehension, and answered mechanically.

'I beg your pardon, Aunt Carrie?'

'I was only saying, would you like to break the spell? I believe that most people are under a spell of some kind,' she went on, 'and are waiting for it to be broken.' She looked round the table; her eyes beneath their lowered lids were questioning and appealing; and I suddenly thought, You're right! I am under a spell – perhaps we all of us are spell-bound. 'And it might happen,' Aunt Carrie was saying, 'that in breaking someone else's spell, one broke one's own. How interesting that would be! And yet what a risk, for oneself

164

as well as them. Because you see, one gets accustomed to one's spell, it's a kind of protection . . .' She hesitated, perhaps feeling she had said too much. 'If Richard stopped Lucy Soames' horse . . .'

'I don't think there's much fear of that,' said Aunt Ada, returning to the charge.

'I can't see a horse or anything else running away with her,' said Uncle Austin. 'I dare say she wishes it would.'

XVI

That night I had a dream about Rookland Abbey. This was not surprising, for it was the subject of many of my day-dreams: I longed to see it restored to its former magnificence. On the back-landing at St. Botolph's hung a print, dark brown with age but showing much more of the ruined part than was left in my day – several tiers of Norman arcading and the doors of the lovely Early English doorway. The print always excited my imagination, and I had got hold of a paper-covered guide-book to the building, by the then Rector, Mr. Le Fevre. I don't know how accurate it was, but it had a ground plan of the Abbey in its original state, complete with transepts, choir, and a huge semicircular apse, all of which had disappeared. Whether the foundations still existed under the tombstones of the graveyard, I had no idea, but I liked to think they did. The ruined nave was, and still is, thick with tombstones too.

I had been reading *Hereward the Wake*, and according to tradition Torfrida, Hereward's first wife, was buried in the nave of Rookland Abbey. Oddly enough – considering I was now seventeen – it was the first novel I had read in which the love-factor didn't seem mechanical and axiomatic: let A be in love with B. Charles

Kingsley was a correct Victorian novelist, bound by the conventions of his time, but he was not unconscious of sex, and Hereward's relationship with the two women – Torfrida, dark and proud, Alftruda, fair and flighty – suddenly became real to me. Imaginatively I lived with the book and in it. I was for Torfrida, I need hardly say: I felt that Hereward used her very badly. Alftruda was nothing but a minx. But the fact that he allowed his weakness for women to come between him and his mission to save the Saxons, thereby wrecking his reputation and his success in after-life, moved me deeply, much as I deplored it. The fascination Alftruda had for him, its strength and sweetness, moved me too, but did not affect my loyalty to her predecessor.

In my dream I was looking for Torfrida's tombstone. It was night, as it nearly always is in my dreams – I have seldom had a daylit dream – and the building, though already a ruin, was much more complete than it is now. My search began to have the urgency of nightmare: I felt I must find Torfrida's tombstone and yet how could I, when it was too dark to read the inscriptions? I peered and peered at them, and at last I began trying to trace the lettering with my finger-tips, but many of the stones were so thickly encrusted with moss and lichen that not a groove was left. At last I found a T and then an O, but was the next letter an R? I scrabbled with my fingers on the mossy covering, I even made them bleed; my frustration mounted and mounted and then I felt I was not alone – I had committed sacrilege, I had disturbed the occupant of the tomb. The ground was rising and breaking and something gathered shape and stood before me – a figure in a clinging white garment – a shroud. 'Are you Torfrida?' I whispered; but the figure glided by me, into the darkness, and as she went, I heard her moan – 'You have broken my spell, you have broken my spell!' But I could still see the outline of her, flitting among the tombstones. 'I have nowhere to go,' she wailed. 'There isn't any place for me now! Nowhere will have me!' 'Come back, come back,' I cried, still standing by the grave; 'I'll let you in again!' Then she came towards me, to within a few feet; and it didn't seem strange to me that her cerements were oozing, almost dripping with moisture. I couldn't see her face, was it Torfrida, or who was it? 'I'll let you in,' I repeated. 'I'll put you back.' Still standing on the broken, gaping earth, I held out my arms to her; she came into my embrace, a sweet, melting presence that turned my fears and frustrations to ecstasy. I had never known such a sensation of happiness. It didn't belong to me, me, Richard Mardick, it was pure bliss, and pure bliss it remained, before, and while, and after, I held her in my arms. The experience couldn't be measured by time, for it was outside time. Yet it was only gradually that I realized that the being I embraced so deliciously was not Torfrida, Hereward's wronged, unhappy wife, but Lucy Soames. 'You have raised me from the dead!' she kept murmuring, 'You have raised me from the dead!' And at those solemn words I was filled with pride and strength and ineffable delight. Kissing her I lost the sense of my identity, I forgot where and who I was. And then I was aware of a change and of the sudden onset of imperfection; I felt myself returning to me, and my senses troubling me with contradictory messages. She was no longer in my arms. Where was she, where had she gone? And then I saw her flittering among the tomb-stones like a great white moth; but she did not come when I called, she seemed to be escaping from me towards the dog-tooth arch where the Abbey ended. I ran after her and caught her, but at first I couldn't hold her, she was so wet and slimy she kept slipping from my grasp. I couldn't bear the weedy, watery smell her clothes gave out, but somehow I managed to keep her by me though it was a clutch, not an embrace. 'Come with me!' I urged, pulling her almost roughly. 'Come with me!' I was overwhelmed by the desolation of approaching loss. 'I can't come with you,' she said. 'There is nowhere for me to go now, nowhere, nowhere!' I felt in her a strength greater than my own, a strength that baffled all my efforts. We were standing by the open grave, and then I knew what I must do. 'I'll let you in, again,' I said. 'I'll put you back.' I pressed down on her shoulders; but as her feet sank into the earthy hole, mine sank too. 'I am going with her,' I thought, and in a panic tore myself away from her, from her arms that were clutching me, and flung myself backwards on the ground, and I still thought I was on the ground long after I knew myself to be in bed.

When I came fully to myself, it was broad daylight. I tried to piece my dream together but could never remember what happened after the earth closed over her.

XVII

I shouldn't, in ordinary circumstances, have made friends with Charlie Wittold, because he wasn't my type, and I was surprised when Aunt Esther asked him to tea. From what I had overheard, she didn't think much of him, either. But she was always anxious for me to amuse myself, and perhaps she was convinced by Uncle Hal's argument that I ought to have a companion more or less my own age. At any rate she clearly hoped we should be friends and I took to him in a way. He was on his best behaviour, as I was on mine. The presence of a stranger, who must be respected as such, had a liberating effect on me. Also at that time, Denys, I was incapable of disliking anyone; I wished everybody well, and I felt they wished me well. Even when my school-fellows tormented me, I didn't bear them a grudge; I felt that was how they were, and so long as they didn't roast me before a slow fire, as in *Tom Brown's Schooldays*, I didn't think I had anything to complain of. Even Aunt Ada's darts, that rankled for a time, didn't really put me against her; I came back for more. I had a Traherne-like feeling that all human beings were likeable and even lovable, and it was up to me to find them so. All this sounds very highfalutin and improbable and unnatural, but it's true. It wasn't until the 1914 War that I began to have doubts about human nature.'

'Do you still have doubts?' asked Denys.

'Yes, sometimes. I've become a sort of Calvinist – I believe in the Elect, a chosen body to which you and I, dear Denys, and our friends belong. The Elect in this world, I mean; I can't answer for the hereafter. I'm not sure that I believe in it.'

'And you still a church-goer?'

'Well, yes. What I meant to say was, I liked Charlie Wittold then, though I might not like him now. There was a fount of friendliness in me, which has since dried up. Not in every case, of course. Charlie Wittold was three years my senior. He was sandy-haired and freck-led, taller than me, and not bad-looking. He knew more about life than I did, and more about the facts of life, though by no means all. This partial knowledge he confided to me. I don't blame him for that; I was just as eager to learn as he was to teach. Like me, he was an only son, but unlike me he was an habitué of the farm-yard, whereas I was only an occasional visitor to it. What did we do? We strolled about, chatting to each other with the camaraderie of youth; being my near contemporary, he could tell me about farming in a way I understood better than when Uncle Austin told me. Farming became something to live with, not to learn. And it was the same with the other things he told me; they ceased to be an academic subject, and a forbidden one, they reached out, tantalizingly, to my own experience, tingling with promise. He told me how an animal would behave, and how I should behave, in certain circumstances. I took a lot from him, without question, because he was an older boy, almost a man to me. And also because I liked him. He gave me what I needed – friendship on equal terms. He didn't condescend to me, or talk down to me: I assumed that he enjoyed my company just as I did his. That there was something about him that my parents wouldn't have liked, I know; under his sandy hair that stuck out almost as if there were straws in it (but there weren't) his yellowish eyes were shifty and even his lean, broad-shouldered figure had a silhouette that inspired distrust. But if I was aware of this, I didn't mind it; I even welcomed it as a change from the high standards that prevailed at St. Botolph's.

Sometimes I went to tea at his house, The Limes, and I looked forward to those visits, boring as they were. His father had a fleshy, rough-hewn face rather like Martin Luther's, and a corporation (I seem to remember that in those days middle-aged men were fatter than they are now). After tea he would fold his hands on the gold watch-chain hung across his ample waist-coat, and drop off to sleep and sometimes snore; while his wife, a handsome woman with dark hair piled in a pyramid on her head, would make conversation with me. Full of curiosity about St. Botolph's, she would discreetly pump me about our way of life. 'I always think your Uncle Austin is such a generous man,' she once remarked, 'as well as a lucky one to have you all with him. Quite a house-full, isn't it? But Mrs. Wright is rather deaf, I hear.'

I wasn't a schoolboy, or ex-schoolboy, for nothing, and knew how to parry awkward questions.

'Oh, Mrs. Wright's all right,' I said, and raised a laugh. 'I mean, she can hear all right when she wants to.' I felt I was being disloyal, and though there was a certain discreditable pleasure in that, I added hastily in a grown-up manner, 'We're all very fond of her, you know.' 'I'm sure you must be. And your Aunt Carrie – what a sad thing that is. Such a brilliant start – such wonderful promise. We were all so proud of her in Rookland. Of course we didn't see much of her – she was always away. She overtaxed her strength in London studying – what a shame that was. Is she any better now, do you think?' 'Oh, I think she's always a little better,' I replied evasively. 'Is that so? We all want to hear that she is *quite* better. And you yourself, Richard? How are you getting on? I should like to see more roses in your cheeks – but there hasn't been much sun to put them there. What a wretched summer it has been, always overcast, and yet no rain, everything dried up. We shall soon be starting harvest – that will keep you busy, I expect.' 'I expect it will,' I said. 'You're looking better this evening but perhaps it's just a flush' (how my heart sank at those words). 'We must get you quite strong and well. In three years (it is three years, isn't it?) you'll be a real farmer. And then, of course, you'll have to think about getting married.'

'Getting married?' said Mr. Wittold, who was only half asleep. 'A man who gets married before he's thirty is a fool.' 'Oh, I don't know,' his wife said, glancing at him. 'You can wait too long . . . There aren't many girls round here, Richard; there seemed to be many more in my day. It isn't a good time for us farmers,' she added inconsequently. 'It was worse ten years ago,' her husband said. 'Well, yes. Your mother, Richard, she was so pretty and so serious, wasn't she? Too good for the likes of us, some people said. Your father came from Yorkshire. Such a clever man; I haven't seen him for years, of course, or your mother; I always thought he was wasted in a Bank – but what can you do without capital? Your Uncle Austin, too, he didn't marry a local girl. She came from the West Country, and had some money, I believe—'

'He waited till he was over thirty,' put in Mr. Wittold. 'Yes, so he did, but I hope Richard won't, and I hope Charlie won't, though he's my one and only son.'

She hesitated, but Charlie wouldn't be drawn. He mostly sat mum on those occasions.

'Well, there is Lucy Soames,' said Mrs. Wittold, and even I joined in the chuckle that followed. 'There is a prize for someone, but a bold man he would have to be. Charlie isn't interested in her, are you, Charlie?' 'Never spoken to the girl in my life,' Charlie said. 'Well, Richard, *you* should have a try. Human nature's the same everywhere – it all depends on how you set about it. But I don't know if your family—'

She didn't finish the sentence. She sometimes spoke of my family in a tone of awe as if it was a caste apart – not socially, for as I told you, Denys, our society in the Fens at that time was simple and democratic. There were no great houses or estates, only two classes, employers and employed, and very few nuances between them. 'Your family' was, I knew, a tribute to our moral worth, to the things we wouldn't do that others would do, and would do that they wouldn't. The Holy Family.

'But it seems a shame,' Mrs. Wittold went on, 'all that money, and the girl's youth slipping by her.'

Here Charlie, who had been showing signs of restiveness, said, 'She's only sixteen, Mother. She's still got plenty of time.'

He crooked his left forefinger at me, a sign for us to go and we went out into the stackyard, taking the terrier with us (everyone had terriers in those days) on a rat-hunt. There were plenty of rats about, in holes in the straw-stacks and hidden in the débris of disused objects, of which all farm-buildings were full; it was hard to believe that the farm – anybody's farm – was a going concern, with all that derelict lumber lying about. Charlie knew where to look, and so did the terrier, who whined and yelped with excitement. I shared in the excitement which, when the quarry made its movements heard, and still more if it came in sight, was breathtaking; but I didn't really enjoy the kill, and could only congratulate Spot in a half-hearted manner.

That day, I seem to remember, we didn't find anything, and, after a while, gave up the search and strolled about, talking of our favourite subject, sex. I don't defend myself, Denys, for the eagerness with which I listened to Charlie; but you can imagine the relief it was to find a compulsive topic to take my thoughts off my own troubles. That Charlie had had all the adventures he claimed to have had, I never doubted; it's still my instinct to believe what anybody tells me. Deliberately, when I got back to St. Botolph's, I would encourage fantasies of sex; they seemed to make a man of me in a way that nothing in my own experience could. The warnings that my father had given me against this sort of thing were so vague that I could pardonably pretend to myself that they had nothing to do with such indulgences, mental and physical, though in my heart I knew they had, and that I was running frightful risks to mind and body by giving way to them. I must have something, I argued, to look forward to and enjoy, and if other people couldn't give it me, I must give it to myself.

Needless to say, these evocations were quite unconnected with the emotion of love – they were purely sexual, if you can use such an expression. They were abstract and impersonal, I associated them with the body, but not with the body of anyone I knew, or was likely to know. The result of them was to make my daily life with my family even more unreal than it had been – I went through the day's routine like a sleepwalker, looking forward to the mental and physical excitements of bed-time, and to my meetings with Charlie, which would give me food for further erotic fantasies.

XVIII

One day I was bicycling along the road to have tea with him. I must remind you, Denys, once again, that our roads were like the divisions of a chess-board; a curve was as rare in them as a straight run would be in other parts of the country, rarer, indeed. The road to Rookland did swerve a little, which was one reason why I liked it, but even there, there was never a bend round which you couldn't see what was coming. The road to The Limes was L-shaped – you forked left to reach it. Before you came to the fork there were two houses, facing each other across the road, The Hollies and The Poplars, each approached by a bridge. But the bridge to The Hollies, on the right over St. Botolph's Drain, was much larger than the other. It was of old red brick, a beautiful arch, a perfect semi-circle. As it led only to the Soames' house, and few vehicles or people ever crossed it, the stone-capped parapet generally showed an unbroken line. But on this particular evening three people were leaning over it, Mr. and Mrs. Soames, and in between them, their daughter, Lucy.

They did not seem to see me, but when I drew nearer, the two grown-ups, as if by agreement, backed away and turned towards the house, leaving Lucy still gazing downwards. Gradually her reflection, elongated on the weedy but unruffled water, began to shorten; I could see her face in it, whereas the original was hidden by the wide brim of her hat. It looked small and sad and pensive, this mirrored version of her face, and had a greenish tinge, borrowed from the greenness of the water.

I wanted to escape from my thoughts; I wanted to do something to help her – I won't deny myself this impulse of knight-errantry. During the last few weeks a great deal had been going on in me that I didn't know about, or I shouldn't have acted as I did. I rode up to the crown of the bridge (one of the few hills in the Fens) where she was standing, jumped off my bicycle and said, 'Good-evening.' She turned to me forbiddingly and said, 'Have I seen you before?'

But I was not to be put off. Was I not a member of the Holy Family? – which was more than she was.

'I think you must have,' I replied. 'I sometimes see you driving in and out of Rookland. But perhaps you didn't see me. I am Mr. Austin Hardy's nephew, at St. Botolph's Lodge.' I pointed to it. 'I came here to learn farming. Before that I was at St. Peter's school in Medehamstead.' I meant to impress her, and perhaps I did, but all she said was, 'I think I've heard of you.' 'I've heard a good deal about you,' I retorted. 'What sort of things?' she asked.

That was a stumper.

'Oh, nothing that I couldn't tell you,' I said airily, but when I tried to think of something I *could* tell her, it wasn't so easy.

'Well,' I said, 'I know that you live here with your

parents, Mr. and Mrs. Soames' (I realized that this piece of information was unnecessary) 'and that you don't see many people, hardly anyone, in fact.' 'My mother and father don't want to,' she said. 'They came here to be . . . well, by themselves. They wouldn't like it if they knew I was talking to you,' she added.

This put me on my mettle.

'But isn't that rather selfish of them?' I ventured. For me as for my mother, selfishness was the cardinal sin: Aunt Carrie exemplified its opposite. 'Aren't you lonely, always being with them?'

She didn't answer, but said, 'I think I ought to go in now.'

She was moving away from me, but I called out, 'Oh, don't go yet! Stay just a moment. I want to tell you something.' I had no idea what it was. She turned unwillingly and said, 'They might be angry with me.'

I realized that we were both victims of parental tyranny, comrades in oppression. The thought was sweet to me, and wheeling my bicycle forwards to cut off her retreat, I said, 'That was what I wanted to talk to you about.' 'Oh, but you mustn't!' she said, looking round fearfully towards the house – a house very like ours in size and shape, but as regards the garden, much less well kept; the holly-bushes, dotted about in round beds of naked earth, looked stunted and forlorn. 'Please let me pass you,' she entreated. 'Perhaps they can see us. I've stayed too long already.'

But I could not let her go; and suddenly I had an idea, and, more than that, a plan.

'Fall down,' I commanded her. 'Fall down and hurt yourself!' She stared at me uncomprehending, her eyes wide with fear. 'Yes, fall down!' I urged her. 'Slip up, stumble, hurt yourself!' It was my last throw; I never thought she would; but all at once, with an obedience which made me proud, she clumsily fell forwards and dropped upon her knees.

'Oh, I *have* hurt myself!' she cried. 'You've made me hurt myself!' and struggling up again she showed me her hands, grazed by the sharp granite, and her knees, which were bleeding through her torn black stockings.

She was crying. I was overcome with self-reproach, and for a moment I thought of riding away; then I remembered my plan.

'I'm sorry,' I exclaimed. 'I'm dreadfully sorry.' And yet I had a sense of triumph. 'I'll take you in to them,' I said. 'I'll say you had a fall and that I helped you up.'

She looked at me uncertainly but I saw that she was yielding and pride rose in me again.

I propped my bicycle against the parapet of the bridge and took her arm. She leaned on it quite heavily for she was pale and limping and needed my support. This somehow banished all the fear I should have felt at the thought of the ordeal before me, and I had enough presence of mind to say, as we were traversing the weedy drive that led to the front door, 'I want to see you again.' 'Oh no,' she answered automatically.

She had stopped crying, but sobs still made her catch her breath. 'They wouldn't like it.' 'They mustn't know,' I said. 'Don't you ever go out by yourself?'

'Hardly ever. Sometimes I take the letters to the post, but they don't often write.' 'Don't you sometimes write yourself?' 'No, hardly ever.' 'Why not write to me?' 'I shouldn't know what to say.' 'Say when you're next going to post a letter, and then I'll meet you at the letter-box. Which one is it?' 'The one up by the Brickfield.' 'Oh, that's the one we use. I'll be there to-morrow at half-past five. You will come, won't you?' 'No,' she said, but I couldn't argue, for by now we were standing at the front door. She turned the handle. 'It may be locked,' she said. 'Sometimes they lock it.' But it wasn't locked, and in we went.

The hall was darker than our hall at St. Botolph's, but in the brief glimpse I had of it, I could see evidence of the Soames' reputed wealth in the furniture, which was stacked and huddled rather than arranged against the walls, as if they had never properly settled in. I knew enough about furniture to realize that it was expensive and good, but before I had time to take in more, Lucy pointed to the door on the left and whispered, 'They'll be in there.' She made no movement to go in, however; it was I who opened the door for her.

Mr. and Mrs. Soames were sitting in silence, one on each side of the fireplace. They rose at our entrance and moved instinctively towards each other. I had often seen a look of the deepest woe on Mother's face and on Aunt Carrie's. A trifling mishap to someone they were fond of was enough to call it up: my father was always begging my mother 'not to look so dis-tressed'. But even so, I was unprepared for the expression of horror and alarm on Mrs. Soames's face at the sight of her daughter's grievous slight.

'*Lucy!*' she cried. She didn't seem to notice me, but as Lucy didn't speak, I spoke for her. 'Miss Soames had a fall,' I said, 'just as I was passing by on my bicycle. I saw she was hurt so I helped her up and brought her in. I hope you don't mind?'

I don't know how I found the courage to say all this: I couldn't have said it a few weeks before.

Mr. Soames, tall – taller than any of my relations – long-jawed and swarthy – came forward and took my hand. 'We are much obliged to you,' he said rather gruffly. Then he looked at me again and said, 'But don't I know you, by sight at any rate? Aren't you at St. Botolph's?' 'Yes, I'm Mr. Austin Hardy's nephew.' 'Learning to be a farmer, eh?'

Mrs. Soames was kneeling beside Lucy, and gazing with such agonized intensity at her broken knees, that even I, who had been brought up to think that health, together with certain moral qualities and a sufficiency of money, and of course love, were the most important things in life, was terribly disturbed. Suddenly she looked up and said, with tears in her eyes and in her voice, 'We are so grateful to you, Mr. . . . Mr. . . . Hardy. Or may I call you by your Christian name?'

'It's Richard,' I said. 'Not Richard Hardy, Richard Mardick.' I was amazed and rather hurt that Mrs. Soames didn't know my surname. My parents had read *The Ordeal of Richard Feverel* on their honeymoon and named me after Meredith's hero, whose father had even more theories than mine. Mother thought Dick Mardick sounded ugly – another instance of the 'M'.

'Well, Richard,' Mrs. Soames said, as though addressing an abstraction. She rose and moved to her husband's side. 'We are very grateful to you, *infinitely* grateful.' Even I, who was used to Mother's sometimes exaggerated expressions ('Don't exaggerate, Chick,' my father would say) thought this rather a tall order. But Mrs. Soames couldn't stem her flow of gratitude. 'We can never be grateful enough for what you have done for us, can we, Henry?'

He cleared his throat, 'No, indeed not,' he said, but without much conviction. He spoke in a deep voice with a slight drawl: all my male relations had tenor or baritone voices. 'You've been a brick, Mardick – Richard, I suppose I should say,' he added.

For reasons that you will appreciate, Denys, I've always liked being called a brick.

'What can we do for you in return?' asked Mrs. Soames. 'May we give you a present?' 'Oh no,' I said at once, having been brought up to refuse *impromptu* presents, though the reason for this I could never understand. 'I only did what anyone would have done. But,' I added, looking at Lucy's parents, not at her, 'may I come and see you sometime?'

Thereupon they exchanged glances.

'I hope I don't sound ungracious, but we don't see people very much,' he said. 'We like to be quiet – that's why we came here. Won't you have a glass of sherry?'

Again I said no. My father sometimes drank claret with his dinner – it only cost one-and-six a bottle then – but Mother was against all forms of alcohol, although as a precautionary measure she used to take a small medicine bottle of brandy with her to Chapel, just in case.

After these two refusals I stood awkwardly, feeling I had been dismissed but not knowing how to take my leave, and still with a strong desire to linger. Then Lucy, who had been struggling with her tears, said in a small voice, 'Do let him come and see us sometime, Mamma.'

I can give you no idea, Denys, how deeply this request affected me. It was the first time, I suppose, that a stranger had ever expressed a wish to see me again; in those days people, even grown-ups, didn't say that sort of thing, at any rate in our circle. And that she should say it – should want it just as I did, and dare to risk her parents' disapproval!

They looked at each other without speaking, then Mrs. Soames said, 'I'm sure that Richard will understand if I take you to your room now, Lucy, and bandage up your knee. Look, it's still bleeding. We have some carbolic, haven't we, Henry? It will sting a little, darling, but you must be a brave girl. Now thank Richard very much for being so kind to you.'

'Thank you very much, Richard,' she said obediently, holding out her hand.

The fruit had been snatched from me, I could only swallow my disappointment. Empty of achievement, but heavy with defeat, I took my leave. How had I come to bungle it, when everything seemed in my favour? With irrational optimism, I had felt sure I should succeed where everyone had failed. As I crossed the garden to the gate, the neglected aspect of the place cast a cloud over my spirits; and I noticed that the monkey-puzzle, which I admired partly because we hadn't one at St. Botolph's, was dying from the bottom up. The serrated foliage along its snaky boughs was brown and dry and knife-edged, and where they had fallen off they left indented circles in the straight, hard bark, as if Nature had tried to 'ring' it. I wanted to get away and yet I wanted to linger. Then I remembered my long overdue appointment with Charlie and jumped on my bicycle and pedalled furiously. For a moment the shame of being late drove other thoughts from my mind. Should I find him, would he have waited for me? I longed to tell him of my adventure and kept going over it in my mind, but when I found him in the stack-yard with his terrier, which was darting to and fro and whining with excitement, I knew I couldn't.

I couldn't tell anyone, that was the trouble. If I could have, everything might have turned out differently. But if I couldn't tell it, I thought about it the more; those few minutes I had spent alone with Lucy obsessed my mind like a recurring tune. I knew I must see her again, my nature would starve if I didn't; the meeting had revealed to me the full extent of my unconscious hunger and the ache of my loneliness – up till then I knew no way of satisfying it except by amorous day-dreams. Now I had the key but could not turn it in the lock.

185

XIX

I suppose one's deepest feelings always find an outlet. It wasn't long, judged by days and hours, before mine did; but to me it was a timeless period, during which I seemed to lose touch with reality and mooned about going through the motions of living while my mind was ceaselessly occupied with the problem of how to bring about another meeting. I knew Lucy wanted to see me, I had heard her say so, and that knowledge cleared a luminous track towards her, like moonlight on the water. But at the same time I was beset by misgivings and the darkness that enclosed that shining pathway. I felt her parents' disapproval like a heavy weight on my spirits, for because of the way I had been brought up, I had hardly ever consciously resisted the will of a grown-up person, it seemed like law to me, so deep-seated was my habit of obedience. And I assumed that the household at St. Botolph's would share the Soames' disapproval. I thought that all grown-ups were in league and that I should never have a happy moment if I flouted them. Or if I didn't flout them; for by now my desires wouldn't accept their unspoken prohibition. Up to now I had lived the life that other people were planning for me, and found such happiness as I had in doing what they expected of me, but now I couldn't. I didn't hate them for their supposed opposition but it alienated me and drove me further into myself. I could see the person they imagined me to be – a boy whose precarious health could only be saved by farming and an open-air life and whose whole future was contained in this – as if it was some other person unconnected with me. I couldn't identify myself with this spineless figure or regard as valid the feelings of gratitude and acquiescence which had so far kept me going. I had no life outside my desires, which by turns tormented and ravished but didn't nourish me.

I could think of no way of communicating with Lucy. A letter might be intercepted. On one pretext or another, I took a stroll every day down the road to The Hollies, at the same hour when I had seen her leaning over the bridge; but she was never there, and I got it into my head that they were keeping her a prisoner, in case she tried to meet me. Wild thoughts of knight-errantry and forcible rescue came into my mind, only to be dismissed, for I have always been more conscious of what might hinder me than what might help me.

I lived with one thought, and that was Lucy. I didn't notice at what moment the hydrophobia cloud lifted from my spirits, chased away by her, any more than I noticed at what point the visits of Stanley, Aunt Ada's swain, dropped off. If Uncle Hal had been with us no doubt he would have remarked on it. Perhaps the young farmer smarted from her pin-pricks, and sought balm and solace elsewhere. I don't know how much she minded his defection, but I remember that she seemed subdued and I wondered why it was.

And if we didn't have many meal-time visitors, we had still fewer to stay. Since Mrs. Wright's advent there was only one spare room, the Lilac Room – with its picture of Tam O'Shanter benighted that used to frighten me as a child. Visitors came seldomer and stayed longer then than they do now. But one day towards lunch-time, I encountered a stranger – James Eldridge was his name. The others seemed to know him or about him; he came from the West Country, I gathered, with which my family had so close a tie. He was a fair, slightly-built man of middle height, already going bald, which made him look old to me; I suppose he was about thirty. He had a kindly, pleasant face, with nothing remarkable about it, and I was rather surprised that my relations treated him with special consideration. Even my Aunt Ada went out of her way to welcome him, she cracked jokes with him and rallied him with gentle teasing; she could do that charmingly when she was in a good mood. Even Mrs. Wright asked him questions and took pains to hear his answers which were generally yes and no. Then Aunt Carrie came in and greeted him with her shy warmth of manner and sat down between him and Uncle Austin – she always sat next to Uncle Austin, so that he might be at hand in case she had one of her attacks – they came of some nervous disorder, I gathered, which wasn't epilepsy. If she had one at mealtimes, she had to leave instantly, and Uncle Austin or Aunt Esther, or sometimes both of them, would go out with her. Once she got up so quickly that her chair went over backwards and she went with it. I was afraid this might happen again – I think we all were. She talked to Mr. Eldridge in her diffident, friendly way and I knew at once that he would never engage her in one of those arguments that my father and Aunt Ada sometimes did, which were bad for her, for she couldn't help taking what was said to her, and what she said in answer, more seriously than most people would have. The meal went on very pleasantly, as always happened when Aunt Carrie seemed better, until a moment came when Aunt Esther said, 'Now what shall we find for James to do?'

This was the first intimation I had that he would be staying for some time.

'Oh,' he said. 'Don't worry about me, Mrs. Hardy, I've got plenty to do. I have some history to mug up for next term.' 'Still, you can't work all the time,' Aunt Esther said. 'Even Richard doesn't work all the time.' She gave me a wink: she was fond of winking. 'He's learning to be a farmer, you know, but he goes for a walk every evening, don't you, Richard?'

'Well, most evenings I do,' I admitted unwillingly, feeling my privacy threatened. 'I go to the Brickfield, to look for caterpillars.' This was true, and on my way I passed the post-box, but Lucy was never there.

'Isn't it odd, James? He goes to look for the Death's Head Hawk Moth,' said Aunt Esther. 'Such a strange taste – I should run a mile if I saw one.' 'I don't go to the Brickfield to look for the Death's Head, Aunt

Esther,' I said, as indulgently as a would-be entomologist could, 'though I should be very glad to find it. You see, *acherontia atropos* is so rare, and so large, the largest moth in Britain. It squeaks if you touch it and the caterpillar squeaks too, fancy that! Just like a mouse.' 'Ugh!' said Aunt Esther and gave an elaborate shudder, and winked at us all. 'The best way to find the Death's Head is when they are turning up the potatoes,' I explained patiently, 'but there are heaps of other caterpillars in the Brickfield, because there are so many plants and bushes that don't grow in other parts of the Fens. There's a bed of gravel there, or used to be, that's why. It's rather like the Garden of Eden, in a way. You might find the Tree of Knowledge, but I don't know what caterpillar feeds on that.'

'Oh, Richard, how you exaggerate!' said Aunt Ada, who had been listening to me with marked impatience. 'Of course you wouldn't find the Tree of Knowledge – you're much too young, for one thing. Don't listen to him, James; the Brickfield's just a sort of wilderness – the Spoilt Acres, they sometimes call it – where some speculators, who wanted to get rich quick, lost a lot of money. I know your father believes in digging clay out of the ground, Richard, but here we are content with farming it, the old-fashioned way. Not that I mind your collecting caterpillars,' she said, giving me a sudden smile, 'though you do seem a bit old for it, and I'm not sure it's really kind to keep them in a box, even with holes in it, for how can they breathe properly, poor things? And sometimes they get out. I found one in my bedroom, and hated having to squash it.' 'Not a Privet-Hawk Moth caterpillar, *sphinx ligustri*, was it? A long green one, with lateral lilac stripes, and a horn on its tail?' 'I didn't notice it particularly,' Aunt Ada said, 'I gave what was left of it to the birds. They collect caterpillars too.'

She laughed and in spite of my grief at the loss of my favourite caterpillar I didn't feel angry with her then, as I should now.

Caterpillar-hunting had been a favourite pastime with the younger boys at school but at the age of sixteen or thereabouts they all gave it up – schoolboys are conventional and slaves to fashion – and I had given it up too. It was a mark of my retrograde progress – my regress, I should say – that I had taken to it again. I found it a more satisfying pursuit than the solitary games of croquet with which I had beguiled my leisure hours. And the Brickfield turned out to be a most useful alibi, as you will hear.

'I won't say anything against the Fens,' said Aunt Esther stoutly, 'but it's not like our Somerset country. No hills, no woods, no hedges, and you can see anyone coming a mile away.'

'That's not quite true, Esther.' Aunt Ada was always ready to disagree. 'There are no hills, certainly, which for walking is all to the good, and as for woods, I never liked them much. Elsie Needham was walking in a wood, do you remember, when she met that man.'

'When she met what?' asked Mrs. Wright.

'A *man*,' shouted Aunt Ada, reddening with the effort and with the shame of the disclosure. 'Oh, a man,' said Mrs. Wright, as if a man was nothing to be afraid of. 'A bear would have been worse.' 'Perhaps she was quite glad to meet him,' put in Aunt Carrie, 'if she was alone in the wood.' 'You don't know the story, Carrie,' said Aunt Ada repressively, 'or you wouldn't speak so lightly.' 'It's not for Richard's ears,' said Uncle Austin, 'he's much too young, and I'm rather surprised, Ada, that you brought it up. However, I don't suppose James would be afraid of a man, either on the road or in a wood. He could always scream.' Aunt Ada put on her sourest expression. 'It's different for a woman, Austin.' 'Yes, no doubt it's more exciting.'

'It was in a wood that I first met James,' said Aunt Carrie. Her words seemed to take the danger out of woods. 'I was a schoolgirl then and he—' 'Was just beginning to be a schoolmaster,' Mr. Eldridge said. 'Well, no harm came of that,' said Uncle Austin. 'Woods have their uses. Pity we haven't one for Richard. The nearest thing we have to a wood is the Brickfield, where he goes caterpillar-hunting.' 'I shouldn't want to go there,' Aunt Ada said with a light shudder. 'You never know what you might find, except caterpillars, and they're not everybody's taste.' 'Plenty of game, or there will be later on,' said Uncle Austin, 'when the caterpillar-season is over. Pity that Richard doesn't like shooting.' 'Don't encourage him,' Aunt Esther said. 'His mother wouldn't want him to, I'm sure. There are other ways of enjoying oneself besides killing things, I should have thought. I wish there were more young people of his age. You like Charlie, don't you, Richard?' 'Oh, yes, Aunt Esther.' 'If only Mede-hamstead wasn't so far away. You could go on your bicycle, of course, but Dr. Butcher thinks—' she stopped. 'Anyhow *you* are looking better, Carrie.'

Aunt Carrie smiled. 'I feel such a *fraud*,' she said.

'Well, you look more of a fraud today than you sometimes do – what do you think, James?' 'It's so long since I've seen her,' Mr. Eldridge said.

I wasn't much aware of Mr. Eldridge – James, as he soon asked me to call him. He spent a lot of time working in the breakfast-room, the room under the bathroom, which I had tended to appropriate for myself. I liked it for its newness and the views it had of the courtyard and the crew-yard. But now, even if he hadn't been in possession, I shouldn't have sat there much – I spent most of my spare time on the roads or in the Brickfield. How well I came to know the land-scape round St. Botolph's! You could go for miles without any sense of change. It would have been as featureless as the sea but for the landmark of Rookland Abbey. It had its moods, just as the sea has; but not this summer. This summer the heavy brooding air and lack of sunshine imposed an additional monotony. I lived with one aim but every hour that passed convinced me I should never reach it.

One day, still possessed by my idea, I came in from driving with Uncle Austin round the farms, and went into the breakfast-room to get a book – I think it was *The Scarlet Letter* which for some reason I had made up my mind to read. James was sitting at the gate-legged table studying history. How I envied him. I said 'good morning' and tiptoed to the bookcase, not wanting to disturb him; but he looked up and said, 'I have a message for you.' 'A message for me, James?' He hesitated. 'Yes, I think I ought to tell you. I meant to tell you yesterday, but didn't get the chance. I went out for a breather – you were out too, I think – and met a girl, she said her name was Lucy—' I came near and stared down at him. '– And she asked me to say, could you meet her at the Brickfield at six o'clock tomorrow. Only I wasn't to tell anyone but you. You would know who she was, she said.'

I still couldn't find words.

'She said it wouldn't matter if you didn't come, you were to please yourself.' 'How did she know you knew me?' I asked. 'She saw me coming out of our gate. She was about two hundred yards away, walking towards me, and when she came up to me, she stopped me.'

And I had gone that way scores of times and never seen her.

'Six o'clock tomorrow?' 'That's what she said. Not at the entrance to the Brickfield, but some way inside, by the chimney-stack. In case you didn't see her, she'd call.' 'Thank you very much, James,' I said. 'But you weren't to tell anyone else, Richard, nor was I.' 'And you won't, James, will you?' 'Of course not.' Afterwards Lucy told me she had known about my visits to the Brickfield; from a window she had watched me going that way.'

XX

Richard paused. 'It all happened so long ago, Denys, that I might be telling you about someone else, really, for I wasn't the same before our meetings and never have been since. I don't remember how long they went on, or what we talked about, because when I think of them, they merge into one. I didn't know I had it in me to be so happy, nor, I'm convinced, did she. Perhaps we didn't meet so very often, she could never count on getting away. It was much easier for me because I had the cast-iron excuse of caterpillar-hunting. 'Time for your walk, Richard,' Aunt Esther would say. 'I'm sure they do you good. He looks a different person, doesn't he?' And whoever was appealed to would agree. And I was a different person, because all my hopes and fears – for I still had them, Denys, even happiness can't change one's nature – were different, in fact reversed. I dreaded the thought that my cough would get better and my temperature return to normal, I dreaded the thought of leaving St. Botolph's. I would stay and be a real farmer, as my mother wished me to be. And with this end in view, I tried to throw myself into the work that Uncle Austin gave me – if you can call it work, for it still consisted chiefly in visiting the outlying farms with him. If he meant to give me any responsibility later on, he showed no signs of it – and I had been a pupil for nearly three months. How long I had been in love, I don't know, though I suppose the calendar could tell me, if I had one.

So our manœuvres for meeting were easier for me than they were for Lucy. My outings were encouraged, hers discouraged – in fact they were only made possible because her governess had left – left the very day before she ran into James. So long as the governess was there, Lucy could not go out alone. But even her parents agreed she must have exercise, and her first act, on attaining this partial freedom, was to go in search of me. All my efforts to get in touch with her would have been in vain, for with the governess she went out in the afternoons, when I was farming with Uncle Austin. Now there was an interregnum: it hadn't been decided whether to engage another governess, or to send Lucy abroad – to Dresden or one of those places. A governess was the more likely alternative, for they couldn't bear the thought of parting with her. A governess would endanger our happiness; the other project would destroy it. We were poised precariously between the two and it was this uncertainty that prematurely ripened our relationship. We felt we must make the most of our time and each meeting brought us closer to each other.

But it wasn't plain sailing by any means, for though I could always get away, Lucy couldn't, even without the obstacle of the governess. Sometimes her parents wanted her at home, sometimes to go for a walk with them. They were more jealous of her than my parents were of me. When she knew she wouldn't be free, she used to leave a note under a heap of granite chips for road-mending close to the Soames' bridge, and on the way to the Brickfield. To hide it she had to make sure that no one was about, and so did I, when I retrieved it. That wasn't difficult; the road was lonely; on the other hand either of us was in view for half a mile each way. Sometimes she couldn't warn me and my journey to the Brickfield was fruitless, except for caterpillars. When she was there, we used to look for them together; she quite overcame her fear of them and would call out to me excitedly when she found one. I have never known anybody, even Aunt Carrie, who could identify her interests with one's own as she did. And she was so amenable to instruction! – which was lucky, for on the subject of entomology I was as eager to give instructions as my father was on almost any subject. She went on foot – her parents wouldn't let her have a bicycle, for fear she should tumble in the drain. She timed her arrival for five minutes after mine, and I left five minutes after she did, for fear we should be seen together. I can still remember how empty and desolate those five minutes were, compared with the bliss of being with her. And the still greater wretchedness of not finding her by the chimney-stack.

There was complete privacy within the Brickfield. Until the shooting-season started, no one ever came. A dyke divided it from the main road, a dyke with a bridge over it. The bridge was said to be, and looked, unsafe for a horse and cart. There were, I suppose, about ten acres – spoilt acres – of the Brickfield, all unfit for cultivation. The company that worked it had dug out the clay. Somewhere towards the centre was a plateau on which stood the remains of the brick-kiln, blackening and ruinous, crowned by its broken chimney and surrounded by pools and hollows, mounds and hillocks on which grew scrub, bushes, and small trees, and here and there a leaning poplar, so characteristic of the Fens. And on all sides miscellaneous objects, pieces of machinery rusting away, piles of bricks which had been left behind when the place was dismantled. Except in the shooting-season, it couldn't be used for anything but what we used it for.

In the ten acres of the Brickfield were to be found more types of landscape than in twenty square miles of the surrounding Fens. And more types of vegetation. In spite of Aunt Ada's disbelief we did find the Tree of Knowledge, with its attendant caterpillar, the Serpent, coiling round it. And we may have found the Tree of Life, too, if life means living, for never before or since have I lived as I did then.

Even the soil was not the colour of the Fen soil – a deep sepia, glistening with richness where the plough had turned it. Here it was many-coloured; in some places red with brick-dust, in others white with lime, in others black with coal-dust, in others the pale grey of cement. Round the kiln still ran the level metal pathway on which the men had wheeled their barrow-loads of bricks for burning. Here and there a slate-blue unfired brick still lay about, as well as those that had been through the furnace. Deep red they were, a prettier colour than the rather ugly salmon-pink of those we made at Fosdyke.

Some of the pools were very deep; rumour gave out that they were bottomless. We approached them warily and hand in hand, peering over the edge until we could see our united reflections looking back at us. Or we would lie side by side under a bush, or scramble up a bank and down again, rejoicing in the differences of level that were as strange to her as they were to me, for neither of us had been about much, we were Fenlanders, as accustomed to the horizontal view as clothes-moths on a billiard-table.

As for the chambers where the bricks were burnt, at first we gave them a wide berth, for some had fallen in and others looked as if they might collapse at any moment. You could still see the holes, tunnelling into the sky, through which the coal-dust had been poured to keep the bricks alight, and the flues through which the fire ate its way from chamber to chamber. This rotation of the fire had always fascinated me in our brickworks at home; inexorably it passed from one chamber to the next, kept alive by the coal-dust and the draught from the chimney-stack. The bricks wouldn't burn off their own oil, I explained to Lucy; they needed outside aid. It was rather fun explaining, after so many years of being explained to, and I was not my father's son for nothing.

The chimney-stack had been a hundred feet high, Uncle Austin said. As a landmark it must have rivalled Rookland Abbey. What a fall was there, for only the blackened stump was left, no taller than the encircling vegetation, and invisible from the road in summer. It was square, not as the brick-chimneys of today are, round, and the summit ended in a jagged spike, like a broken eye-tooth, on which the very sky seemed to rest uncomfortably. Death must have been due to natural causes; for if the chimney-stack had been 'felled' (unpleasant word) the workmen (at Fosdyke we used to call them 'brickies') would have made a neater job of it.

We used to speculate about this and take a curious pleasure in following the ruins of the chimney-stack where they lay in serpentine coils on the roof of the kiln. Had the works closed down in such a hurry that the workmen had no time to tidy up? Had some of them been hurt or even killed when the chimney fell? Did they rush pell-mell through the opening on to the road, as if something was after them? Bankruptcy: the word was often on my father's lips, as almost the worst thing that could happen. I was never very clear what it meant, and even at seventeen was sometimes visited by the childish notion that it was a physical phenomenon, dangerous to life and limb. The Dutch-built bank that held the Welland in bounds had broken once: my mother remembered voices crying through the night: 'The bank's bruck! The bank's bruck!' – while a dark wall of water swept through the low, broad, ancient streets of Rookland. And another bank broke too – the London, Boston and Spalding Bank. Breaking, it ruined thousands, and the crash was still spoken of in tones of awe.

Perhaps that was how the Brickfield met its end – through lack of cash. My uncle would have told me but I didn't ask him. I didn't want to draw his or anyone's attention to the Brickfield. In it we had the secrecy we needed and I didn't want that secrecy endangered, even by a word. For I had an inkling that our feeling for each other would only thrive in an exotic setting: it was to be Love among the Ruins.

What did it mean to us, that love? you might ask, Denys. Well, it gave us something that we both lacked. It was the same kind of lack. She had suffered from it longer than I had, but not so consciously, for she had never known any other kind of life than the one her parents had made for her, nor any other kind of love. The existence of someone to cherish and adore, at one's own choice, and by one's own volition, was as unsuspected by her as it was by me. A skin had grown over her, which nothing had penetrated or even scratched until the day when at my command she fell down on the bridge and broke her knees. Yet all that time beneath the isolating tegument, desire had been growing with her physical growth, fed by a strength and singleness of purpose it might not have had if she had been exposed to the competing and compensating influences that affect other girls more normally brought up. She had no experience to compare her emotions with, or to dilute them or to take the edge off them: they were all for me.

And mine were for her too, for though I had a background of school life, and of a much more unrestricted family life than she had, I had suddenly been deprived of my natural context by what was thought to be my illness, and drawn into an isolation less complete than hers, but perhaps more painful, since I had known a richer, more varied existence, with outside interests to fill my day and the promise of a future which at one time seemed bright. And I had learned something about sex from Charlie, though not sex combined with love. Now those two forces had been united, and the effect on me was overwhelming.

And so our twin solitudes had been fused and the sense of loneliness, for me at any rate, had disappeared so completely that I couldn't even remember what it felt like. And she told me it was the same for her. She still loved her parents, but that love was a combination of many things – habit, gratitude, a sort of automatic unthinking response to all they had done and were, for her. She couldn't give them anything of herself that she hadn't already given. She was always the recipient, never, consciously at any rate, the giver. She couldn't expand herself with them or be otherwise than she had always been. Whereas with me beside her, she could indulge the wish to give that every woman has, with me she could be all that she had it in her to be.

She didn't tell me this, of course, but it came out of what she said – the feeling that she had the freedom of another heart and was no longer shut up in her own.

What we talked about I don't remember. What could

we have had to talk about? For subject-matter, I had more than she, for my life, restricted as it was, had been fuller and more eventful. She had little to tell that in imagination I didn't know already; it was contained in the legend that had grown up about her; she only filled in the details. There were other details, as I afterwards found out, that she didn't know. If she had known them, she would have been better fitted to face the world – and me. I suppose I told her something of what I have told you, Denys, not all of it, by any means. I must have done quite a lot of editing, but unconsciously, I'm sure; I never had the feeling, when I was with her, that I was holding something back; our communion seemed complete. Nor do I recollect when our embraces started, though I remember when they ended.

Inwardly my life was utterly transformed but outwardly it went on much as usual. Naturally, however, I saw less of Charlie. This was embarrassing because until then I had been glad enough of his company, and I couldn't help feeling that, though he never showed it, he was doing me a favour by giving up so much of his time to someone who was three years his junior in age and much younger in experience. My general sense of redundancy may have accounted for this: I felt that wherever I was, I was in the way. Actually, I now think Charlie was quite glad to see me, for he was lonely too, and perhaps enjoyed relating his experiences, real or feigned, to a member of the Holy Family. (As I told you, Denys, the Fen farmers weren't socially snobbish but a certain moral cachet attached to us.)

I made the excuse that my uncle sometimes wanted me to go out with him in the evenings, but Charlie chose not to believe this and said he was sure I had found a girl somewhere. This, of course, I denied – it was almost my first deliberate lie, and put me out of humour with myself, and incidentally with his company, for I had been brought up to be conscientiously truthful. Whether he believed me or not, his conversation became increasingly salacious, and this at first grated on my feelings which were romantic and poetic, and much more concerned with the marriage of minds than with the mutual appeal of bodies. Moreover it troubled my image of Lucy whom, consciously at any rate, I hadn't thought of in that way, though I suppose I had in some part of my make-up, for since my meetings with her, my sensual dreams and evocations stopped almost completely. Her presence exorcized them. But as time passed, under Charlie's promptings, they came back again, with Lucy as their object, and I was aware of the new element in my longing for her. I won't pretend, Denys, that it made me unhappy, but it made me restless and excited.

One evening when I was riding back from an encounter with her, I saw two figures on the road and wondered who they were – road-users in our parts were quite an event. When I recognized them – James and, of all people, Aunt Carrie, I was still more surprised. Never before had I seen her outside the garden of St. Botolph's. So engrossed were they in talking that they didn't hear the slight scrunch of my tyres. I jumped off my machine, as we called it then, in a small cloud of dust, for it hadn't rained for weeks. They seemed just as surprised to see me as I was to see them; and for a moment none of us could think of anything to say. Then James said something like, 'Coming back from your caterpillar-hunting, Richard?' and I said yes, and Aunt Carrie said, 'Don't you think it's clever of him, James, to find his own amusements?' For some reason I blushed furiously at this, and James, who wasn't the most tactful of men, drew Aunt Carrie's attention to it. She gave him a reproachful look, and then reddened herself. 'I daresay we should all look rather warm if we had been bicycling as Richard has. You won't overdo it, will you, Richard?' I mumbled something about changing for supper and then jumped on my bicycle, partly from embarrassment and partly because, after I had been with Lucy, I liked to be alone with my thoughts – they had an indescribably sweet after-taste. I thought I had been hasty and I turned and waved, and saw that they were walking arm in arm.

I didn't think this strange: I suppose I was too much concerned with my own affairs and dazzled by the glow of happiness, my private illumination, which, in a way, shut me up in myself almost as much as my unhappiness had. My happiness was like a rainbow; I knew there were dark clouds behind it, but as long as I kept my eyes fixed on it, I didn't heed them. I did notice that Aunt Carrie now came much oftener to meals – sometimes even to breakfast – and there had been no recurrence of her attacks for a long time.

One day Aunt Esther who, unlike me, could always find a moment when no one was about, said, 'I've got some good news for you, Richard. Dr. Butcher says Aunt Carrie is better – not as well as she once was, perhaps, but really better. We are all so thankful. It's been years, hasn't it? And she has something that she wants to tell you – I dare say you can guess what it is?'

You may not believe it, Denys, but I couldn't guess.

Aunt Esther gave a little sigh. 'Well, Richard, you're too young to be thinking about such things. But I've got another bit of good news for you – for you yourself. Can you guess what *that* is?'

Again I couldn't, but a shadow crossed my mind, for with so much good news in my heart, how could any other news help being bad?

'Why, bless the boy, Dr. Butcher says you're better, too. In the last few weeks you've made great strides, he says. You *must* have noticed that you don't cough so much?'

Strangely enough I hadn't.

'Well, all of us have noticed it,' Aunt Esther laughed. 'Even my mother has, and you know how deaf she is! And Dr. Butcher says your temperature is nearly normal now – it was under ninety-nine yesterday! So you see what Rookland air can do!'

I was thunderstruck. The fact was that since I began to see Lucy, I had almost forgotten about my health, which had been my chief concern, and the languor which the idea of my imminent demise engendered in me. All the backwaters of stagnant feeling had been swept away by the torrent of my love for her. 'The bank's bruck! The bank's bruck!' It had indeed broken, and breaking, swept me into another landscape.

So for a moment Aunt Esther's announcement – her two announcements – didn't register as she thought they would. The penny, as they say now, didn't drop. Then all at once it did – I almost heard the click. I was back, in imagination, in my pre-Lucy phase. I felt, I almost saw, the cloud of illness hanging over St. Botolph's – stultifying, retarding, making all we did of no effect – the dreariness, the greyness – brightening in sunshine. Where was it? I looked up – the clouds still lowered. And then, so brief is happiness to those who are not constituted for it, a cloud began to gather about my mind, too.

'Why, you don't seem pleased,' Aunt Esther said.

I pulled myself together.

'Of course, I'm pleased, Aunt Esther,' I said as heartily as I could. 'And specially about Aunt Carrie.' (This was true: I had been conditioned to believe that her welfare came before anyone else's, even my own.) 'The only thing is,' I went on, 'does it mean I shall have to go away from St. Botolph's?'

I couldn't have said anything that pleased her more.

'Why no, of course not, unless you want to, or unless your mother wants you to,' Aunt Esther said. 'We should all miss you very much, you can be sure of that. *I* should, and so would Austin. He was only saying yesterday how much he enjoyed your company – and how you are coming on as a farmer – more interested in it, too. I know you always tried to seem so, but we couldn't help thinking you were really longing to go back to your books, when you were doing so well at school.'

How perceptive she was, under her rather practical exterior.

'Of course I don't want to go back,' I exclaimed, and indeed at that moment the thought of going back to school seemed drearier than the prospect of farming had ever been. 'Besides, Aunt Esther, if I went back I might get ill again – it's being here that has made me better.'

'We shall have to hear what Walter and your mother say.'

A few days later Mother and Father came over to St. Botolph's. Mother was so delighted by the news that she shed tears of joy, as much for Aunt Carrie's recovery, I suspected, as for mine. There was a tremendous feeling of *détente* and relaxation, for though St. Botolph's had never been an unhappy house, in spite of all there was to make it so, its cheerfulness had been a little forced. I didn't know how to adjust myself to the new state of affairs; depression is an infection of the mind and can't be thrown off in a moment. But I remember how we all walked about the garden, Aunt Carrie included, instead of being shut up indoors, behind closed doors, where conferences took place. My mother, too, found it hard to believe that the calamities of years were lifting. She said more than once that Aunt Carrie ought to see a London specialist, perhaps two, and so ought I – she had a great belief in London specialists. We all paid court to James, more, I thought, than he merited, for to me he seemed a kind and well-meaning, but fundamentally a rather dull man.

A conference there must have been, however, and about me, too. Even when my health wasn't in question, they didn't talk about me, in my presence; they retired to what was the equivalent of a doctor's consulting-room, leaving me outside. All this secrecy gave me the feeling that I did not really belong to myself, but was the creature of a destiny too dark for me to know about.

Soon the trap came round to take my parents to the station, for Mother wouldn't hear of being driven the whole way back. But before it came, she drew me aside and took me for a little stroll down the road I knew so well. She was still tearful and made no effort to disguise it. She kept saying how thankful she was that Aunt Carrie and I were better. But I wasn't sure if she quite believed we were, and she had some other reservations, too. 'I do hope Carrie will be *happy*,' she said. 'I do *hope* she will be.' And when I said, 'Of course she will be, now she's better, she'll be just like she was before,' Mother shook her head sadly, as if there was something I didn't and mustn't know. 'And you, my darling,' she questioned me, 'are *you* quite happy?' I said of course I was, I had never been so happy – which was the truth. 'We never meant you to be a farmer,' she went on, 'it wasn't what we had planned for you, and

Daddy was always against it.' I was afraid they really meant to take me away and adduced every reason I could think of for staying at St. Botolph's. My health was my strongest argument; I went on and on about it. I knew my mother's temperament; she couldn't look for long on the bright side; she was braver and, in a way, more cheerful, in adversity than in prosperity; no one has ever been more conscious of the crumpled rose-leaf. She admitted this and said, 'Don't think me ungrateful, I thank God all the time for you, and even for Carrie. Oh, I do hope she's *really* better.'

Someone came out of the gateway to call her; she kissed me fervently and we went back into the garden where a group had gathered round the dog-cart. Uncle Austin was the driver and my father was holding Minnie's head – the flies were worrying her and, like Dr. Butcher's Princess, she wouldn't stand. 'Come along—' he called out to Mother, in one of his fits of irritation, 'don't keep us here all night.' I was afraid of him in these moods, but I managed to say, while James was helping Mother up the steps – such small slippery footholds – on to the dog-cart, 'I'm so happy, Daddy, here, you won't take me away, will you?' I rather hoped my words would also reach the ears of Uncle Austin, who was looking so smart and dapper, as he always did when he was associated with a horse. 'You must ask your mother about that, my boy,' Father said a trifle curtly, trying to give his attention to the horse and me at the same time. 'We can spare you if Uncle Austin can put up with you.' I knew him too well to feel hurt by his bluntness – his 'Yorkshire' way of talking, and I took his place at the horse's head, which was not a position I really coveted, while he jumped up on the back seat. Minnie started with a rush, as she always did when she had been kept waiting, and I remember we all trooped out on to the road and waved and waved until they were out of sight.

XXI

I did not see Lucy that evening, of course, but I did see her the next, and for many evenings following. They had decided not to send her abroad, at any rate for the present, she told me; a new governess was coming but hadn't been chosen yet. Her parents were so particular, they had to have references and interviews, and it all took time, but she might come at any moment.

This gave our meetings a new urgency, for if she went abroad, they would have to stop, and if a governess came, they would be fewer and even more precarious than they were. We spoke of these eventualities as little as we could, and when we did she clung to me, to keep away the thought of parting.

Yes, she clung to me, Denys, and I – well I was not the boy I had been even a few weeks ago. The doctor's verdict – for he had now told me, as well as them – had given me a confidence and pride in myself that I had never had before, when I seemed to live only by his favour, and to know less about myself than almost everyone else knew about me. Somehow – it isn't difficult to see how – this knowledge that I was well and whole like other boys – like other men – changed my conception of myself. I felt grown up at last. It got into my consciousness and through my consciousness into my blood, that I was a free agent now and able to do what I wanted to do without asking anybody's leave, and I didn't ask it, Denys. I did ask her leave and she gave it, not knowing what it meant, not knowing in the least, as it turned out. *I* knew something, because Charlie had told me, but I still thought children only came with marriage.

And so we clung together, as all lovers have, and I thought that what happened had to happen, though it doesn't seem so inevitable now as it did then. You see, the sense of release was overwhelming. It seemed to spread from me into every nook and cranny of St. Botolph's – the Cosy Corner had a great many nooks and crannies – it went right through the house, as if a hospital had been turned into a dance-hall. All the pro-hibitions and inhibitions under which we had laboured, Aunt Carrie and I – and because of us, the others – the life-destroying routine, none the less destroying because its object was to cure us, had been swept away, leaving a marvellous sense of space and freedom in which all things seemed possible. Anyone who has recovered from a long illness knows what this means, and I knew it at that time, though I shan't know it again. Dr. Butcher isn't here to tell me I am better, no doctor is.

In the Brickfield, freedom reigned. I still remember what it felt like and I think Lucy shared it, for the threat of being sent abroad, now partially lifted, had been a weight on her spirits, too. We had to celebrate our free-dom; we had to explore it to its furthest limits. Even if we didn't at first know what they were, we felt something was lacking, and yet for fear of the finality of fulfilment, we kept away from it, seeking the perfect moment, the moment when all feelings should converge. At last it came, and others followed, each more ecstatic than the last.

Does one bear the mark of such experiences on one's face? Or did James break his promise to Lucy? Nearly everybody has one confidante to whom they tell their secrets. Or was Aunt Carrie gifted with second-sight?

One evening, returning from the Brickfield, I was told she would like to see me. I suppose I had an uneasy conscience, for though Aunt Carrie was the least alarming of mortals, I felt as if I had been summoned to the Headmaster's study – and not to receive a prize. She was at her usual place in the Cosy Corner, under the convex mirror gripped in the eagle's talons; when I think of her, it is nearly always in that setting. She hadn't lost her rapid, nervous gestures or the spot of high colour on her sallow cheeks; but underlying them I seemed to detect a new confidence, as if life had opened its arms to her at last. Of course I had already told her how glad I was that she was better, but only in a brief, formal way; I never found it easy, when I was with her, to show her the strong feeling that I had for her, and more than ever difficult just then, when a stronger feeling was competing with it. And perhaps she felt with me as she did with Mother – that our solicitude for her expected a return she could not give.

She made room for me beside her and began hurriedly:

'I wanted to see you, Richard dear, to tell you one or two things which you probably know already, and some that perhaps you don't know. I'm much better – that you do know, you were sweet to me about it. And perhaps you know that I am going to be married – no, I see you don't—' for I had registered open-eyed surprise. 'Well, I'm glad I told you and I hope you will be happy about it, as I am, though it's something I can't talk about much, even to you. You have been so nice to James. Everyone has been, and welcomed him and made him one of the family – which isn't easy when we are all so devoted to each other. He was rather nervous when he came here, but I began to feel better when he came – well, some time before that, when I knew he was coming. I have known him for a great many years, but somehow he never came to stay with us, he was so busy at school. We have so many things in common, besides memories, music chiefly – I wouldn't have liked to marry someone strange to us all.'

She stopped. The old hesitation which wasn't a stammer but a kind of hold-up in her utterance, seized her, and I was afraid, but it only lasted for a moment. Tears came into her eyes and seemed to relieve the tension.

'So you'll be leaving St Botolph's?' I said.

Aunt Carrie smiled. 'Yes, my dear, two of us would be a tall order, even for Esther and Austin. In a way it will be better – better, you know, to start again, in a new place. I think it might be better for you, too.' 'Better for me, Aunt Carrie?' 'Yes, Richard dear, it might be better for you too.' 'But don't you want me to be a farmer, Aunt Carrie?' 'No, I don't think I do, not here at any rate. You're not really cut out to be a farmer.' 'Uncle Austin thinks I am,' I protested. 'I know he's very glad to have you,' said Aunt Carrie. 'Everyone is. But this is a lonely place for someone of your age. You shouldn't be too much on your own. And may I tell you something else – something I wouldn't say to anyone but you?'

I stared at her uncomprehending, but in the depths of my mind I heard the thin whisper of misgiving.

'You shouldn't be too much with one person,' she went on. 'I was, Richard, and I wouldn't have had it otherwise. And if I could, I'd do the same again. I think I told you that. But everything I've been through, and everything that other people have been through on my account – how long is it, five years? – all came from this, that I was too much attached to one person. You know about it, I think, I asked your mother to tell you. I was too fond of him, and when he died I couldn't get over it. *That* I could have borne, but what I couldn't bear was being a trial and a burden to everybody. Not only to Austin and Esther, who have been angelic to me, and whose lives I have cramped, but to your dear mother, who feels for me more than she does for herself – as you know. Instead of being what I should have liked to be – someone who lent a hand' – she shook her thin vein-blue hand at me, and with the other fidgeted at the tight sleeve at her wrist – 'I've tied everybody's hands. How could Esther and Austin live a normal life – I'll be frank with you and say, how could they have children even, when I was like a millstone round their necks?'

I knew she ought not to be talking like this – I could feel and see the agitation it was causing her – but the imp of perversity is strong and I saw a weakness in her argument. If I had been older, I should have let it pass. 'But you're going to do it again,' I exclaimed. 'You're giving yourself up to one person! You're going to marry James. If he died! – If he died!' I stopped, appalled.

Aunt Carrie took it more calmly than I feared, embarrassed though she was to find an answer.

'My dear,' she said, 'I trust you absolutely, otherwise I wouldn't say this. If James died, it would be a great grief to me – I don't deny that. But not a grief like the other. Please believe me, I love James dearly – it's he who's made me better – but, I can't explain it – it isn't a love that excludes other feelings. It doesn't dwarf or drown them, and besides—'

She stopped again and began to tremble.

'Don't say it, Aunt Carrie,' I cried. 'Don't say it. Leave me to guess.'

'No, I'd rather say it. I shall be going away quite soon, very soon.' 'But you can't be going away,' I argued. 'You aren't married yet, you're only engaged.' She smiled. 'I shall be married next week,' she said, 'the quietest wedding, but you'll be there, I hope.' 'But does that matter so much? You'll just be married and then—' 'And then we're going to Australia. James has got a post there, quite a good one.'

I don't know how it happened – I suppose our conversation had worked on my feelings more than I had any idea of – but I burst into tears.

'Oh, don't do that,' I pleaded, 'don't do that! Think of us all——' 'I *have* thought,' she answered, with a gravity in her manner that was new to me. 'That's partly why I'm going.'

I was too much upset to take in the meaning of her words. It was only afterwards I realized that something – Heaven, Fate – had found her an outlet for selflessness. Or did she really *want* to go away? That I shall never know.

During that time of stress and excitement – the preparations, the wedding, the packing, the farewells, the departure, I lived a double life. The Richard of St. Botolph's wasn't and couldn't be the Richard of the Brickfield. Oblivious as I can be to what is going on round me – you know how oblivious, Denys – I couldn't be oblivious to Aunt Carrie's leaving us. It was at once so joyful and so sad, to my mother more sad than joyful, for as I learned many years afterwards, she never quite believed that Aunt Carrie was in love with James, or that she was really strong enough to undertake married life, especially in Australia. She wept throughout the wedding service – but she is not the only woman to have done that. My father, who might easily have been impatient with, and perhaps resented Mother's inordinate affection for Aunt Carrie, was kindness itself to her, trying to engage her interest in the practical as well as the emotional aspect. What would they *do* when they got to Australia? How would they live? Would they have a bathroom? Would the groceries be delivered, or would they have to fetch them? Would they acquire an Australian accent? My father, who often took a different view from other people, hoped they would. They would be thought stuck-up, he said, if they kept their English accent, which in any case, he added, warming to his subject, was not a true English accent, for only in the Pale of Dublin was English spoken as it should be. They were lucky to be going to Australia, he said, Australia was a healthy place; many people would give their eyes to be going to Australia. Getting heated, as he sometimes did, with an imaginary opponent, he enlarged on the merits of Australia.

My mother, despite her intense belief in love as the be-all and the end-all, was by no means deaf to the call of the practical. She tried to enter into his state of mind, and indeed corrected him about details of household management, of which he knew very little. But he couldn't reassure her about certain things, the climate, the length of time letters would take, the possibility of finding a specialist. 'I don't suppose they have them there,' she said wistfully. 'Much better for them if they don't,' my father said. 'The ancient world tried to make medicine a science, and failed, the modern world has made it a business, and succeeded. Didn't you know, my dear, that the wrong diagnoses made by doctors are the second principal cause of death?' He didn't tell her what the principal cause was.

But when the time came for the wagonette to take them to the station at Willow Drove to start the long train journey for their brief honeymoon in the West Country, he didn't worry her with arguments, for he was moved himself.

XXII

You have stayed in so many large houses, Denys, with lots of servants, and people coming and going – I have myself, for that matter – that you can hardly imagine the change it made at St. Botolph's when James and Aunt Carrie went away. It should have been a relief to everyone, the cook and housemaid especially, for on them had fallen most of the extra work an invalid makes. But I think they minded more than anyone – more obviously at any rate. For days they went about red-eyed, and Annie the housemaid said to me, 'Of course we mustn't say so, Master Richard, but he isn't worthy of her, he isn't really. And her to be an ordinary schoolmistress in those outlandish parts, when she could have been anything she liked in England!'

It was news to me that Aunt Carrie was to be a schoolmistress, and sad news. Our meteor that had flashed so brilliantly! That was one of the things she hadn't told me. I asked for confirmation and found that Annie was right.

Aunt Carrie's appearances among us had been few and she made no noise at all; yet when she had gone, the house seemed empty and silent. I didn't like the sight of her closed door and when I went to my room, turned my eyes away from it. I had never suspected that the removal of a burden – for she had been a burden, on our thoughts, at any rate – could cause one so much sadness.

But it didn't last, of course. When Aunt Esther and Uncle Austin came back from seeing them off at Southampton, the household moved to a new rhythm, and a gayer one. And yet I missed her in a hundred ways. Why had I seen so little of her, I asked myself, when I might have seen so much? The school-children of Australia would see more of her in one week than I had seen in months.

All these happenings curtailed my visits to the Brickfield. They began again with a new ardour, carefree and winged by love. In Lucy's arms I gradually forgot the flaws, the grains of grit that life so often puts in the mood of complete happiness. My sky was clear, and in the egoism of bliss, it didn't occur to me that hers wasn't.

Little things began to show it to me. Not a lack of warmth; our caresses hadn't become automatic, quite the opposite; she embraced me more fervently than before. She seemed as though she could not have enough of me. But whereas once our meetings and our acts of love had seemed an end in themselves, unrelated to other people and to what was going on around us, now they seemed to take place in spite of something, to be rifts in a cloud that was hanging over her, like the clouds that still hung over the sky.

One hates to ask someone what is the matter; it so often sounds like a criticism and suggests that whoever it may be, isn't happy with one. 'What have I done?' one feels like asking – and yet dreads to ask, for fear of the answer. One can't believe that any other agency except oneself has brought about the change. But at last when her smile didn't meet mine as readily as it used to at some joke I made, I asked her.

'What is it, Lucy? Have I done something? I couldn't always get away last week or the week before, but you know why that was.'

Then she told me it was nothing to do with me at all, but my relief on hearing this was tainted by a twinge of jealousy. How could something not to do with me upset her? Was I not all in all to her? In my own case I knew that events at home had altered the pattern of my behaviour; it couldn't be helped. I had forgotten that her home life, which was so much more exacting and intense than mine, might have affected hers. Our seeming conquest of her disabilities made me forget they still existed. Life took its own course at The Hollies no less than at St. Botolph's, regardless of our wishes.

'It's the new governess,' she said. 'She's coming tomorrow and I know I shan't like her.'

'Why not, Lucy?' I could never say her name often enough.

'Because I know her. She taught me once before – I don't remember how many years ago – and left because she was ill. She was always asking questions and trying to find out things – not that there was anything to find out, then. Mamma, too, thought she was prying and didn't like her manner, she was rather cheeky, you know, and thought she knew more about children than Mamma did. I was so thankful when she fell ill and left! Papa liked her, because she had such excellent references, and she was a good teacher, I have to own that, and I could have learned a lot from her if I had liked her. He didn't mind her being strict with me, nor did Mamma, for that matter – they were strict with me themselves. I suppose love makes people strict – their sort of love, I mean, not ours. But, oh how I wish she wasn't coming! She won't want me to go out alone, she never did.'

Lucy began to cry; I comforted her as best I could, and said, as much to convince myself as her, 'She'll be different now you're older.'

With that Lucy seemed satisfied, for she had a great belief in me, so blind and so unquestioning that she made me share it. I was much younger than my years in many ways, but not with her, for love is a quick teacher. Emotionally and physically, she was mine. What would be the next step? Marriage, of course. It had been so easy in the case of Aunt Carrie and Uncle James, and they had not been lovers in the sense that we were. Of that I felt convinced. But I had no money to get married with.

For the first time I began to think seriously about our future. How long could this state of affairs go on? September was at hand, harvest would soon be in full swing. I should have to take part in it like any other able-bodied male; and I was able-bodied now, Dr. Butcher said so. I couldn't play truant and run off to the Brickfield whenever I felt so minded. At some date in

September – I took care not to find out what date – the Brickfield would become a nest of partridge-shooters. Uncle Austin once said, alluding to my caterpillar-hunting, 'Richard would make a brace of partridges, wouldn't he? or perhaps two brace – he's grown much plumper since he was here.' In imagination I would hear the shots whizzing, round her, round me, round us. Where should we find shelter? And if we were discovered— 'What on earth are you doing here, Richard? And this girl, too? Why, she's Lucy Soames!' Sensation; and then the curtain would come down on our world – our world of make-believe, as in my saner moments I still knew it to be, though it was more precious and more real to me than any other world.

In normal circumstances I should be going back to school, to spend my last year there. What prospects had I? None; I had no money, so how could I support a wife? Would my parents give me some, to start farming on my own account? I knew they couldn't. Hers could, but would they? Would they consent to a long engagement, until such time as I was in a position to marry? But how could I ask them, when they knew nothing about my relationship with Lucy, and would be appalled if they knew?

And yet something must be done, I felt, to ensure a future for us in the real world. The summer weather, gloomy as it was, had favoured us. What would happen in winter, with the Brickfield, as like as not, deep in snow? Where could we meet then, where could we find the privacy that was so precious, so essential to us?

If I did go to Mr. and Mrs. Soames, what should I say? Should I burst the bubble, and tell them that their daughter and I had been keeping company for – for how long? For ever, it seemed; I could not think of it in terms of weeks or months. For her sake, if not for mine, I couldn't tell them. In my own family life, I knew to what lengths feelings would go. From what she had told me, and from what I had seen myself, they were much stronger at The Hollies, with its prickles turned against the world. I had forced my way in once; but they had made it clear they didn't want a second visit. Yet they had nothing against me personally, nothing that they knew of. I was a member of the Holy Family, which even they must look on with respect.

At last I went. I didn't tell Lucy I was going. I didn't want to involve her in any way. They mustn't know, they must never, never know, that we had ever met since the framed 'accident' on the bridge.

Six o'clock then, six o'clock now – it was the best time, I thought, to find them in, and not find Lucy, whose hour it was for walking. I had left a note under the stone-heap to say I hoped to be at the Brickfield, but might be late. Would she wait for me? I knew she would.

So the coast was clear, and with a beating heart I led my bicycle down the weedy drive, past the decaying monkey-puzzle and the unkempt holly-bushes. With a beating heart; and yet somehow I persuaded myself that my mission would succeed.

They greeted me, not warmly as they had the first time, but with the reserve I suppose they kept for visitors, for visitors they must have had from time to time – they couldn't have kept their isolation absolute. They hadn't forgotten me, they said how kind I had been to Lucy; they remembered how long it took – ten days, I think – for her knees to heal. They asked me if I would have some sherry, and when I refused they began to talk of other matters – harvest prospects and the like – with the air of playing for time.

I knew that my visit was unwanted and an intrusion on their privacy, and I suddenly realized how hopeless it was to expect that I, a mere lad who had only met them once before, could break down the plan of existence they had laid down for themselves so many years ago. When I came into the room they had towered above me. Now that we were sitting – they side by side on a sofa, I on a chair some distance away – I still found their united physical presence, backed by money, age, mystery and other intangibles, almost overwhelming. But I had grown up a great deal during the summer.

I knew what I wanted, and when the conversation seemed in danger of petering out, I suddenly heard my voice saying the sentence I had prepared:

'I came because I fell in love with your daughter Lucy the first time I saw her, and I want to ask you whether you will let me ask her to marry me.'

They stared at each other, and Mr. Soames jumped to his feet. 'And have you never spoken to her from that day to this?' he asked. 'No,' I lied. 'And she knows nothing about your feeling for her?' 'Nothing.'

He sat down again and turned to his wife and many expressions that I could not interpret passed across their faces. 'My dear,' she said to me, 'how old are you?' 'I shall be eighteen in May.' She nodded to something in her thoughts, and said to her husband, 'How old were you, Henry, when . . . ?' She blushed and didn't finish the sentence. 'About his age,' he answered imperturbably.

They said no more for a moment, when the silence was broken by Mrs. Soames. 'If Richard will excuse us, we will go into the next room. Do you mind waiting a little while?' 'Oh no,' I said. I was so used to people going into the next room to talk about me that it seemed the natural thing.

They left me staring at the dark wallpaper and ornate wooden overmantel, in the recesses of which stood many china cups and saucers, but I didn't take in much of what I saw. Nor do I know how long they were away, but they came back with the stiff solemn faces (with which I was so well acquainted) of people who had come to some decision about me. They sat down on the sofa and each waited for the other to speak.

'Well, perhaps I ought to talk to you,' he began, 'since I'm Lucy's father.'

At that his wife made a little movement with her hands and turned away. I thought: She doesn't want to see my disappointment.

'You must forgive me,' he said, 'if what I say sounds rather personal. But you haven't been well, have you? You came to Rookland for your health?' 'Oh yes,' I answered eagerly. 'I had a cough you know, and

Mother thought—' I broke off feeling it would be safer not to say what Mother thought. She had never told me, but I knew. 'But I'm much better now, in fact I'm quite well. You can ask Dr. Butcher. He said I was blooming – it's the Rookland air.'

Mr. Soames smiled. 'You certainly look better than you did the last time you were here,' he said in his deep grating voice. 'I never thought of the Fens as a health resort, but something has done you good. Now Richard, what you've just asked us, Miriam and me, can be answered in a moment – I expect you realized that?'

Crestfallen, I agreed.

'You didn't expect us to say yes, did you?'

I had to confess that I didn't.

'Well, we both think it was plucky of you to come and put your cards on the table. It isn't only that I fell in love at first sight myself, when I was just your age.' I expected his wife to make some acknowledgement to this, but she didn't. 'And it isn't because you tell me you now have a clean bill of health, though I'm glad to hear it for your sake. And it isn't because your uncle is a neighbour of ours and well liked in the district. It's because – don't think me patronizing – I've heard such good accounts of you and from people you've never heard of, I dare say, people you've met on market days with your uncle. I don't see much of them, but I see them there. They say you're a boy to be trusted.'

I must have looked bewildered when he said all this, for it wasn't the practice in our family to repeat compliments. I felt that everyone in Rookland must have as poor an opinion of me as I had of myself, and rate my gifts for agriculture as low as I did.

'But don't think,' he went on, 'that because we haven't said no, it means we shall say yes. You're much too young, for one thing. Well, so was I' (here again I thought his wife would have made some sign of agreement or dissent, but she did not). 'I was young too, and I fell in love with my wife at first sight, as you did. But before we were engaged, we'd seen a great deal of each other, which you and Lucy haven't.'

I blushed, I couldn't help it.

'Yes, you may well turn red,' he said, 'and it does you credit. But you must realize this, young fellow, Lucy is the apple of our eye, she's the only thing we've got, and that is why we've kept her to ourselves – if people call us selfish, well, let them. But there comes a time in a girl's life, or a boy's for that matter, when things change for them, as Miriam has just reminded me. We thought of sending Lucy abroad – we might still send her – but we didn't think we could stand the separation, and we didn't think that she could. Because if anything happened to her, Richard, it would be the end of us. This life we've built up for ourselves, it may not be conventional, but—'

He cast his eyes down on to the carpet and Mrs. Soames said, speaking with less intensity than he had, 'Yes, Richard, she's our ewe-lamb, but there comes a time . . .'

'But that time isn't yet,' he said roughly, 'that time's a long way off. But what I'll do, Richard, is I'll see your mother and father, and ask them what they think. That's one thing; but first we must ask Lucy.'

I knew this was coming.

'Oh yes, of course you must ask her,' I said.

'And if she wants to see you, well, she shall see you. Here and in the garden . . . that sort of thing, you know, if you want a quiet chat. Or at St. Botolph's, if they agree to it.'

He rose abruptly – he was trembling with emotion and could hardly speak.

His wife looked up at him as if he was a stranger.

'Well, run off now,' he said, 'that's quite enough for one day. Soon you'll be hearing from us one way or the other – one way or the other. Lucy will be here at any minute, and there's the governess coming too.'

I said my good-byes as quickly as I could, mounted my bicycle and pedalled furiously to the Brickfield. Supposing she hadn't waited, supposing she had come home another way (there wasn't another way, but that didn't allay my fear).

She was in fact on the point of starting back. I was just in time to tell her of our amazing, unbelievable good fortune, and to warn her on no account to say we had ever met since the bridge accident. 'But what *shall* I say?' she asked. 'Just this, that you remember meeting me and would like . . . would like to see me again. Oh Lucy, this is the great day of our lives – of my life, at any rate.' We clasped each other, disembodied, unable to think of anything but our joy.

XXIII

That was the last time I saw her, Denys – no, not the last time, but the last time I saw her as she used to be. The next day I found a note under the stone-heap, saying she couldn't come; the following day another. I was beside myself with worry; I would have called at The Hollies, but the second note implored me not to. I thought she must be ill; but how could she be really ill if she was able to go as far as the stone-heap? I left notes for her, begging her to tell me what was the matter. 'It's the governess,' she said in her third note, written in a handwriting that I scarcely recognized; 'she doesn't want me to go out alone, and she asks me so many questions.'

When Dr. Butcher paid me his weekly visit, he looked at me rather hard, and still harder at the thermometer. 'Have you got something on your mind?' he asked. I couldn't tell him, Denys; I have never told anyone from that day to this.

At last, after nearly a week, I found a note saying that she would be at the Brickfield the next day, but I should find her changed. Changed in what way? I asked myself as I went to keep the tryst. Appearance, manner, what? Had she put her hair up? But all the alterations I could think of seemed too trivial to warrant the word *changed*, that final, irrevocable word. Some changes are for the better, people go in search of change, change of air, changes of scene, change of food: but when they say that *they* have changed, they mean it's for the worse – or that the person they are speaking to will think it is.

The moment I saw Lucy, I knew she had changed, though I couldn't have said how. She kissed me and then moved away from me and said hardly a word. 'What is it?' I kept asking her. 'Please tell me.' For a long time she wouldn't, and we wandered about our old haunts, up and down the hillocks, in and out of the chambers of the brick-kiln, almost without speaking. 'You must tell me,' I said, 'you must tell me, I shall go crazy if you don't.' And then she did say something. 'It's the governess,' she said, 'she's been talking to me.'

'What about?' I pressed her. 'Anything about me?' 'No, not about you,' she said, 'she doesn't know about you.' I was almost painfully relieved. What was there for her to worry over? 'Oh, it was dreadful what she said, I couldn't tell you.' 'Couldn't tell me? Why, we used to tell each other everything.' 'But I couldn't tell you this.' 'Do your parents know?' I asked her. 'No, but she said she'd have to tell them.' 'Oh what is it, Lucy? What *could* she have said?' 'She asked me a lot of questions,' said Lucy slowly, 'the day after she came – all sorts of questions that no one had ever asked me before – even Mother hadn't.' 'What right had she to ask you questions, Lucy? It's no business of hers.' 'She's my

233

governess: perhaps she thought she ought to.' 'I don't see why. She's just a tiresome, interfering busybody.' 'Please don't say that, Richard; it doesn't do any good.' We bandied words and came near to quarrelling, I was so indignant for her and so miserable myself. But soon I realized that she wasn't arguing or putting forward a case; the words themselves meant nothing much; they were forced out of her, as screams might have been, by the torment of her spirit. Indeed, I wished she would scream or cry: it was as though her wretchedness had paralysed her feelings. And she was cold to me, she held me off; she wouldn't embrace me or even kiss me: she kept away from me. I tried to make conversation with her; I asked her if her parents had seen mine, as they said they would; because if they had, Mother hadn't told me. She said she didn't know; she rather hoped they hadn't. 'But why?' I asked her, horrified, 'why, Lucy? Don't you want us to be together?' She didn't answer, except by a sad shake of her head. She seemed to have grown away from me, even in years, and to be like one of those older people, who wouldn't tell me something they knew about me, because they thought it better for me not to know. Then I got really angry and said all sorts of things I didn't mean, to break down her stubbornness. But she kept aloof from me and it was only when we parted that she kissed me.

Well, Denys, I'm coming to the end now. I don't remember much of what happened during the next days. Misery takes the individual content out of things, makes them seem alike. I waited for news, news from home, news from The Hollies, news from under the stone-heap. Had she told her mother and father that after all she didn't want to see me? It would have been easy for her to say that. But I didn't think so, I didn't think she was sufficiently in control of herself to take that final step. Every day I visited the Brickfield, in case she had left a note I hadn't found: I can't tell you how melancholy it was, wandering about those familiar places by myself. They weren't familiar, they were strange and hostile, without her to see them with me. I thought of what Aunt Carrie had said about not giving oneself too much to one person: such an odd thing for her to have said, and on the eve of her marriage!

I didn't think that anything could surprise me, but one day I had a surprise. The stone-heap wasn't there! All that was left of it was a scatter of granite-chips, and in a moment I saw why: a little further on, the road was being mended: a steam-roller was drawn up on the verge. My first thought was that if Minnie saw it, she would shy at it: she couldn't pass a steam-roller without making a fuss. And then the dreadful fear assailed me – if the stone-heap was gone, we were finally cut off from each other, we couldn't communicate any more! I stooped down and began to look under the remaining pebbles, one by one, quite without hope – it was just a routine proceeding for the sake of certitude. And then I jumped back as if I had been stung, for there *was* a note. Had it been there on other days, and had I missed it? I had to overcome a momentary reluctance to read or even touch it – but I got over that. Here it is, Denys, the only note of hers I kept.'

Richard pulled out his pocket-book, fumbled in the compartments and brought out a slip of paper. He smoothed it on his knee and read in a neutral voice, deeper than his own: 'I will be at the Brickfield tonight. Love, Lucy.'

He returned the note to his wallet and the wallet to his pocket. After a few seconds he began again:

'I went there, Denys, as she asked me to, and made straight for the chimney-stack, our meeting-place, but she wasn't there. I wandered this way and that, still sanguine with the hope that flickered in me. I went to the entrance in case she should be coming down the road, but she wasn't. Then I went back and stood under the chimney-stack for I don't know how long. Then impatience seized me, and I walked about, always in sight of the chimney, calling her, as I had done the first time we met, but never since. I hadn't had to. I called and called until the sound of my own voice frightened me and the thought that if she didn't hear it, someone else might. So then I began to prowl about the ruins, and up and down the hillocks, where we used to scramble, hand in hand, and that was how I found her, lying face downwards in the pool that was said to be bottomless, quite near the edge, in a few feet of water – oh Denys—'

It was an appeal, a cry, not an exclamation.

'Yes, Richard?'

Richard closed his eyes, and said weakly, 'Those tablets – you know where they are.'

Denys got up from his chair slowly, as he did everything, and went to the chimney-piece.

'I don't see them here, Richard.'

'On the bureau then, and a glass of water.'

After a moment Denys said: 'They don't seem to be on the bureau.'

'Perhaps in my bedroom then . . . or just bring the water.'

Denys went slowly out and came back with a glass of water in one hand and the phial of tablets in the other. He took a tablet out and held the glass to Richard's lips, watching them change colour.

At length, Richard said, 'Ah, now I feel better. But I could have sworn those tablets were on the chimney-piece.'

'We must put a chain on them,' said Denys, giving his friend a long, speculative stare.

'Oh, but they're always there, Denys – it was just this once, unless the daily woman moved them. But I'm feeling all right now.'

'All the same, you'd better go to bed.'

'I think I'd rather finish, if you don't mind – it was just when I got to that part – I knew it might happen when I got to that part. I often think about it, without getting so worked up, but it was saying it – the effort, you know that upset me. But on that evening I was calm, like a landscape when a high wind has died down and nothing moves. I told Uncle Austin – it was the first time I had ever broken the news of a death – and he did what had to be done. It haunts me still that I never saw her face – I had seen it so often reflected in the water.'

'Didn't you try to pull her out?' asked Denys.

'I did, I did, I got into the pool. I put my arms round her and tried to haul her out, but she was too heavy for me and kept slipping through my hands, or dragging me down, my feet sank into the mud, right up to my thighs, under my weight and hers. I couldn't . . . I couldn't turn her over. And I was afraid of getting drowned myself – my mouth was only just above the water-line when I gave up trying and scrambled out. I lay a long time on the bank, trying to get my breath.

I couldn't go back to The Hollies, I didn't know where to go. The whole world seemed closed to me, especially the world within, for I could not bear my own thoughts. I might have thrown myself into the pool beside her, but what good would that have done? Besides, I knew how to swim, and she didn't, there were so many things she didn't know, until this governess came, and told her one of them.

When I got over my physical exhaustion, I sat up, and looked about me, still dazed and only half there, and it was then I saw, without taking in its possible meaning, the muddy skid-mark, deep and two or more feet long, beginning from below where I sat and reaching to the water's edge. *I* hadn't made it; I could see the spot where I got in. All my life I have remembered that dark, oozy groove, and forced my conscience to remember it, too. She *might* have slipped in, Denys, she might have slipped in! In the state of mind she was, she might easily have slipped in.

My Uncle Austin thought so, when I brought him to the place, and the police thought so, and the Coroner thought so; it was something the governess said that made them order an autopsy.

But Lucy was found not to be pregnant. Nothing came out at the inquest that inculpated me. I had a perfectly good reason for being at the Brickfield: my quest for caterpillars. Did I often go? Yes. Had I ever seen Lucy there? No, not till that day. Did I think she had been coming to meet me? She might have been, I said. But when the Coroner asked me 'Why?' I broke down and could only say, 'Mr. Soames knows why.' And Mr. Soames, whose face was blotchy and almost unrecognizable, told the Court of my second visit to The Hollies, all of which you know, Denys, and how he and his wife had consented for Lucy to meet me from time to time. 'We saw no harm in it,' he said. 'They were lonely young people, and I had heard such good accounts of the boy. I am almost as sorry for him as I am for ourselves.' He explained, what I did not know, that he had been to see my parents, and they raised no objection to my seeing Lucy, though they agreed with him that we were too young and ought to wait. 'And did your daughter take kindly to the idea?' the Coroner asked. 'She did at first,' said Mr. Soames; 'she seemed as pleased at the thought of seeing him as he was to see her, and mentioned the Brickfield as a place where they might meet. But a day or two later,' he added, 'she didn't want to see him; she was listless, and wouldn't go out. We thought she must be ill, but she said she wasn't. She didn't like Miss Froxfield, the new governess, and begged us to send her away. Our daughter was very precious to us and we did as she asked, giving no reason but incompatibility of temperament. We paid Miss Froxfield a month's wages and she left. My wife thought she was a jealous, possessive woman, who wanted to gain an ascendancy over Lucy.'

He sat down beside Mrs. Soames, who was very pale, but more composed than he was.

Last of all the governess was called. She had a pale face and dark grey eyes, hair parted in the middle and drawn tightly back. She said she had felt it her duty to ask Lucy certain questions which no one, apparently, had ever asked her. They were questions which any responsible person, in a position of trust, would have asked a girl of Lucy's age. She hadn't meant to frighten her, she had only meant to tell her what the symptoms she described *might* have been caused by. 'As a governess,' she said, 'it is my duty to enlighten my pupils, and I wonder that this had not been done before. A child can be sheltered too much. I don't think any sensible person, or any one who had the child's welfare at heart, would blame me for what I did. When I found out that she had missed a period, I told her what it meant, or might mean. How could I have guessed that Lucy would jump to a conclusion which I assured her was in any case only a remote possibility, and in her case, an impossibility? What reason could she have had for thinking such a thing might happen to *her*? Did I do wrong? I have not been a governess all these years for nothing; and I know that at a certain age, girls are almost as nervous as boys, and almost as likely to get ideas into their heads. But why should Lucy, who, as far as I knew, had never seen a boy in her life? If I had told her that in South America there is such a thing as a boa-constrictor, I couldn't have expected that she would fancy she would meet one, here, walking out of her front gate.'

Once a governess, always a governess, I suppose, whatever the circumstances may be. Perhaps the Coroner resented Miss Froxfield's over-confident manner, which may have masked a lack of confidence, for he said mildly: 'Wouldn't it have been better to ask the girl's mother before you spoke to her on such an intimate subject?'

To which Miss Froxfield replied: 'I would have, if she had had a mother.' 'What do you mean?' the Coroner asked. 'I mean that Mrs. Soames isn't her mother,' the governess answered, and burst into tears.

That's all I remember of the proceedings, Denys, except that the Coroner brought in a verdict of Accidental Death. I had been an ardent and impetuous wooer, but not an experienced or proficient lover; Lucy's poor body bore no mark of my embraces, and I left the Court without a stain on my character. Indeed, my mother told me afterwards that the Coroner expressed sympathy with me, as well as with the bereaved parents, parent rather, for the governess was quite right, Mrs. Soames was not Lucy's mother. Much, much later my mother explained to me, with tears in her eyes, that the lady who passed for Mrs. Soames was really Mr. Soames' deceased wife's sister. That was why they shunned society and lived to themselves. How the governess discovered their secret I never knew, or why she revealed it; perhaps from spite at having been dismissed. The general feeling was that Lucy's death served them right, it was a judgment on them. As soon as they could they left the district, and The Hollies passed into the hands of other tenants.

XXIV

I left the district, too. It was my mother who took me away. A few days after the inquest – I don't know how many – I was wandering about the garden, in search of scents and smells, I suppose, for I could still respond to them – when I saw her, all by herself, between the gate and the house. She was zig-zagging along aimlessly, poking the gravel with the tip of her umbrella, for she always carried one, in case it should come on to rain. I ran up to her, and said something like, 'Oh Mother, what are you doing here? You never told me you were coming.' I could hardly believe that she had slipped in unbeknownst, for at St. Botolph's arrivals were made almost as much of as departures. 'Where's Daddy?' I went on. 'Isn't he with you?' for the idea of Mother coming alone was inconceivable to me.

She put her hand over her mouth, a gesture she had when she was embarrassed, and then said, 'Daddy wouldn't come with me.' 'Why not?' I said, and all my guilty feelings rushed to one point. 'Was it because of Lucy?' Everything seemed to be because of Lucy. 'Lucy?' she repeated. 'Oh, you mean the poor girl who was drowned. I'd forgotten that her name was Lucy. No, my darling, it was nothing to do with her, she

243

wasn't a relation of ours, was she? It was very sad, very unfortunate, but not as if it had happened in the *family* – I mean the Soames' were nothing to us, were they? I'm sorry it was you who had to find her, for I know you minded, but think how much worse it would have been for Carrie! I'd always hoped you wouldn't have to see someone who was dead till you were much, much older. It is something we all have to face, but it should be put off as long as possible. But it's much more painful if whoever's dead is someone you have known and loved. I felt deeply for Lucy's parents, even though Mrs. Soames, as I expect one ought to call her, wasn't the girl's mother. That somehow made it sadder – you wouldn't understand why, my darling, but you will, in later years.'

I realized that Mother had been talking to gain time, she wasn't making for the front door, as I supposed she would, but drifting round the blind side of the house where I had come from on my smells-crawl. 'But, Mother,' I said, 'don't you want to go in? Do they know you're here?'

She looked guilty and frightened, like a child that has been caught doing something wrong.

'No, my darling,' she confessed, 'they don't, and that is why I feel so unhappy. Daddy didn't want me to come, he wouldn't come with me. He even said he wouldn't pay for the carriage. Oh, Richard, he was *so* cross with me.'

Her tears began to flow, and though I knew they came quite easily, they never failed to move me.

'He was so cross with me,' she repeated. 'He said I was a . . . a *fool*.'

If it had been the strongest expletive ever used, she couldn't have uttered it more tragically.

'A fool, Mother?' I said. 'He couldn't have meant it!' 'I'm afraid he did,' she said. 'And he didn't love me just then, but perhaps he will again . . . You see, he thought me very silly to have come here. He thinks you ought to stick to what you say, and so do I, of course. But he didn't realize how much I minded you being away – perhaps you didn't either, my darling. But I have missed you *so* much. I tried to be brave about it, because I thought it was for your *good* – to come here, I mean, and learn to be a farmer. I didn't know what it would be like – losing you for three years, and perhaps for ever, because you might marry and settle down here. But there isn't the same reason for it now, because you're so much better. And so I asked him to write to Uncle Austin and say he wanted you back. But he wouldn't, and he wouldn't let me – he said we should make ourselves a laughing-stock if we changed our minds so often, which wasn't fair, because we should have only changed them *once*. And so we argued to and fro about it, and finally I said I would go over by myself, and ask Austin, *very nicely*, if he minded your coming back to us – I'm sure he won't, but somehow I don't like to ask him, after what Daddy said.'

At this point Mother stopped, and looked at the west side of the house in terror, as if it was an angry animal and might bite her. I think that of all my emotions relief and happiness were uppermost, but also I was shocked by her having defied my father, and by her extravagance of driving all the way – why, it must have cost nearly a pound, and I didn't think of Mother as having any money of her own.

'Why didn't you ask Uncle Austin to meet you at Willow Green?' I asked. 'He meets everybody there, he would have met you, if you had been a servant.' 'I didn't like to,' Mother answered. 'I didn't want to put him to the trouble, especially when Daddy was so much against my coming.' 'Where is the carriage?' I asked. 'Has it gone away? If it has, how will you get back?' 'It's waiting on the road,' said Mother. 'I didn't like to drive up to the door – it would have looked, well, peculiar. Daddy said that if they saw it drawing up, they would think I had taken leave of my senses. Carrie would have understood! But the others! Of course I love them all, but Ada is so sharp-tongued, sometimes. And I shall have to tell them that I came against your father's wish. Oh, I feel so unhappy! If only you were a little *older*, my darling, then you could help me. I feel they would listen to a *man*.'

'But won't they listen to *me*?' I objected. 'After all, it has to do with me.'

My mother shook her head. 'You are still too young to know what is best for you, my darling. Your father *thinks* he knows, but he isn't *always* right. You see, he didn't want you to come here in the first place, and he kept reminding me of that. But he was wrong, the Rookland air *has* done you good – he can't deny it, and there's no harm in telling you. And I'm sure he's wrong, too, in not wanting to take you away. You came here for your *health*, much more than to learn farming. Uncle Austin understood that: we haven't *deceived* him. And I hoped you would be company for Aunt Carrie, but she has left us now, so you can't be any comfort to her.'

Mother spoke as if Aunt Carrie was dead; she was in a mood when every thought was painful to her. 'I've told Daddy over and over again, there's no reason why you shouldn't come back to us, and every reason why you should. But he won't listen – he's like so many men, he thinks that because you've once said a thing you must abide by it, however unwise it is. It's not a sign of weakness to change your mind, it's a sign of obstinacy not to, and I know that if I asked Uncle Austin *very nicely*—'

'Then why don't you?' I interrupted, passionately hoping that Mother would get her way, though my sense of justice still sided with my father. 'Why don't you? It's almost tea-time, and Uncle Austin will be in, they all will be, and they'll be so glad to see you.'

'You think so?' Mother said, and it was one of the few times she asked me my opinion. 'I'm not sure. Daddy was so strong against it, and Austin won't like his plans being interfered with. Richard, if I didn't *know* that I was right, I should ask the cabman to drive me straight back to Medehamstead. That was another reason why I wanted him to wait outside, where they couldn't see him, in case I changed my mind at the last moment. They may think me as silly as your father did. I haven't the courage of a water-rat – I never had.'

I was afraid that Mother was turning tail, and I tried to urge her on. 'But Uncle Austin can't kill you!' I exclaimed, using an argument that had some weight with schoolboys. 'And why should he mind my going? It will be one less millstone round his neck.'

'My darling, you're too sweet,' said Mother indulgently. 'Do you really want to come back to us? I've sometimes thought you didn't.'

This was a totally unexpected attack.

'Of course I do,' I said indignantly.

'Well, that does make a difference.'

By this time we had turned the corner of the house: the front door showed green beneath its awning.

'You *will* say you want to come back, won't you?' whispered Mother. 'But you must say it *very nicely*—'

We both said it as nicely as we could, and Uncle Austin and Aunt Esther also said, as nicely as they could, that they didn't want me to go, but they quite understood that in the circumstances it might be best. If they were surprised, they didn't show it, and they certainly weren't angry. Aunt Esther thought up some pleasant things to say about me – how they would miss me, how dull they would be without me; and Uncle Austin said that when I was no longer sitting beside him on our visits to the farms he would start talking to himself.

Tea went its way in an atmosphere of increasing good-will. Aunt Esther's silver tea-kettle, which I so much admired, hissed and puffed like a benignant dragon, and I couldn't understand why Mother had got herself, and me, into such a state of panic. It was a little difficult to explain to Mrs. Wright what was afoot. In answer to repeated shouts she said, 'But why is he going away? He's like one of the family!' 'He *is* one of the family!' said Aunt Esther, who could always make her mother hear. 'But you see his parents want him back.' 'His parents?' quavered Mrs. Wright, as if I had been an orphan. 'Yes, Mary, you know Mary? she's sitting opposite you, and you know Walter, Richard's father, only he doesn't happen to be here.' 'What I don't understand,' broke in Aunt Ada, with the air of someone who has kept silence for too long, 'is why Walter *isn't* here. It looks very much to me as if he didn't like what Mary's doing – taking Richard away. Why didn't he come with you, Mary? Thursday is his half-day, isn't it? He *could* have come. Farmers don't have half-days off, but they do in Banks. Why did he let you come along, and *how* did you come, anyway? You haven't told us that.'

Mother, whose youth had come back to her since tea began, suddenly looked years older. 'I took a cab,' she said. 'You took a cab!' exclaimed Aunt Ada, as appalled as I had been at Mother's extravagance. 'You took a cab! And how much did it cost, I wonder? Well, I'm glad you have the money to throw away – *we* have to save up our pennies. But I think there's more in it than that—'

'It doesn't matter much *how* Mary came,' Aunt Esther interrupted. 'What matters is that she *has* come, and given us all such a delightful surprise. It would have been nice if Walter could have come too, but he is a very busy man—'

'Surely not on Thursday afternoons,' said Aunt Ada, sticking to her point.

'We don't know, Ada, do we, what calls men have on their time? For you and me Thursday afternoon is like any other afternoon – perhaps we work harder then. Did I see you weeding in the garden?'

Aunt Ada didn't answer.

'Anyhow, let's enjoy ourselves till Mary has to go. What would you like to do, Mary? Take a little turn with Richard? You must have so much to say to each other.'

So it was arranged that I should leave St. Botolph's. Mother must have had a private word with Uncle Austin, for when we were clustering round the cab, admiring it – 'It must have been *very* expensive, Mary,' said Aunt Ada – I heard him say, 'Then Walter will be writing to us, won't he?' Mother got in, looking self-conscious but a little proud, and drove away. What would my father say to her when she got back? Would she win him round? Would she persuade him to pay for the cab? I felt sure she would.

The knowledge that she had incurred his displeasure by coming, that she had missed me so much, that her feelings were stronger than her principles, endeared her to me, melting the core of resentment that had been hardening in my heart.

But in spite of my reconciliation with her, I wasn't reconciled to myself. A gap had opened in me that she couldn't fill: I couldn't go back to that blissful state when my mother's love, and my response to it, satisfied all my emotional cravings. I had found a way of giving that was new to me, and a way of receiving that was new too. The rôle of protector, which is an essential ingredient of love, had been aroused when I was with Lucy: I protected her, or thought I did, whereas with Mother, the protection was all on her side: she couldn't have conceived our relationship otherwise, nor could I. Grateful as I was to her for coming to my rescue, and touched as I was (for I was old enough to appreciate other people's motives) by her having violated two of her strongest instincts – obedience to my father and economy over money – by coming to St. Botolph's, I couldn't transmute those feelings into terms of love – the sort of love I had for Lucy.

But guilty they made me feel, as any love does that one can't meet on equal terms. In that interim period, so Mother told me afterwards, Dr. Butcher was quite concerned about me: he told her I was highly strung and might even have a breakdown. 'I didn't like to tell you at the time,' she said, 'because it was better for you not to know that you were highly strung.' So bewildered was I, I could hardly take in the meaning of what was happening to me: it seemed to be happening to someone else, as indeed it was. I lived so much in other people's conceptions of me, that my own personality, if I had one, was hidden from me. I only knew that I was not the boy they thought I was, but somebody quite different, of whom they wouldn't approve at all.

I tried to black out the whole of the Lucy episode and forbid my thoughts to approach it, but approach it they did, sometimes under cover of comforting unrealities. I would pretend to myself that the tragedy had never taken place, that everything was as it had been, that I should meet her tomorrow. Or if I did face up to it I tried to lighten my load of grief by fixing my mind's eye on the long skid-mark on the verge which, as the Coroner had said, pointed to accident, not design.

All the folk remaining at St. Botolph's were extremely kind to me – they showed it not so much by word of mouth as by putting on special faces when they spoke to me. I was a victim, as Aunt Carrie was, and needed special treatment. Aunt Ada did once say, 'I think your mother is wrong, Richard. She should have let you stay with us, as I'm sure your father would have liked you to. But she's ambitious for you, just as she was for Carrie, and look how that turned out!' A most unfair remark, for Mother was always for holding Aunt Carrie back. Aunt Ada didn't impute blame to me but she was always tilting at my mother: perhaps she couldn't forgive her for being the first of the family to marry.

Aunt Esther, with her practical bent, said, 'If you have got tired of caterpillars, Richard' (I had in fact lost interest in them since Lucy's death), 'why don't you go in for croquet-practice? It can't be much fun for you, but you used to like it.' And I, for whom an older person's word was still law, obediently fetched a mallet and four balls out of the Chinese-pagoda summer-house, and started those interminable games against myself in which, as blue and black, I waged sado-masochistic wars with red and yellow. What humiliations I devised for them! And I think this civil strife on the green battlefield of St. Botolph's lawn was my best solace.

How interminable, even on the parade-ground, a spell of marking-time is! But one day Uncle Austin said, 'Well, my boy, I'm afraid we're going to lose you shortly.' He stopped, and gave me one of his old-fashioned quizzing looks. 'I'm sorry, I can tell you. You would have made a farmer, I'm sure of it, and I shall miss your company, we all shall. But perhaps, as Esther said, it was lonely for you not having anyone of your own age to hobnob with, except Charlie, and he's not everybody's choice. But remember you will always be welcome here, if that cough should start again. Butcher doesn't think it will – he says you'll be as right as rain.'

Why rain should be right I've never understood. I was grateful to Uncle Austin for his speech, though I felt he had rehearsed it, and by giving me so much the benefit of the doubt, he had undermined the bulwark of self-pity I was trying to build up. If most people are sorry for you, how can you be sorry for yourself?

My mother came the day before I left, to help me pack: she didn't think I could do it, and perhaps she was right. She wore an air of subdued triumph. 'Daddy was so sweet to me,' she said. 'He really wants you back as much as I do – or nearly as much. He even said he was sorry he had tried to stop me coming, and it's very difficult for men to say they're sorry, they nearly always think they're in the right. And also – but you mustn't tell anybody – he not only paid for the carriage, but gave me a little present as well, something I'd *always* wanted.' But she wouldn't tell me what it was.

She had the Lilac Room, I remember: there were three spare rooms now, and would be four when I quitted.

XXV

My feelings were so mixed I couldn't disentangle them. Relief was uppermost, but underneath were stirrings of regret. Who knows, Denys, in any interplay of the emotions, which is the leading one? I didn't realize that at St. Botolph's my inner life had reached the highest pitch it could, and the house and its surroundings had grown into me in a way that no place since has. Now that I was leaving it I had lost my dread of it, but there was no part of it that didn't recall some thought or feeling. I could hardly believe it would go on existing when I wasn't there.

There was one thing I wanted to do but couldn't, and the conflict turned my mind into a battlefield. Sometimes guilt, sometimes grief took charge; sometimes an ignoble feeling of self-congratulation that I had got off as lightly as I had. Yes, I had got off with flying colours – with everyone's support – a miscarriage of justice so flagrant that it shocked even me.

The battle grew more intense as the day – my last day at St. Botolph's – wore on. Lucy had been buried in the Abbey churchyard. I felt I must go and stand beside her grave. It was a compulsion and my conscience, that dubious ally, backed it up. But repulsion

255

was equally strong; and the thought came to me that if I went, Lucy might take possession of me, just as I had of her. I knew now by experience that I mustn't try my nerves too far. Yet not to go was cowardice, and worse than cowardice. Action was a better anodyne than thought. I jumped on my bicycle and rode off.

Twilight was falling though night was still an hour or so away. I propped my bicycle against the Abbey porch and walked through the Early English gateway into the nave. The churchyard lay at the end of the ruin, beyond the dog-tooth arch that had no doubt helped to support the central tower before it fell. There were no new graves in the nave; for centuries perhaps, no one had been buried there. My dream had been an anachronism, somehow mixed up with the legend of Torfrida. I went on into the churchyard, graves all round me; how could I tell which was Lucy's? By the headstone, of course; but nowhere could I find it. I was unversed in the sad arrangements of mortality, and it was a long while before I realized that there wouldn't have been time to put up a headstone to her, and without its aid, I could not discover where she lay. Relief surged up in me, to be beaten down at once by disappointment, for now I should never be able to take my last leave of her. Then quite suddenly I came upon two newly-made graves, side by side; two long mounds, each turfed over, and each smothered in flowers. One of them must be hers, but which? At first the uncertainty made my search seem useless, then a kind of peace stole into my mind. Someone else had died as well as she. Hitherto, in my eyes, she was a solitary victim; all the rest of the world survived, she only had been singled out for death. Now my responsibility was lessened; I shared it with Fate, which had struck down somebody quite unknown to me. I said a prayer for Lucy over one grave, then I stepped across and said it over the other. I can't remember what I said. I think I prayed for myself as much as her, for I needed prayers and she did not. I felt that I had done my duty and that things were better than they had been, not only for me but for the world. And the superstitious nerve that had quivered almost physically at the thought of being alone with her was muted if not silenced. For I hadn't been alone, another spirit kept her company and shared my communion with her. A shadowy third! I had never wanted one while she was alive.

That night I asked if I might have a bath. A bath was not taken for granted then as it is now. Someone else might want a bath, and besides, the boiler had to be stoked up. Aunt Esther agreed at once; it was something for Richard to do! – and since Lucy's death my every whim had been met more than half-way. To them, I, the corpse-discoverer, was the real victim. So I said good night and took my candle from the gate-legged table in the hall, choosing the tallest, as out of selfishness I sometimes did, and hastened to the bathroom. The bathroom had been done up by Uncle Austin, when he added on the room with the hot and cold wash-basin next door, for we had no downstairs 'cloaks'. It hadn't lost its air of novelty for me, or even the slight smell of paint which the varnished pitch-pine panelling gave out, and there was still on the chimney-piece – for like many bathrooms of that date this one was furnished with a fire-place – the bottle of Anzora Cream that testified to Uncle Austin's unexpected streak of dandyism. The brown water gushed in bringing its heavy smell of rust and other natural products, so different from the smell of today's chlorine; and I lay there quite a long time, counting the knots in the airing-cupboard door, as I used to years ago and regaining, or trying to regain, the feeling of innocence I had then. Vaguely I felt that this immersion was a lustral bath, a ritual, which would do more than cleanse my skin. The experience seemed to sum up what was essential to my time at St. Botolph's, though I could not analyse it then any more than I can now.

My departure wasn't triumphal, as Aunt Carrie's had been, with her James; the shadow of defeat was on it. It was rather hurried, and Minnie the mare, who had no sense of an occasion, pawed the gravel and seemed to share our wish to get it over. I had a good deal of luggage, carefully packed by Mother's loving hands, so we needed the wagonette to take us to the station. There were the usual farewells and wavings, without which no departure from St. Botolph's was complete. Oh how we clung to each other in those days, much closer than we do now! But for once these demonstrations of affection ceased before we were out of sight, and I had an uneasy feeling that my aunt and uncle, who had done so much for their relations, might be glad to see the last of me. We drove in silence, my mother and I, down the long straight stretch of road that turned to the left so dramatically when it reached St. Botolph's bridge; and silent we remained till we drew level with the north side of the Abbey. I was staring out of the window with unseeing eyes. Mother was sitting beside me in the glass-lined embrasure, with her back to the horse. Her face, which had been sad enough before, suddenly put on its most distressed expression.

'Don't look at it, my darling,' she said.

I started. 'Don't look at what?' I asked.

'At the "M",' my mother said. 'The "M" on the side of the tower. It's so *ugly*, you know. The Abbey used to be so pretty. They've spoilt it by putting up that dreadful thing. It wouldn't have mattered if they'd been *flying* buttresses. Don't look at it, my darling. You must never, *never*, let yourself get used to ugly things.'

I had always felt that Mother's objection to the 'M' was captious, a sign of feminine caprice which (for I had something of my father in me) must none the less be borne with. But now I saw what she meant. Those hard straight upright lines – the two long ones – made of cement or some such lifeless stuff, embossed on the old but living walls of the grey tower – they *were* an eyesore, something mechanical and functional imposed on what was hand-made and heavenly. And it moved me that in the midst of all my mother's other cares and anxieties – myself just then the chief – she could mind so much a thing being ugly. And flying buttresses? Why should they be better? There was nothing for them to rest against, for one thing, and for another they were French in origin. My mother, in her timid, diffident way, liked French modes and styles: I didn't.'

XXVI

'That's all, Denys,' said Richard. 'You know the rest, or most of it. There's nothing more that counts.'

'Nothing more that counts?' Denys repeated. 'I should have thought there was a lot more that counted, Richard. Your money from the bricks, for one thing.'

'Oh that? Yes, it did count, and still does count, thank goodness, or where should you and I be? My father was a better business-man than Mother's relations gave him credit for. He was nobody's fool. Through thick and thin he held on to the brick-works, and it didn't let him down, as the Rookland Brickfield let me down. For nearly forty years it paid its way, and then it paid my way. I've been its pensioner for thirty years – I'm the same age as it is. We were both my father's children, and he made me a director of the Company, but I can't say I ever helped him with it, any more than I ever helped Uncle Austin with his farms, though he, too, did very well with them, better than he would have, I'm sure, with my assistance. How the pattern of life repeats itself! I was the fifth wheel of the chariot in both cases, but the chariots rolled on, or have done until now. Everyone thinks I have been very lucky, and no doubt they're right.'

'You say the pattern repeats itself,' said Denys, slowly stretching his long arm towards his glass. 'Don't think me inquisitive, Richard – your story moved me very much – but has there been a repetition of the Lucy episode?'

'No,' said Richard, 'nor will there be – I'll see to that. "My life closed twice before its close." You remember those lines? Well only you could make it close a second time. Dear Denys, I hope I haven't bored you with this long recital? But I wanted you to know the whole set-up, in case, in case—'

'I felt impelled to write about it,' Denys said. His round baby-blue eyes smiled, then grew more serious. 'As for the pattern being repeated, you needn't be afraid that I shall drown myself – I'm not that type.' He gave Richard a sly look. 'You're not disappointed, are you? You don't expect me to commit suttee if—'

Richard looked a little hurt.

'Oh, I didn't mean *that*,' said Denys quickly. 'You would have seen it was a joke if you hadn't been tired. You must be tired, Richard – it's twelve o'clock, long past your bed-time.'

'Tired, yes,' said Richard. 'Not ill, though, like I felt before. If I hadn't stopped then, I couldn't have got going again. There are some things you can only say in the context they belong to, otherwise they peter out in shame and silence. And I wanted to get this off my chest, or heart, or whatever organ it was pressing on. You're too young, Denys, to know how suddenly an impulse flags, especially when you've had to beat it up,

262

but when you get to my age and begin to slow down, the things that worried you in youth re-assert themselves, and your mind hasn't the same resilience. You haven't anything to worry about, I'm sure, but I have – or had, until I told you of my double life. Trying to square the opinion people have of you with what you're really like, is quite a problem.'

Denys fixed on Richard his long, disconcerting stare. 'How much do you value other people's opinion?' he asked. 'What does it mean to you?'

'Everything – and nothing,' Richard answered. 'Nothing, because if I try to identify myself with the mind of God – ha-ha! Denys – and at times I am capable of that presumption – I know that most people's opinions don't matter. They are made up of all sorts of considerations which, I assure you, could never influence the mind of God. At times I know it is so – but those times are rare, and at other times I am oppressed by the view the world takes – not by the view that I conceive it takes of me, but by the much harsher view it would take if it knew . . . well, what you know. I don't respect its judgments but I mind them, indeed I dare say that my whole inner life is conditioned by my dread of them. What would the world think, I ask myself, what would it say? I resent its power to affect me, and yet I can't ignore it. I would rather die (that's no great boast) than have this episode of my early life made public: it falsifies the image I have tried to build up in people's minds. But equally I couldn't die without telling someone about it, not only for the sake of confession, but for the sake of truth. As I told you, I would like the shadow of it to be thrown on anything that might be written about me. The shadow of the fact, but not the fact itself. Never the fact! Could you manage to convey the one without the other, Denys?'

Denys rose and began to pace about the room.

'I don't see why you want the shadow adumbrated, if that's not tautological,' he said. 'I told you I should be flattered to be your father-confessor. But now you've confessed, doesn't that satisfy your conscience, or whatever it is that's worrying you?'

'Not quite,' said Richard. 'I do feel better already, much better, but not so much better as I should if you had been a hostile auditor, an imperfect witness, quite out of sympathy with me, as Turgenev was with Dostoievski! Or as if I'd taken some sort of risk by telling you. No, it's the principle of justice, abstract justice for which I have a reverence, though how one can revere it I don't know, without revering the human beings for whom, I suppose, it was conceived. I don't think "they" have a right to know anything about me whatsoever, except what they can find out; yet all the same I feel that justice does demand a debt from me which I should like to pay. A slight blot on the 'scutcheon – you mustn't say what, you wouldn't say what, would you?'

'Of course not,' Denys said.

'That's all right then. By the way, where are those pills?'

Denys stopped in front of Richard.

'Do you want another?'

264

'No, I just wanted to be sure where they were.'

'I thought I put them on the chimney-piece,' said Denys, raking it with his eye. 'No, they aren't there, where *did* I put them?' He sauntered about the room with his back to Richard and stopped in front of a little table.

'Ah, here they are!' he said.

'Good,' said Richard, 'good. Give them to me, would you, Denys? They are my life-preservers, I suppose. I do feel a bit tired – I wonder if, for once, you'd give up your own downy couch and sleep in the other bed in my room?'

Denys hesitated.

'Is it made up?' he asked.

'No, and there are my books and things on it, I use it as a sort of table, as you know. But between us we could make it. I do feel a bit tired.'

'Well, so do I,' said Denys. 'But if it's any consolation to you—'

'Well, just this once,' said Richard. 'It won't need airing, will it? We can take the clothes off your bed.'

'That's an idea,' said Denys. 'But what will Mrs. Cuddleston say?'

'Oh, she knows about my frail state – she won't think it's a woman friend.'

'Don't you be too sure,' said Denys. 'These daily women get all sorts of ideas in their heads, especially about nightly women. But I'll oblige you this once.'

Together the two friends went into Denys's room and set about dismantling his bed.

From Byron, Austen and Darwin

to some of the most acclaimed and original contemporary writing, John Murray takes pride in bringing you powerful, prizewinning, absorbing and provocative books that will entertain you today and become the classics of tomorrow.

We put a lot of time and passion into what we publish and how we publish it, and we'd like to hear what you think.

Be part of John Murray – share your views with us at:

www.johnmurray.co.uk

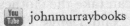 johnmurraybooks

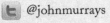 @johnmurrays

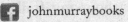 johnmurraybooks